ALAYAH WEAVER

The Chilling Secrets of Cherry Hill High

First published by Self publish 2025

Copyright © 2025 by Alayah Weaver

All rights reserved. No part of this publication may be reproduced, stored or transmitted in any form or by any means, electronic, mechanical, photocopying, recording, scanning, or otherwise without written permission from the publisher. It is illegal to copy this book, post it to a website, or distribute it by any other means without permission.

First edition

This book was professionally typeset on Reedsy. Find out more at reedsy.com

Contents

	Acknowledgments	iv
	Prologue	1
1	Chapter 1	4
2	Chapter 2	22
3	Chapter 3	31
4	Chapter 4	45
5	Chapter 5	54
6	Chapter 6	64
7	Chapter 7	76
8	Chapter 8	90
9	Chapter 9	110
10	Chapter 10	126
11	Three Months Later	140
12	Chapter 12	152
13	Chapter 13	165
14	Chapter 14	181
15	Chapter 15	209
16	Chapter 16	233
17	Prom Night	246
18	Chapter 18	259
19	Eight Months Later	273
20	Jackson	286

Acknowledgments

First and foremost, I want to thank my mom—your constant love and support have always been my foundation. Your belief in me and my dreams is the reason I'm here today.

To my manager, KK, thank you for giving me the opportunity to work on this book and for your unwavering support. Without your flexibility and encouragement, this story wouldn't have come this far.

To Don, I'll always be grateful for your advice.

A special thank you to Mariam—for always believing in me, even when I doubted myself.

This book exists because of the love, support, and inspiration I've received from all of you. Thank you for being part of my journey.

Prologue

In the small town of Cherry Hill, nestled by the big mountains of Oregon, I lived in one of the wealthiest neighborhoods. Cherry Hill looked like a postcard town—old brick streets, cozy cafes, and friendly people waving hello as they passed by. But if you take a closer look, you'll see things that aren't quite as perfect. Beneath the town's charm, there's a darkness hiding in the cracks. Secrets are whispered in corners, and behind every smile, there's a story you might wish you hadn't heard.

My story began in high school—Friday night football games, Monday morning gossip. Teachers dating students, cheerleaders slipping out of class to meet their older boyfriends. What if I told you those boyfriends were college seniors, maybe even recent grads?

At Cherry Hill High, bullying was so normal nobody even questioned it. It got so bad that some kids dropped out, and some even took their own lives. And drugs? Yeah, they were everywhere. It's easy to act like you're above it—until it finds you. And it found me.

Now, I hate a lot of things. I hate football games. I hate the sound of forks scraping against plates. I hate crying babies in diners. I hate the smell of brown sugar vanilla perfume. I hate gray clothes, rain, fake smiles, crowded rooms, and silence. I hate pretending everything's fine when it's not. I hate the lies I told, but I hate theirs even more. I hate muffins, coffee, steaks, and oatmeal. I hate my mother, my dad, the sound of glass breaking. I hate suits, needles, penthouses, schools—maybe even art.

But nothing makes me hate prom night even more. That night changed everything for me.

I'm locked away in a place called Dooms Institution. It's cold, quiet, and smells like bleach. The walls are a dull gray, and the windows are covered with thick bars that let in just enough light to remind you there's a world outside. I don't like talking about what I've seen, but they make me. They say it's part of the process, part of getting better.

I was always into crime, serial killers, and the twisted psychology stories. The way their minds worked fascinated me—the motives, the patterns, and the dark corners of humanity they hunted. It wasn't just about the crimes themselves, but the questions they left behind. Why did they do it? Could it have been prevented? Were they born that way, or did the world mold them into monsters?

I would spend hours poring over documentaries, reading case files, and analyzing every detail of infamous cases. From the Zodiac Killer's cryptic letters to Ted Bundy's chilling charm, each story felt like a puzzle waiting to be solved. Sometimes I wondered if I could've done it—if I could had gotten away with the crime better.

People know who I am. Everyone does. I'm the *"school killer."* That's what they call me. The cops, the news, the kids who whisper my name like I'm some ghost that haunted their memories. I try to block it out, but it's there, always there, like a stain I can't wash off.

The night they found me, I was covered in blood—my hands, my clothes, even my face. None of it was mine. I tried to tell them that, but no one believed me. Not the cops, not the teachers, not even the kids who used to be my friends. Her body was there, twisted and lifeless, and I was the only one standing over it.

Every day, I sit in a circle with other kids my age. We're all here for different reasons, but no one really says much at first. Some stare at the floor; others pick at their sleeves or fidget with the cheap plastic chairs. When it's my turn, all eyes are on me. My stomach knots, and my hands get clammy. How do you tell people you're not a monster when even you start to wonder if maybe, somehow, you are?

What if I told you the true story? Would you believe me?

1

Chapter 1

I never understood how my Mom could afford to live in Cherry Hill. I wondered if she had been a prostitute or an exotic dancer when she was younger. Or maybe, back at the age of forty-five. All I knew was that she worked at a local restaurant and wanted to become a nurse.

On Sundays, before school started again, we'd go to a restaurant to celebrate my *"accomplishments."* I hated those dinners. It wasn't just the attention, but because I had to pretend school was going well.

Mom dabbed her mouth with a napkin, then said, "Do you want to know what my son did today?" She smiled, waiting for her friends' reactions. "He walked outside to take out the trash just so some girl would notice him, but she never does." The whole table laughed.

I forced a smile onto my face. Deep down, I wanted to flip over the table. "Her name is Lyra Barns, by the way, and it's just a coincidence," I said.

I remember Lyra Barns with a kind of ache. Every time I saw her, my heart would race, my stomach would twist, and that

CHAPTER 1

hot rush feeling would course through me, like I might burst. It was love, or something like it, but sometimes I wished it could just fade away.

A woman sitting next to me whispered, "My daughter would love to date you." She ran her hand up my arm, and I pulled away with a smile. She visited my Mom often after work. I hated the smell of her flat ironed hair, her red nails, and her too pale skin.

Mom spotted her smudged lipstick in the reflection of her wine glass filled with sparkling water. She took a napkin to fix it. She loved five-star restaurants and often stole their soft napkins and spoons. The spoons were sterling silver, and she'd turn them into rings, wearing them until her fingers bruised.

"My son is finally a senior. Acelin, tell us how school is going so far!" She moved her short brunette hair off her shoulders.

I clenched my jaw, knowing I was about to lie, which made me nervous. "I love everything about being a senior. High school is a dream, and I don't want to waste a single second of it." I was bullied almost every day and was called the school shooter. "I made many friends last year." I cleared my throat.

Mom looked proud. "My boy is getting older day by day," she smiled, sitting across from me.

I went to therapy sometimes. I didn't like talking about why I went, but it helped in some ways. I just wanted to prove to Mom I was trying. Trying to get over the past. Either way, after that dinner, I met with my therapist, Dr. John.

"Good afternoon, Acelin. I'm glad you came back," he said, settling into his chair.

"It's not like I choose to be here."

"Well... I'm happy you are here," he replied, crossing his legs.

I smirked, but I felt annoyed. "Sure." I clenched my fists so tightly that my nails dug into my palms.

"How have your night terrors been lately?" he asked.

The nightmares were terrible. The sweat, the dry throat when I woke up. The dreams always got worse. There was one dream that kept repeating. I could still picture the blonde-haired boy sitting on the living room floor with me, playing with toys. It was cold outside, and my dad had just gotten home from work. I could hear screaming, glass breaking, and my dad packing his bags. The boy stopped coming around ever since my dad stopped. That's how I remembered the dream.

"Most of the nightmares just go back to my dad," I said. "Like when he used to beat me." I wiped my eyes quickly. "The rice. I remember that. If I didn't clean the yard right or make my bed, he would make me sit on uncooked rice until my knees bled."

Dr. John stopped writing and glanced at me, rubbing his fingertips together. "It's okay, Acelin. You don't have to talk about it if you don't want to." He noticed the shakiness in my voice. "Would you like to talk about something else? School, maybe? Is the bullying stopping?"

I ran my hands through my hair. "Nope, it doesn't get better," I said. "Nothing's changed."

"You're only seventeen. It's okay to feel this way, but things will get better. They will."

"When?" I looked him in the eyes, my head tilted slightly.

"When you allow it to," he said, squinting a bit. I stared down at my shoes, and the timer went off, signaling the end of our session. Dr. John closed his notepad and popped a mint into his mouth. I could hear the crunch of the candy as he said, "I'll see you again."

I was already at the door. "No, you won't," I said. He didn't turn around. He just stayed in his chair with his back to me,

CHAPTER 1

smirking as I closed the door behind me.

*　*　*

I always woke up two hours early before school started. I still couldn't believe those kids had been murdered—Tommy Graves, Seulgi Sew, and two others. Though I didn't care much about the others, the popular ones mattered more. Their deaths felt heavier, like a part of the school had been ripped away. I wanted to be the first to find the killer. Maybe then the bullying would stop. Maybe I'd finally be seen as someone who mattered. A hero.

Most mornings, I fixed my hair with the gel Mom made, slicking it back perfectly in ten minutes flat. Then I rode my bike to the diner, where breakfast always came with a side of serial killer podcasts I couldn't stop listening to.

"Do you need a refill on your coffee, sir?" a soft voice asked.

"No thanks. I was just heading out." I packed my bag, slipping the half-finished blueberry muffin into it. It was wrapped with a napkin.

"Cherry Hill High?" she said, picking strands of hair off her apron. She looked at my uniform. We had to wear white shirts, navy blue jackets, ties, and nude casual pants for the boys. The girls wore the same thing, just had to wear skirts.

"Ya, that's my school," I smirked.

We wore a pin on the left corner of our jackets with *"CH"* circled in red. If we wore the symbol on the right side of our jackets, we would be called unprofessional. That was the only way we could enter the school building. "Well, I hope you have a good first day," she smiled.

"Thanks… and for the meal, again," I walked out of the door.

On the school radio, I heard a follow up on Tommy Graves. He was last seen at the bus stop late at night, carrying his football bag. Rumors were circulating around town that he'd been acting strangely, possibly due to drugs. They said it made him lose his mind. But I didn't think his death was a suicide, as they stated. His body had been found a day later on the school football field, after a game. It was in bad shape, like it's been there for longer. His veins were black, and brown blood had formed from his mouth, ears, and nose.

He was a charming young boy. Blonde hair, a face as a model with his brown eyes that were smooth like honey pools. All of that was gone in the hands of a school we called a second home. They saw the signs of his mental health and didn't think to help him. They failed him. They failed all of us.

Nick Adonis, the football captain and quarterback, had been Tommy's best friend, and he was the reason I hated going to school. I was scared for my life. He dated Lyra Barns, the girl I'd been crushing on since middle school. Once, he grabbed my camera and smashed it on the ground because I was taking pictures of her for the school yearbook. I never reported him for doing that to me.

I slid through the gym doors and ducked down by the window, watching as he passed by with his teammates, laughing about how the freshman girls looked dull and unappealing this year. I took a deep breath, clutching my camera, waiting for him to pass by. If Nick wasn't the one I was worried about, it was Lyra Barns. I searched for her everywhere, almost like I had been stalking her my whole life. She didn't know I lived down the street from her. She didn't know that sometimes, I watched

CHAPTER 1

her through her window at night before she went to bed. She always slept with a lamp on—just like me, afraid of the dark.

I knew she got her hair trimmed every month to keep it healthy. She was strict about her health—never eating before practice, and afterwards, only apples and Diet Cokes. She wasn't dealing with an eating disorder; she was just picky. The pictures I took of her for the yearbook always ended up stashed away—some in my drawer, some in a small box in my closet.

By the bleachers, I snapped a few pictures as she stretched, applying lotion to her soft, shiny legs. She was the captain of the cheer leading team and the most beautiful girl I had ever seen. Her brown skin, pinkish lips, and thick lashes coated in mascara. I'd let her ruin my life again if she wanted to.

The moment our eyes met, she asked, "Are you taking pictures of me?" Her voice was a soft shout. She stood up and wiped the lotion off her hands onto her shirt. Her nipples were hard; I could see the outline of them, through her white shirt.

Being that close after observing her from afar felt weird, like meeting someone new. I saw things I had never noticed before— the tiny freckles dotting her nose, the way her teeth sat perfectly in her mouth, and the little eye squint she did. Her scent, that familiar brown sugar vanilla perfume, filled the space around me. I was left speechless, my mind racing with no words coming out of me.

I hesitated to speak. "What?" My heart skipped a beat. I stuttered over my words, noticing her smile dropping at my awkwardness. "I'm just taking pictures for our... school yearbook. Would ya like to see what I took of you?" I tried to show her on the camera.

"Of course, but if you got my ugly side, I swear, I'm going to kill you." She tilted her head. "I'll just... give you my number, and you can send them to my phone," she bit her lip. I followed her to the other side of the bleachers, my nerves on edge. She reached into her bag, which looked like it had been crafted by a third grader on arts and crafts day. It was filled with colorful buttons and glitter.

She handed me her phone. "Today is going to be a long day for me. I have to stay after until my boyfriend gets out from practice," she said, sounding upset.

My hands shook uncontrollably. Lyra Barns, the girl I had been scared to talk to my whole life, was giving me her number? That familiar feeling was coming back—the butterflies in the pit of my stomach.

"I thought ya guys already broken up." I heard rumors about their relationship from people in my classes. Nick always cheated on her, and she took him back every time she could. I thought they had an open relationship, in my opinion.

"Um, no," she frowned.

Lyra was always in and out of school. She had left middle school early because of the trauma she was going through. That's why I had developed a crush on her. I barely saw her, and she remained a mystery to me. I heard that her dad killed himself because of depression. I guessed such things like that ran deep in her family. Her mom seemed like a psychopath to me. She was crazy, in other words, not normal. I always thought she was capable of killing people. She would stand in the middle of the yard watering the grass, staring into space during freezing weather while wearing her nightgown in the middle of the day.

Lyra continued as she twirled her ponytail. "Me and him are like the school's favorite couple. This year for prom, hopefully, we'll win King and Queen," she said with a smile. What I loved

CHAPTER 1

most about her hair was the slicked back ponytail, with the strands of hair she always left hanging down—her signature style.

"Sure," I said.

There was a silent moment between us. I could hear the gym floors squeaking from the shoes that aggressively hit the floor. I looked around, avoiding eye contact with her. She started biting her nails. I didn't know what to say, so I just stood there, waiting for her to continue bragging about her horrible relationship, but she didn't. She looked at me with disgust and boredom, standing up and down on her tippy toes. "I've got to go back to practice, and I love your camera, Acelin," she said as she walked away, swaying her ponytail back and forth.

My eyes widened at the fact that she knew my name. But that was likely because I was known as the school shooter, all thanks to stupid Nick. He had spread many rumors about me, saying I was stealing people's pictures from the red room and jacking off to them in the bathrooms. The red room was where I edited the school photos before making the yearbooks. That all started in tenth grade. But that didn't stop me from smiling. "Get off the fucking court, creep!" shouted one of the boys playing basketball, pointing towards me.

On my way to class, I spotted Seulgi's brother. His name was Drew Lu Sew. He came to school occasionally to visit her locker. Seulgi was one of the students who had drowned in the school pool, hitting her head when she dived in some odd way. I watched as he cleaned her locker, removing the flowers that had turned brown and lifeless.

He gathered all the note cards from people who had slipped them into the cracks. He carefully placed them in a plastic bag, wrapping it twice before tucking it under his arm. I could see the pain in his eyes, her memory still clinging to him. What could I say? I had never lost a sibling.

"Hey you," a voice hissed from the bathroom door as I stood there watching Drew. A boy stepped forward, pushing his curly brown hair out of his face. "Want to buy or what? I've got the best offer for you."

I nodded, stepping into the bathroom with him.

I had forgotten about the druggies who liked to hang out in the freshman hallway. I tried to avoid them whenever I could, but this time, he'd caught me. He held out pills in both hands. One hand was filled with blue pills, each marked with a smiley face, while the other held red pills, each with a sad face. I had two choices: I could take them and avoid looking like a wimp, or I could turn him down and deal with the bullying for not going along with it.

He leaned against the cold, tiled wall, a grin on his face. "You can take the blue ones for now. Only since class is starting soon."

I hesitated, then shrugged. "It's fine, I'll go with the red."

He frowned, clearly surprised. "Oh shit, you seriously want to get fucked up before school starts, huh?" He chuckled. "I'll just give it to you for free, it's on me." He noticed my awkwardness as he raised an eyebrow. "You seem like you really need it, bro."

I swallowed hard, trying to keep my hands from shaking. "Thanks." I took the pills from his hand, feeling the weight of them in my palm.

"If you need something more, I got you," he added with another grin. "I'll be here till the end of the day."

The bathroom felt suffocating, like the walls were closing in on me. Guilt hit me hard, and I couldn't shake the feeling as I rinsed my hands under the cold water. I thought about my

CHAPTER 1

Mom—how she would flip if she ever found those pills hidden in my room. She still did my laundry every week, always checking my things, never giving me the privacy I used to have.

I twisted the small pill bag and placed it inside a little zipper compartment in my bag, making sure my books covered it.

Pushing open the library doors I felt all eyes on me. I was too nervous for the first class, so I skipped. Especially since what happened in the bathroom earlier with the drugs. The smell of book dust and quiet whispers of students studying calmed me. I reached into my bag and pulled out a sketchbook with a set of wooden sharpen pencils. Drawing had always been an escape for me, a way to pour my jumbled thoughts onto paper.

Time passed, marked only by the steady ticking of a clock. The soft breeze of a fan brushed against my neck, the only thing I could feel. My face was down on the smooth, rounded, cool table. My hands, once active, were now still. My cheek was left red, as if I had been smacked. The same dream happened again with the little blonde-haired boy, and I realized it occurred when I was under a lot of stress. My restless dreams showed visions of a future I didn't want to live, but I knew it was just a dream. The house, once mine, now belonged to someone else. My dad crossed my path once more, but Mom remained missing.

The bell rang for the last hour of the day. The lights were turning off as I walked down the hallway, I heard a panic whimper. I stopped to listen. No one was left after hours except for janitors or teachers staying behind to grade work. From a distance, a light flickered off and on down the hallway. After hours at school were the worst. I thought around this time was when the school spirits came to light, the spirits of students who had died here. In fact, I did believe in ghosts.

In the boys' bathroom, I saw a petite girl slumped against the wall, with white foam forming at her mouth. Her eyes had rolled to the back of her head. Her head slowly fell down to her knees. I screamed for help, tapping her face to try to keep her awake. I took water from the sink, cupping my hands to splash it on her face. She didn't wake up.

I froze as a hand clamped over my mouth from behind. My body tensed as I struggled to break free. I could feel his breath on the back of my neck, the smell of cheap cologne mixed with something harsher. It was the boy who sold drugs to me earlier that day.

He was new this year, on the football team, trying to fit in with Nick's crowd. I could tell he didn't like the attention, but he didn't want to be bullied either. He had gotten into drugs to fit in at his old school, and now he was hooked. He had tried to quit before but couldn't. He didn't believe in getting help, so he kept dealing to stay connected to others in the same mess.

"Shut the hell up!" he said, dropping hand towels next to the girl. His feet slipped on the water I had splashed.

"What are you doing to her?" I asked, barely holding back the panic in my voice.

"She bought drugs from someone, but not from me!"

I helped him drag her into a stall. "How ya even got her in here?" I froze, waiting for an answer.

He glanced at me, as if surprised I was asking. "You never heard of hookup hours?" He shrugged. Then he snapped, "You think I did this to her?"

I didn't answer. I put her book bag under her head. We waited it out as he stuck his fingers down her throat, trying to make her throw up. She was sweating, twitching, but he kept a hot rag on her forehead.

CHAPTER 1

He sat next to her, breathing heavily. He then brushed her hair from her face. "My name's Jamie Day," he said, holding out his hand.

I shook it, unsure if I should. "Acelin."

"No one can know about this. If they do, I'll be kicked off the team and expelled," he said quickly.

"Expelled," I repeated.

"Yeah," he nodded. "Her name's Julie Forster, by the way. But I swear, I'm not trying to hurt her."

I looked at him, feeling like he was lying. He tapped the back of his head against the wall.

"Right," I said, keeping my eyes on him.

"They warned me about the drugs," he said quietly, "I just never thought it would be this bad."

Reporting him would've been insane, especially knowing she was the one who took the pills. Was she trying to impress him? Honestly, I didn't care about her. As long as we didn't get caught, I kept my mouth shut.

* * *

A car rolled past me, then stopped quickly. She reversed back to where I stood, her window lowering with a hiss.

"Do you want a ride to the party?" she shouted. Her pale skin stood out with her red, chapped lips, which she nipped on nervously. Her hair, bluntly cut to her neck, shaped her face.

"Moe Hart?" I recognized her from school. I never saw myself being friends with someone like her. She had grown up in a tough environment. A hellhole. When her mom got hooked on drugs, her dad stepped in, but only to use Moe to keep the family business running. As her mom aged from the drugs, she became less attractive, her face marked with scars that looked like pimples. Her dad hated seeing the dirty needles the mom hid around their house, so he kicked her out on the streets.

She gripped the steering wheel with both hands, ready to drive off. "Are you coming?"

I raised an eyebrow. "Why would ya think I want to go to a party?"

"The uniform, stupid. Everyone from Cherry Hill High is going. Do you want a ride or not?"

If I had gone to the party, it might have made people start to think I was normal. "Um, sure," I said, though I didn't think she was capable of kidnapping me. If she did, I wouldn't mind. She wasn't horrible looking, but there was something about her pale skin that I didn't like.

When I stepped into Moe's house, the smell hit me first—weed mixed with something like cleaning supplies. She went to a table, casually scooped some white powder with her pinkie, and rubbed it on her gums. She seemed satisfied, like this was something she did every day. I just stood there, watching her, feeling disconnected from everything around me. Her sister stood next to her. They looked alike, though her sister's hair was longer. She had a tired look, like she hadn't slept in days. Her body was covered in tattoos, some visible up to her neck, giving her a rough, worn-out appearance.

Around seven, students from school started arriving. They brought beers and board games, the kind you play while drinking. A boy from Burn Wood showed up, took off his varsity basketball jacket, and folded it to hide the town name.

"Truth or dare, Acelin?" Moe asked.

CHAPTER 1

"I'll go with truth," I replied, clapping my hands together lightly.

"Is it true that you killed those students?" The boy from Burn Wood interjected.

"That's not fucking funny," Moe quickly defended me, addressing the boy.

I smiled, lowering my head before looking at the boy. "I've never heard of you before. Don't ya live in Burn Wood?"

The room fell silent. Mumbles of laughter and whispers spread through the group. Moe bit her lip, drawing blood from the anxiety, waiting for his response.

He kicked his feet up onto the table and leaned back on the couch. "At least I'm not called the school shooter. We all know what you did last year."

Anger burned beneath my skin. "I know about you... that you're gay and using Moe to cover it up."

Moe cleared her throat, her voice tight. "Okay! Next game!"

He slowly stood up without responding, then stopped Moe from getting up. "Wait," he said, grabbing the liquor bottle from the table and gulping it down like it was nothing. He seemed more intrigued than angry. I had him figured out in less than two seconds—he didn't look or act gay. I could tell by the way he had eyed me when I walked in. "How about we play seven minutes in heaven? Whoever doesn't want to snort a line has to go in the closet with Moe," he suggested, clearly looking for revenge.

All eyes turned to me, and I could feel their stares. The party felt less like fun and more like an embarrassment. "I'll go in the closet," I said, trying to sound confident. "I'm the only one here who doesn't do drugs."

"Fine," Moe replied, grabbing my hand and pulling me

towards her room.

She led me to her closet, which was large enough to fit a whole lobby inside. It had a couch and a TV she barely used, and the fluffy white rug was buried under scattered clothes. I kept my eyes down the entire time, feeling nervous. I had never been alone in a room with a girl before.

Moe's eyes drifted up and down my body, making me feel exposed.

"Where are you from originally before you moved to Cherry Hill?" she asked, studying me closely.

"The Southwest," I said, clasping my hands together to hide the nerves.

"I can tell from the way you speak. Why'd you move to a small town like this?" she asked, frowning slightly as she waited for my answer.

"Why so many questions?" I shot back, matching her curious tone.

She ignored my question. "You never had a girlfriend before, right?"

I shook my head. "Why do ya care?"

She looked puzzled. "I just don't get it," she said, huffing. "You're perfect." She stepped closer, adjusting my tie. I took a deep breath, gripping the edge of the table to steady myself. "If I was interested in you, I would date you," she added, tapping my cheek lightly.

"Okay," I muttered, my face turning red. I wasn't sure how to respond. What if she was my first kiss, not Lyra Barns?

Moe lifted my chin, a smile on her lips as she bit them. "I think we're going to be best friends," she said.

After that, I decided to leave the party early. All they did was drink, smoke, and gossip about the new freshmen, and I had

CHAPTER 1

enough. I waved goodbye to her quickly before leaving her house. She smiled, rolled her eyes, and shut the door behind me. I stood there for a second, feeling the cold air on my face, before I started walking away.

* * *

I blew into my hands, trying to warm up as I waited for the green light to come into her room.

Finally, it happened. Lyra Barns had asked me to come over. She'd called me at 2 a.m, crying about something Nick had done to her, her voice trembling like it was the worst thing that had ever happened.

I threw small rocks at her window to get her attention, but she wasn't in her room. I knew her window was always slightly open at night because her mom kept the house too hot, even when it was warm outside. My heart pounded as I climbed up to her room, nervous. When I reached the top, broken glass cut my hand deep, almost making me lose my balance. Blood dripped down my hand, staining the sleeve of my gray hoodie. I gritted my teeth, pushed through the pain, and climbed into her room.

Her room smelled like her favorite perfume. The brown sugar vanilla. Pink was everywhere—on the walls, the bedding, and little decorations. Cool posters of eighties rock bands covered the walls. Everything was neatly organized, from the books stacked carefully on her desk to the baking recipes filed away in a folder.

On her computer screen were pictures of a girl named Remy

with Nick. He had his arms around her neck, kissing her forehead at a party. Remy used to be Lyra's best friend. Every Friday night after cheer practice, they would have sleepovers. Remy started to be more independent, exploring her own interests instead of staying in Lyra's shadow. Whether it was fencing or basketball, when she wanted male attention.

Lyra's footsteps echoed as she entered the room. "I'm so happy you're here," she said, wrapping her arms around me in a tight hug.

I tried to hide the blood by slipping my hand behind my back. "Did he cheat on you with Remy?" I asked, my voice gentle. She ignored me, tearing down their old group photos. "Lyra, ya can tell me," I stepped closer to her.

She grabbed my arms, her hands shaking slightly as she wiped away the tears from her puffy eyes. "Yes. I knew they had something going on," she whispered, her voice cracking. "I hadn't seen Remy around school for a while and started to worry about her, until someone sent me the photos." She paused, her hand hovering near her face as she wiped more tears away. Her eyes dropped to my hand, the bloodstain now more obvious.

"Your hand?" she asked, her voice sounding worried. She examined it.

"It's fine, seriously." I pulled away. "I just want to know if you're okay."

Rage rose in her eyes. I saw it clearly. She didn't have to say much more for me to get it. I could feel the sting of betrayal in her voice, the way her chest tightened with the rawness of the pain. That suffocating feeling when someone you trusted broke you down, left you in pieces, and you were left wondering if you had ever even been worth it. The desire for revenge wasn't

CHAPTER 1

just about anger; it was about getting back something that had been taken from you, making the other person feel the same emptiness, the same twisted sense of loss. I knew that feeling too well.

"I want him to hurt. I want him to feel how I feel," she pouted.

In the back of my head, I was happy Nick had broken her heart so I could heal it. "How would ya do that?" I asked, barely able to breathe.

With an evil smirk, she said, "By smashing his favorite sports car."

Chapter 2

Three sports cars were parked in Nick's driveway, but his most prized possession was locked away inside the garage. The neighborhood had a watch system in place, and Lyra knew the pass code to access the garage. If she entered it incorrectly twice, Nick would be notified, and the plan would fall apart.

Her watery eyes and chattering teeth from the cold made me question her state of mind. She gripped a bat in her hands, trembling, seemingly oblivious to the consequences of what we were about to do.

A mechanical noise startled me as rust from the bottom of the garage door fell into my eyes. The car was an old classic named Hellfire. Its bright red color was marked with white double stripes on the front bumper, freshly painted. A family picture hung on the wall beneath a trophy sealed in a glass container. It was the trophy the football team had won against Burn Wood last summer. My fingertips hovered over the names leading to Nick Adonis, leaving a smear of blood on the glass.

Without hesitation, she smashed the car window. Each strike

CHAPTER 2

released her frustration, denting the car and shattering the glass. The noise was deafening, stirring memories from my childhood—the sound of wine glasses shattering in the kitchen. Tears streamed down her face as her rage grew. I grabbed a pocketknife from a nearby table, its blade lying next to shriveled orange peels. One by one, I slashed his tires. Pain shot through my hand, blood trickling from the cut as it started to throb again.

Lyra was supposed to be sweet, innocent, and fragile—the version of her I had created in my mind. But no, she showed a different side. Even so, I still believed we were a perfect match.

The lights in Nick's room flicked on, sudden and bright like a flash of lightning. Through the dusty old garage windows, I saw him peeking through the curtains. My chest tightened, panic clawing at me. My eyes shifted to Lyra, waiting for her to react, to run—but she didn't. Her face stayed calm, her breathing steady, like she'd done this a hundred times before. It unsettled me more than Nick's shadow in the window. How many times had she done this? With who?

"We need to leave," I hissed, grabbing her arm. She yanked it free but followed anyway. We ran from the garage, the tall grass of his neighbor's lawn tangled around our legs, slowing us down. Lyra tripped over something—a root or twig, I wasn't sure—and fell hard onto the sidewalk. She gasped, wincing as her knees scraped against the rough concrete. A hole tore through her black leggings, showing raw, red skin beneath. She cursed under her breath, trying to push herself up.

The front door burst open with a loud crash. Nick's voice filled the doorway, and for a second, I could've sworn he was looking right at us. My breath caught up to me. He stormed out, holding a baseball bat. "Whoever did this, I swear I'll kill you!"

he yelled, his voice loud and hunting. He stood in the middle of the street, turning his head slowly, scanning for movement. My heart slammed in my chest as I pressed lower onto the ground. Beside me, Lyra stayed perfectly still, her eyes locked on him with that same cold, unfazed look. Like she was daring him to find us. My chest ached with something I couldn't name—fear, maybe, or something closer to denial. How could she be so steady while I was shaking?

The night mist thickened around us as we crawled low and slow, like soldiers sneaking past enemy lines. The wet grass clung to my hoodie, the dampness seeping through to my skin.

Finally, we made it to Lyra's parked car at the end of the street. We slid into the front seats, ducking low, breathing hard. Her hands were still trembling, gripping the wheel even though we hadn't started driving. I glanced at her, watching the rise and fall of her chest. Her eyes were glossy, like she was holding something back, but she didn't look at me. She just stared straight ahead.

Nick slowly walked back inside. He didn't even slam the door—just closed it quietly, the kind of quiet that felt more dangerous than the shouting. We didn't say anything as we drove away. I kept glancing at her, noticing how her fingers tapped against the wheel like she was trying to shake off nerves. I wondered if she was thinking about what she'd done—or about Nick—or maybe about nothing at all.

Later, she appeared behind me in the mirror. Her reflection caught mine, and she said, softly, "I don't want you to think I'm crazy." There was something vulnerable in her voice, like she was ashamed of even needing to say it.

But even then, there was something about her that kept me hooked. Maybe it was the way she could change from storm to

CHAPTER 2

still water in a matter of seconds. "Your secret is safe with me," I responded. She sat down on the toilet seat, rubbing her knees anxiously, trying to hide the pain. "Do you have a med kit?"

She sighed. "I do." She retrieved one from her bathroom cabinet.

"Can I help patch you up?"

"Yes." She removed her leggings, revealing her underwear. Her brown skin appeared cool under the bathroom light, speckled with goosebumps. I wiped both of her knees down with an alcohol packet. She squeezed my hand tight, letting out a big sigh. I stopped, glancing at her to make sure she was okay. She frowned, biting her lip. I noticed how close we were, how her breath came in shallow bursts.

"Sorry," I panicked, placing a Band-Aid on her knee. She didn't look at me, just kept her eyes on the floor.

"Thank you," she said. "Could I give you a new shirt?"

She looked at my hoodie and saw how dirty it was with blood stains.

I chuckled. "I can't fit your shirts." I watched her dig into her dresser for my size.

She held up a shirt, examining it. "Okay, some of my shirts are medium. I don't wear all extra smalls."

"Is it okay that I change in front of ya?"

"You act like I've never seen a boy without a shirt before. I have a boyfriend, Acelin."

I laughed, though it felt more like a knife in my chest. If they got back together, she'd tell him I ruined his car—it was only a matter of time. I slipped the shirt on and something in me sank. She was using me, just like she always did—getting people to fix her mess, then walking away without a second thought. She knew how to make me feel like I mattered, just enough to get what she wanted, but I was always left holding the pieces.

I decided to go home. What she said lingered, not sitting right with me. "I'll see you at school tomorrow, Lyra."

"Acelin," she called before I reached the window.

"What?" I asked, frustration edging my voice.

"I'll never tell him you were with me if he finds out, I promise."

I nodded as I left out.

The next morning, I rushed out of the house, toast hanging from my mouth. My hair was still damp from the shower, and my uniform was wrinkled. I fidgeted with my tie, trying to make it perfect, but only made things worse, tying small knots. I looked at the time on my phone. I was late for the first hour.

A car caught my eye—Moe, driving down the street slowly. I never told her where I lived, but somehow, she figured it out.

She parked on the curb. "Hey, wanna ditch school today?" she shouted from the car window.

"No. It's okay, I'm heading to school now!" I yelled back, ready to ride off on my bike.

"Come here, please!" she said, giving me those puppy eyes.

I walked over to her. The smell of weed lingered from her car. "Why are ya stalking me?"

"Stalking you?" She laughed, carefree. "I see you walking home from school all the time."

As I looked down the street, I saw one of Nick's cars, the same one I'd spotted in his driveway the other night. I had no choice but to get in the car with her. Without thinking, I opened the door, ducked down, and waited until the car drove past.

"Why the hell are you hiding in my car?" she asked, taking her hands off the steering wheel.

"I'll explain everything, just drive!"

We arrived at a bar—a place for underage teens to sneak

CHAPTER 2

into. The bar was called The Trope, owned by Moe's sister. The windows were blacked out, and thick vines crawled up the sides of the building, making me anxious. Tall, thin trees surrounded us, their branches stretching out by the entrance door.

Inside, the man I had seen in Moe's kitchen marked an X on my fist. He went by Knuckles. His black eye told me all I needed to know about this place. My body stiffened, and I felt a wave of fear wash over me.

I turned to talk to Moe, but she was gone. Motorcycle men from Burn Wood crowded the door, making it hard to spot her. I was shoved inside and found a seat at the bar. There was a drink in front of me, barely touched. Nervously, I sat in another seat, my eyes scanning the room. The men around me were tough intimidating, bearded, and reeked of trouble and stale beer.

"There you are." Moe slid her hand across my back and handed me a drink. I realized if I didn't drink, I wouldn't fit in. The low music and laughter in the bar almost made me forget about everything else. "So, what was it that you wanted to tell me?"

"I forgot," I said, pulling her stool closer with my foot.

She laughed, not taking it seriously. "Do you ever remember anything Acelin?"

"I don't know anything Moe," I said, my eyes locked on hers. My mind felt scattered, unsure if I was saying the right thing. There was something about the way she looked at me, like she knew I was hiding something, but maybe she didn't care. Maybe that was the problem—I wasn't sure if she ever cared.

"Drink this." She handed me another glass. I stared at it, took a deep breath, and drank.

By the time night fell, Moe and I had talked more. She wasn't the person I thought she was. Her life was a mess, but she was kind to me in ways I hadn't expected. She didn't judge me, not like everyone else did. Her company made me forget about my own problems, even if just for a moment. It was easier to lose myself in her presence, to let her distract me from my inner thoughts.

Maybe it was just a platonic feeling we shared. I wanted to believe it was more, because I needed it to be. I wanted to be loved. It didn't matter if I was setting myself up for disappointment.

But as the night went on, my eyes kept going to the entrance door. There was so much noise, people coming and going, that I couldn't focus. I couldn't shake the feeling that something was about to happen, that it was coming for me.

I picked up a shot glass, unsure if it was mine. "To our friendship, we'll always be there for each other, no matter what," I said as I raised the glass.

"Cheers," she said, taking a drink. "No matter what."

The strong liquor burned my throat, and I coughed. I held my chest as a strange sensation washed over me. My breathing grew uneven, and a wave of dizziness made my head spin. Something wasn't right, I started to feel funny. Moe's face blurred as she tapped my legs. "I'll go play a song," she said.

"Wait, I should come with you—" My voice trailed off as my legs felt like they disappeared. My vision blurred with each blink. My chest tightened, like I was being crushed. I looked at my hands, trying to pull myself together. My legs wouldn't move. I grabbed the edge of the bar to steady myself.

The bartender noticed. "Are you okay, sir? Do you need water?" His face twisted into a blur of colors, and his voice faded as he spoke.

CHAPTER 2

I started to hallucinate. The murmurs around me turned into a strange symphony of sounds. The people around me stretched and twisted, their faces turning into something unrecognizable. Moe rushed over with water, forcing it into my mouth. My shirt was soaked, and foam dripped from my lips.

The music seemed more intense, and I could hear Nick's voice shouting, filled with anger. He'd found out about me breaking into his garage with Lyra.

"Where's Acelin?" Nick shouted.

Moe's face frowned with confusion. She didn't know the whole story, she didn't know why I was running—but she understood enough to cover for me.

"He's not here," she said, trying to sound confident.

My chest felt weak, and each breath was hard to take. I slapped my face, trying to clear my head, but nothing worked. Whatever I drank was messing with me, making me see things I didn't want to think about.

The noise around me blurred together until a voice shouted, "That's him! I can see his feet!" Nick's friend said, pointing at me.

I tried to push myself further behind the bar, but my body wouldn't move. All I could do was watch as Nick came to me. He dragged me by the leg, his grip tight. The doors to the bar slammed open. I tried to resist, my hands dragging as I clung to the door, but it was useless. Outside, he punched me in the face—again, and again. My mouth filled with blood and foam, and I coughed uncontrollably, the taste sickening in my mouth.

Moe screamed, her voice shaking as she struggled against Nick's friends holding her down. "Let him go!" she yelled. I heard the fear in her voice, but I couldn't bring myself to look at her. I couldn't do anything. The world was spinning, and all

I could feel was the constant pressure of Nick's fists, landing with force onto my face.

It wasn't anyone's fault but mine. I had brought this on myself.

3

Chapter 3

My fingertips were cold, and my body pulsed with pain, as if something was cutting into me over and over. My face was numb and swollen, like a thousand stings had left their mark. I was shaken by uncontrollable shivers, but I knew I had to wake up. I forced myself to move, starting with my hands, little by little.

I had smelled mint, a leafy scent mixed with Lyra's perfume. A hot rag had been pressed onto my forehead, soothing the shivers throughout my body. My vision had still been blurry as I tried to open my eyes. Lyra was there, she sat near the bed, her hands resting lightly on a teapot. Steam rose into the air between us, twisting and curling like it didn't belong in the same space as me.

Her eyes locked onto mine. Her smile was soft, like nothing had happened, like she wasn't the reason I was here.

"Hey," she said. "How do you feel?"

I didn't answer right away. My throat burned, and my tongue felt too thick to form words. I tried to sit up, my arms shaky beneath me, and every movement pulled at the bruises on my ribs and face.

Lyra brought the cup of tea to my lips. "Go slow," she said, like she cared. I took a sip as she held the cup steady.

I watched her, waiting for her to say something real, something that showed she understood what she'd done. But she didn't.

Moe stood near the doorway, arms crossed and scowling. "You were drugged, and Nick beat you half to death," Moe said, her voice cold.

Lyra winced but didn't look away from me. "I didn't mean—"

"You didn't mean what?" Moe snapped. "Didn't mean to fuck him over? Didn't mean for him to take the hit of what you started?"

As they argued, I tried getting up again. The room was too warm. The tea in my hand smelled sweet, but it made me nauseous. I shoved it back at Lyra and forced myself to stand. Moe moved to help me, her grip tight on my arm, steadying me as I stumbled into the bathroom.

When I saw my face in the mirror, I froze. One eye was nearly swollen shut, dark bruises spread across my cheeks, and my lip was cracked and raw. A hand shaped bruise circled around my neck. I stared at myself, barely breathing. I didn't look like me anymore. The bruises and swelling made me feel like a stranger, someone broken and weak. Looking at myself hurt more than the punches.

Moe's voice wavered as she stood beside me. "I'm sorry, Acelin. I should've stopped it before it gotten this far." Her hands hovered, unsure whether to help me stand or give me space. Her words faded in and out. "Maybe I should take you home?"

I walked past Lyra without looking at her and headed outside

CHAPTER 3

to the car. I pulled my jacket tighter around me, hiding my face as Moe started driving.

When I got home, it was late, and the rain had just stopped. The house was dark when I went inside. Mom wasn't home yet. Maybe she was still at work, or out, or even looking for me. Lately, it seemed like she cared more about me, but I wasn't sure if it was real or just guilt. I missed how things used to be—movie nights, her laughing at my bad jokes, just the two of us, always.

Her car pulled into the driveway, and I heard the door slam shut. She rushed through the front door. "Acelin Jones!" she yelled, her voice shaking. "Where have you been?"

I stayed where I was, in the kitchen, unsure of what to say. I pulled my hat down, trying to hide my face. "I'm sorry," I mumbled.

Her eyes were red, like she'd been crying. "Sorry? You've been gone for almost a week, Acelin. Do you have any idea how worried I've been?"

I sighed and took off my hat, letting her see my bruised face. Her eyes went wide, and she looked at me like she didn't recognize me. "I got into a fight," I confessed. It wasn't a lie, but it wasn't the whole truth either. Telling her everything felt impossible.

"Who did this to you?" she asked, her voice shaking even more now.

"It's my fault," I said quietly.

She reached out to touch my face, but I flinched. "Acelin, I need ya to be honest with me. What happened? Who were you fighting with?"

I leaned against the counter, staring at the floor. "I told you. It was my fault. It doesn't matter," I muttered, trying to end the conversation. I shook my head, not wanting to explain.

"Don't walk away from me!" she yelled, but I went upstairs anyway. I closed my bedroom door behind me, leaning against it to shut everything else out. I couldn't face her. Not now. Her footsteps thundered down the hallway, then stopped outside my door. She banged on it like it was the only thing standing between her and the truth. "Let me in! We need to talk!"

The knocking barely registered as I thought back to that night. The sound reminded me of the punches from Nick, the way he dragged me. I couldn't shake the memory. "Open the door, Acelin! Now!" she shouted again.

My hands shook. "Just leave!" I shouted back. "I'm fine, just leave me alone!"

I covered my ears, hoping that if I ignored her long enough, she would give up. I couldn't bear the thought of her seeing me like this, knowing I had been beaten up over a girl who lived down the street. It felt too much, too embarrassing to share.

The silence stretched on, but then I could hear her breathing outside the door, soft but steady, like she was trying to listen for something. I wondered if she could hear my heart pounding.

When morning came, the house felt cold. When I woke up, I saw that Mom had left scar cream by my door. My heart sank, guilt flooded in me at the thought of still not wanting to talk to her. I sat on the couch, still shaken by the argument from the night before. She didn't even glance in my direction as she passed by, as if I wasn't even there.

The doorbell rang, breaking the silence. It was Grandma, visiting as she did almost every year. She stayed for a couple of days before heading to visit her son, but she never mentioned him. Sometimes, I wished she'd slip up and say his name, so I could ask—what was he doing now? Where did he live? Who

CHAPTER 3

was his wife? But it seemed pointless to wonder about him. My dad didn't exist to me anymore.

Grandma looked surprisingly young for her age, thanks to her skincare routine and all the injections that hid her wrinkles. "Hello, my angel," she said, wrapping me in a hug. Her face froze in shock at the sight of the bruises on my face. She didn't say anything, but I could see the worry in her eyes. I smelt the wine on her breath—dark cherry, the same kind Mom used to drink. Drinking ran deep in my family. Mom had stopped when she realized how much it was affecting her and me.

I used to find her passed out, sprawled across the floor in her room. The bars had been her best friend, and I'd clean up after her, missing school some days to take care of her. It felt like a secret I couldn't share with anyone. I hated bringing it up to my therapist, it felt too recent.

I held the hug longer than usual. "I missed you!" I said, pulling back slightly. "Let me help with your bags." I took them from her hands and carried them upstairs to the guest room, where I set fresh towels and soap on the bed.

Grandma met Mom in the kitchen. "So how is everything?" Grandma asked.

"Great," Mom replied, avoiding eye contact.

"I know there's something bothering you. You can talk to me."

"I only called you for Acelin. Nothing more than that," Mom said, placing her hands on the counter.

"Christina, is this about his father?" Grandma placed a hand on hers. "He's doing better now, but after his—"

"Don't bring that up around Acelin. He's dealing with enough already." Mom pulled her hand away quickly.

"I think it's time to tell him."

Mom tilted her head at Grandma. "I have this under control. I'll tell him when I'm ready," she said.

"Tell me what?" I asked, coming back into the kitchen.

Grandma's eyes widened. "Nothing, sweetheart. Let's start making the soup. My famous dish—"

"Our famous dish!" I smiled. But as I looked at her, I couldn't help but wonder how my dad had turned out the way he did.

We were halfway through making the soup. The bread was almost ready to come out of the oven, golden and buttery. The soup, a tomato base with chopped carrots, bell peppers, celery, and small bits of beets, was seasoned with garlic powder and pepper. The smell filled the house, making my stomach growl.

"You have a girlfriend?" Grandma asked, gently bumping my arm with her elbow.

A laugh slipped out before I could stop it. "Well, I kind of like someone, and I've liked them for a while now."

"Have you told her... or him?" Grandma's smirk widened.

I raised an eyebrow, confused for a moment. "No, it's a girl. Her name's Lyra. Lyra Barns." Admitting that I still liked Lyra, after everything she had done to me, made my stomach turn. But despite it all, I still loved her.

We sat around the table, and Grandma took a seat next to me. Under the table, I saw her pour wine into her cup, hiding it beneath the surface. She then straightened up, smiling brightly as she said, "Let's eat." My smile faded as I watched her drink. She glanced at me, like she was about to say something.

I quickly looked away and started eating. The table fell quiet for a few moments, the sound of silverware the only thing breaking the quiet. Then the conversation shifted back to school, just like it always did.

By the time night came, Jamie showed up. When I opened the

CHAPTER 3

door, his nervous smile greeted me, but there was something in his eyes that made me question why he was really here. I wasn't sure what it was, but I didn't feel like asking.

"Listen, about what they did to you…" Jamie started, his voice hesitant. "I talked to them. They want to make it up to you."

I didn't want to hear it. I didn't care what they wanted to do or how sorry they were. I wasn't in the mood for their fake apologies. "I don't care," I muttered, closing the door behind him.

He followed me upstairs to my room, like he always did, and it felt almost normal. Almost. I didn't know why I still let him in, why I still let him sit beside me when all he ever did was pull out something to get high. As if that made everything go away.

He sniffed a substance up his nose, looking like he was about to pass out. He leaned his head back against the bed, his eyes unfocused. "You know I like you, man," he said with a grin. "You cool. I don't get why they mess with you."

I glanced at him, his words dull in my ears. "I don't get it either," I said. "I really don't."

"I just don't want you to end up like those other kids who…" He trailed off, his words fading as if he didn't want to finish the thought. "You know, die in some weird way."

I froze, my pulse racing. The mention of death hit me harder than I expected. "I wrote an article about them last school term," I said, trying to brush it off with a nervous laugh. "I was obsessed with figuring out who really killed them. I studied everyone in their inner circle."

Jamie stared at me, his eyes wide, like I'd just said something insane. "Yeah, I didn't even know Seulgi and Tommy were dating until Nick mentioned how weird it was that they died so close together."

"I never saw it that way," I said quietly, staring at my hands, unable to shake that thought. For a moment, neither of us spoke. We both shifted, looking around the room, as if the right thing to say was just out of reach.

Jamie walked over to my desk and started looking at the pictures pinned to the wall. It was just another reminder that this house, this room, didn't feel like mine anymore.

"You wear glasses?" he asked, running a finger over the edge of one of the frames.

"Come on… do ya really have to go snooping around?" I snapped, the irritation flaring up before I could stop it.

He didn't seem fazed. "Why don't you wear them?"

I ran a hand through my messy hair, letting out a sigh. "I don't know. I just… I hate who I used to be." The words spilled out before I could stop them, like saying them out loud made them more real.

Jamie threw a soft ball at my head, an attempt to change the mood, but it didn't work. "You need therapy," he said, his tone calm but somehow serious. "Oh, and I forgot to tell you. Seulgi's brother, Drew Lu, works at our school now as a swim coach."

My eyebrows shot up. "He works where his sister died?"

"For real, it's crazy. Everyone was talking about it yesterday at school." Jamie said it like he was thrilled by the gossip, but his eyes were half opened.

I couldn't help the smile that spread across my face. "I think I have a better chance of finding out who the killer is now. Maybe Drew can give me something about Seulgi's last moments."

Jamie snickered, shaking his head. "I heard she was pregnant with Tommy's baby."

I blinked. "What the hell?" We both fell silent for a moment, and then, without saying a word, we both cracked up laughing.

CHAPTER 3

"Wanna smoke?" Jamie asked, pulling a blunt from his pocket and offering it to me.

I stared at it, unsure. "I don't smoke."

Jamie raised an eyebrow. "Come on, just a hit. It'll help you forget everything for a while."

He opened the window and sparked up, the scent of weed filling the room. I watched him, wondering if I should take the risk. His hair fell into his face as he stared out the window, his shoulders slumped with exhaustion. There was something else in his eyes, though—something that felt too heavy to ignore. But I didn't ask. I wanted too badly.

"Come here," he said, motioning for me to come closer. I moved, pressing my head against the wall beside him. "You can get high off secondhand smoke, you know. Just breathe it in."

I hesitated, my thoughts scattering like leaves in the wind. "Okay," I said finally.

But before I could breathe it in, I heard Mom's voice. "Acelin, what is that smell?"

I stiffened. The footsteps came closer, and panic dropped through me. Jamie flicked the blunt out the window, and we scrambled to open the window wider, trying to air out the room. By the time Mom rushed in, we were lying in bed, pretending to sleep.

"Acelin!" Mom flicked the light on. She tapped my shoulder, but I didn't respond. "Jamie, I know you guys are awake.'"

Jamie laughed first. "Sorry, sorry! It's my fault. I didn't know he couldn't smoke in the house." He sat up, but the nervous giggles were impossible to hide.

"Of course he can't," Mom said, hands on her hips. She looked at us with that disappointed look that made me feel like a child again.

I pushed myself up in bed, trying to look more innocent than I felt. "I didn't smoke anything," I said, my voice weak.

Mom glared at me, the irritation in her eyes barely contained. "Acelin Jones, we're going to talk about this in the morning," she said, pointing a finger at me. Then she turned and slammed the door shut.

I threw a pillow at his head, and he laid back down, still chuckling under his breath. "Good night, Acelin."

"Good night," I said, throwing the covers over my head.

* * *

Days passed, and my face started to look better—not perfect, but not as bad as before.

Mom got me a job at a diner through one of her friends. She thought working would keep me out of trouble. I wasn't a troublemaker, but she always seemed to catch me at my worst.

The diner had recently become a popular spot for students. Rumors had spread that I was secretly handing out free muffins. The rumors were true—it all started when Jamie told the football team. A few of them passed it onto the cheerleaders, and now the diner was chaotic.

At school, a lot had happened while I was gone. During lunch, I went to the library to browse the crime and horror section. As I flipped through books, I overheard whispers about Jackson White, a new transfer student who was joining the football team.

"He's here for a fresh start," one boy said.

"Yeah, right. That boy is trouble," another replied.

CHAPTER 3

"What happens in Burn Wood stays in Burn Wood," someone joked.

"Yeah, hopefully no one finds out about him and Mandy," another boy added with a grin.

Rumors were also floating around about students using drugs in the bathrooms. It all started when Jamie was caught high after school. Apparently, the principal walked in during his rounds and found Jamie stumbling out of a stall. Jamie's drug use seemed to be getting worse.

In class, he was often slouched in his chair, his eyes half closed. I covered for him, saying he was just tired or going through a rough time, but the red eyes and sluggish movements told a different story. It was clear he was struggling. *Bad*

After the bathroom incident, the principal ordered Jamie to meet with a counselor to talk about his addiction. Even so, I wasn't sure it would actually help him.

Meanwhile, the race for school president was in full swing. Students were eager to have a say in planning events, setting rules, and reporting troublemakers. Julie Forster won the election by the end of the day, though it was obvious she'd cheated her way in.

Standing at the podium, she forced a smile. "I'm so happy for everyone who voted for me!" she said, her voice full of excitement. It didn't match the quiet room, and it was clear not everyone was on her side.

Nick shouted, "How about you worry who's fucking yo boyfriend!" His words drew laughter from the students and shocked gasps from the teachers.

The principal took the microphone. "Settle down, everyone," he said, waiting for the crowd to quiet. "Julie, congratulations." The auditorium sank into an uneasy silence again.

I rolled my eyes at Nick, his attempts at humor fell flat. His charm did nothing to excuse his behavior. It was bad enough watching him tease the girl in front of him—he kept tugging at her hair, a smug smile on his face.

Moe tapped me on the shoulder, her question catching me off guard. "Has Jamie ever mentioned me to anyone? Like, that we're dating?" she whispered.

I turned to her. "No. Why?"

She hesitated. "His mom wants to meet me, but... I don't know where I stand with him."

"I think you should talk to him," I said, studying her expression.

She smiled slightly. "You think so?"

I nodded. "Yeah. I do."

Nick's eyes locked onto mine. I quickly looked away, but he got up, and before I knew it, he was pushing past people to get to me. Moe sank back into her seat, avoiding the scene. Nick plopped down in the empty chair next to me, leaning in with a smirk.

"Should I report you? You and Jamie, doing drugs in the bathroom?" His voice dripped with mockery.

"Why?" I asked, narrowing my eyes. "What's ya point?"

"You two have been hanging out a lot lately. He missed football practice yesterday because of you."

Out of the corner of my eye, I saw Moe watching us. Now she probably thought I was part of the rumors, tied to Jamie in a way I wasn't. She didn't know the truth—that I never touched the stuff Jamie offered me.

I stood up slowly, wanting to escape Nick before he caused more trouble. But as I made my way out, he followed, forcing both of us to stumble over people's legs. The hallway felt colder as I stepped into it, only to find Nick's teammates surrounding

CHAPTER 3

me. I took a deep breath, trying to prepare myself for the worse.

"What do ya all want?" I asked. "It's Jamie's problem, not mine, if he misses practice."

Nick snorted. "Then why run like a coward?"

From the end of the hall, Drew leaned casually against the wall, watching the scene. His voice cut through the question. "Says the guy whose dad took his car," his accent cut deep.

Everyone turned to Drew. He pushed off the wall, walking towards us. Some of the boys started backing away, clearly not wanting to be part of whatever was coming next.

Nick clenched his jaw. "Because I was drinking and driving," he snapped.

Drew stopped in front of him, standing calm. "You should've crashed," he said with a smirk.

Nick's face frowned, and he turned to me. "I'll see you later besto," he muttered, shoving my shoulder as he walked off.

Drew gestured for me to follow him. My nerves tightened, but curiosity won, so I followed him to his office. "Have a seat," he said. Once I sat, he perched on his desk, arms crossed. "Nick and his guys tried to set you up," he said bluntly. "They planted drugs in your locker, hoping the police search would get you caught. I took care of it, though."

My stomach dropped. "I could report him," I replied, tempted by the thought of turning the tables on Nick.

Drew chuckled lightly. "But that's not why I called you here," he clapped his hands together. "Your article was impressive."

My heart raced. "How did you find it? I threw it out," I said, nervous.

He clicked his tongue on his teeth. "It was under a pile of papers."

His lies felt real, his energy dark and oddly comforting. I

didn't know how to react. I didn't want to admit how much he scared me. But I loved it—I loved that feeling. It was intoxicating, though I couldn't quite explain why.

"You're just as curious as I am about who killed my sister," he continued, his voice satisfying.

"I—" Before I could respond, the fire alarm went off. He didn't flinch, sipping his coffee like nothing had happened. There was something unsettling about him, something dangerous.

And at that moment, I couldn't shake the question: who *was* Drew Lu Sew?

4

Chapter 4

Drew Lu Sew had flown into this small town to settle down about two years ago. His parents, Marco Sew and Kim Sew, had returned to Japan after the tragic loss of Seulgi. To protect Marco's reputation, they'd chosen to keep their family secrets hidden. Marco had been involved in the drug trade back in Tokyo, a business that was still thriving.

Over the past week, I'd been digging deep into Drew's life. He lived in a penthouse spanning three floors near the mountains, an hour away in the big city. A massive portrait of his sister hung above the crackling fireplace. Her eyes seemed to hold answers I was desperate to uncover. I'd follow him after school like a shadow, piecing together the details. During the weekdays, he worked at the school, while weekends were reserved for parties and self-reflection.

By 5 a.m., he would start his self-care routine, a choreography of steps he seemed to follow religiously. Drew sought perpetual youth. Creams, elixirs, and serums lined the shelves of a mini refrigerator in his bathroom. He maintained a beauty standard of a high nose, wide eyes, and a sharply defined jawline, chewing gum constantly, convinced it would keep his jaw sharp.

The smell of expensive chlorine hit my nose as I stepped into the swim room. There was never enough air circulation in the humid space. Drew's office was located towards the back, near the laundry room. He arrived there every morning at seven sharp, reading books on how to become a great leader. He was on chapter eleven.

I hesitated before speaking. "Hello," I said. "I thought about what you said." I placed a batch of cookies on his desk.

His face softened a little. "What was it that you thought about?" he asked, his accent thick. He picked up a cookie and took a bite. Chocolate stuck to his teeth, and he licked his lips. Then his expression changed—his eyebrows drew together, and his lips pressed into a line.

The chlorine made my eyes water. "I want to know more about your sister," I said.

"Hmm," he murmured with a nod. He slid a small red stamped letter into his drawer with care. "How about we get to know each other better first?" he said, bowing slightly.

My voice carried with curiosity. "What made you want to work here?" I asked, sitting on a small bench in the corner, trying to match his energy.

He sat on top of his desk, towering over me. "The swim competitions," he said, running a hand through his silk short hair.

A glimpse of a tattoo peeked from under his sleeve, inked on his wrist—a small square inside a larger one. It caught my attention, unlike anything I had seen before. I wanted to ask about it but held back, not wanting to come off as intrusive.

His office was small but just the right size for him. A bookshelf stood against the wall, holding about three hundred

CHAPTER 4

unevenly stacked books.

"I wanted to get your permission to publish the article about your sister and the other students who passed away here," I said.

"Um, excuse me." He pressed a hand to his forehead, eyes closed. Then he smiled faintly. "I think that's a wonderful idea."

"What will I get in return?" I asked carefully, watching him.

He leaned forward, his eyes glinting with amusement. "Whatever you want."

I took a deep breath. "I want the bullying to stop."

"Okay," he said without hesitation.

The unexpected response surprised me. Relief washed over me, easing the burden I hadn't realized I was carrying.

I stood up, a little awkwardly. "That's all I wanted."

But something in my gut twisted. The way he leaned back in his chair, his eyes watching me, that half smile coming and going—it didn't feel right. He looked at me like he was sizing me up.

Since he became our swim coach, we'd won many games at Cherry Hill. Why? Was it his charm, the way he used his words? People said he was strict and mean. The swim team was second in the league. Moe, the captain, was removed for not following the team diet. Julie Forster replaced her. He was strict about what his team ate, drank, and did in their free time.

Practice was today for the football players. I pushed my way onto the field to take pictures for the team, assigned to capture moments for the yearbook. Nervousness stuck to me, like the mud on my shoes. Days passed, and I hoped they didn't care enough to hurt me again. The field grew muddier the further I went, the wet ground splashing onto my pants. I wiped at the stain, pressing harder than necessary.

"Yo Acelin!" Nick called out to me. "Meet me in the locker

room," he said, calmly.

A tall, stubby boy added, "We got a surprise just for you."

I fixed my glasses as they slipped down my face, wiping the last bit of dirt off my shoes. "Okay," I stuttered, feeling uneasy. A knot tightened in my stomach, and my palms grew sweaty. Something didn't feel right, but I forced myself to go anyway.

The hallway smelled strongly of sweat, the musty odor following me into the locker room. The lights flickered on and off, adding to the uneasy feeling. As I stepped further into the locker room, it was empty. The boys were nowhere to be found. I could hear the ice machine dropping new ice every few seconds. I set my camera down on the bench and called out, "Where's the surprise?" I walked into the shower area, the floor already wet, soaking my feet.

I flipped the light switch on, but water splashed onto my face from water guns aimed directly at me.

Some of the water guns were filled with red soda, the cherry flavor staining my skin. I covered my face, slipping on the wet floor. They threw water balloons filled with hot water at me, making me stumble back. My glasses flew off, and I scrambled to grab them, my hands shaking. They shoved my head down onto the wet floor. I gasped for air. "I can't breathe!" The laughter grew louder as I struggled, knees digging into my spine, pain shooting through me.

When the laughter finally faded, I laid there in shock. "Guys, chill, he's not moving," Nick said, kicking my feet. "Acelin, wake up!" I heard fear in his voice.

"Just leave him, come on," a voice mumbled as they pulled Nick away from me. I watched as they scattered, picking up their water guns and emptying them, acting like nothing had happened.

CHAPTER 4

The thing about getting bullied was that I've learned to coexist with it. It started as a one-time thing, then turned into an everyday reality. I've grown so accustomed to it, both mentally and physically, that it almost felt normal. The jabs, the taunts, the stares—they were just part of my routine now. It didn't even surprise me anymore. I'd built walls around myself to block it out, but deep down, I knew the bullying would always be there.

I felt a tug on my wet shirt. "Acelin... Acelin, can you hear me?" Drew stood over me, shining a flashlight in my face. The halls were empty. It was eight at night, and practice had ended at six. Mom wouldn't be home until eleven.

I made my way to Drew's office. He poured me a cup of hot tea, preferably lavender. The warmth of the cup chilled my fingers. I wrapped myself into a thin cotton cover that was used for his swim students after games. He also gave me his swim jacket that was heated inside. Shards of glass embedded into my hand. I didn't feel it from the adrenaline. The frames of my glasses were fragile, very cheap. The first time I thought I should wear them again just to be reminded not to.

"I'm glad I stayed behind," he said, reaching for my hand. He used a lamp to look for the shards using tweezers to pick them out. Looking at the blood made me feel nauseated and lightheaded. "I can't even image what they could've done to my little sister."

I closed my eyes as he extracted each shard. "Ouch!"

He looked at me seriously. "Don't be a baby about it," he said, wrapping my hand with a bandage. "Show no fear and never let pain take control."

"They still find a way to hurt me."

He threw the bloody tissues away. "Because you allow it."

I fidgeted with the bandage. "How do I not allow it?"

He smirked. "Getting revenge."

When I got home, I collapsed on the living room couch, lost in thought. My hand throbbed with pain, blood still seeping through the cotton bandage. It was the same hand that had been cut climbing through Lyra's window. To ease the pain, I searched Mom's room for painkillers to stop the aching.

A car pulled in the driveway. She was finally back home from work. I could hear her on the phone with one of her friends, talking about the gossip at work. I placed the pills back in her drawer. I sprinted down the stairs making my way inside the kitchen, tucking some of the pills inside of my pocket.

She pulled the phone away from her ear. "You okay?" She rubbed my back.

I sat at the table, exhausted. "Just had a long day."

"Your hand... what happened?"

I took a deep breath, pressing my lips together. I squeezed my eyes shut, trying to hide the pain. "I was cutting apple slices," I said.

"Make sure you put cream on it," she said, giving my forehead a quick kiss. "I made cookies, but don't eat too many. I added my detox mix to them, and it's no joke."

Detox? Revenge? Tomorrow's football game? The pieces fell in place. I thought about using the cookies for the football players and claim they're a gift from their coach.

I stayed up all night, mixing extra doses of her detox medicine into the dough. Tomorrow would be my moment—the night I'd finally show them who's better. I baked three fresh batches of chocolate chip cookies, imagining their humiliation when they'd have to rush to the bathrooms, only to find the doors locked. Luckily, I knew exactly where the janitors kept their keys.

CHAPTER 4

When school ended, I slipped into the locker room and left the cookies out, arranged neatly for tonight's game. Then, I hid in a bathroom stall, waiting for the perfect moment to lock both the bathroom and locker room doors.

Someone walked in, and soon I heard the water running. I held my breath, my heart pounding as I listened intently.
Drew was on the phone, he said, "I'm taking care of it now! I think I've got someone." My foot slipped off the toilet seat. He paused, then slowly approached my stall. Another student entered, and Drew quickly looked away, exiting the bathroom. I let out a relieved gasp, holding my chest.

Later, the fog hung thick in the late-night air as the game stretched into overtime, down by one point. The students cheered and I waited for the detox to take effect. Just one point, that's all our team needed to secure a spot among the top five football teams in town.

Jamie sprinted off the field, tossing his helmet aside, and rushed to the bathroom. He didn't deserve it, but what could I say—wrong time, wrong place? Another player vomited uncontrollably. The coaches jumped from the bench, trying to figure out what was happening. The game continued, though. Nick lunged at an opponent, only to suddenly clutch his stomach. He struggled to hold it in as he dashed off the field, pushing past the cheerleaders. He reached the bathroom, but the doors were still locked.

Burn Wood secured a win. They made the final touchdown. The crowd laughed as they whipped out their phones to record the players vomiting everywhere and clutching their stomach, racing towards the bathrooms. I sat on the bleachers, front row, laughing until I locked eyes with Drew. He stood alone, hands crossed, near the cheerleaders, leaning against a light pole. His head tilted, a slight smirk playing on his lips. My smile waned as he walked away.

When the game ended, the news spread quickly before sunrise about what had happened with the football players. Everyone was talking about it, but no one knew I was the one who had laced the cookies—except for Drew. It felt like he was always watching me, like a wildfire waiting to catch my next move. He seemed to know everything, almost as if he was waiting for me to slip up, ready to expose whatever I did next.

That night, rain tapped steadily against the windows, the sound helping me relax and draw. I laid back on my bed, my legs propped up on my pillow, with only the bedside lamp lighting the room as I sketched.

A soft knock broke the silence. I looked up to see Mom standing in the doorway, arms crossed. "Before you go to bed," she said quietly, "I just wanted to remind you, today was ya dad's birthday."

My heart tightened at the mention of Dad. What was I supposed to do with that? Call him and say, *"Hey, Dad, it's me, your son. Happy birthday!"* The thought felt ridiculous.

"I have nothing to say to him," I mumbled, turning away and pulling the covers over my head.

"Acelin," she persisted. "I'm trying to get you guys back on talking terms, okay."

"I hate him," I said before I even realized the words were out. I looked at her, hoping for some kind of answer, but she just stared back at me, blank and distant, like she didn't know what to say.

After a pause, she spoke. "He's your dad at the end of the day."

"A dad who's never here?" Maybe I was wrong. Maybe I shouldn't have said that. But I couldn't escape it. I was stuck

CHAPTER 4

with these feelings, and there was no way around them.

She sighed, shoulders dropping. "You need to get over it."

Get over it? The words hit me hard. How could I? After all the years he hurt me, all the birthdays he didn't call. All the times he walked away without a second thought. It wasn't fair.

She walked away before I could say anything. I wanted to run after her, make her understand my pain, but I couldn't.

Was I supposed to forgive him?

Chapter 5

"How are you?" Dr. John asked, writing in his notepad. His cursive was hard to read. The smell of mint candy hung in the air as he chewed it.

"I feel like I'm getting worse," I said, staring at the timer ticking down. The room was neat and modern, with white walls and no distractions. It felt strange being back here, like I'd failed myself.

I started coming to Dr. John in eighth grade, after I stabbed a kid in the hand with a pencil. He used to steal my glasses and hide them in his locker. Mom said my anger started long before that—when my dad left. But I don't believe it.

One time, I liked a girl. Maybe it wasn't love—more like jealousy. She had something I didn't: popularity. At summer camp, she got her first period. She bled through her white shorts and tried to hide it from everyone. So, on the last day of camp, I went into her bag, took those shorts, and threw them into the pool. Everyone saw them. Everyone knew they were hers. Back at school, she was bullied constantly. She started cutting herself, and I reported her to the school counselor. They

CHAPTER 5

sent her to some institute. I never saw her again after that. I never told Dr. John about it. Sometimes, I wish I could just get it off my chest.

Dr. John nodded but didn't say anything. He tapped his leg and watched me. "How do you feel about your Mom asking you to call your dad for his birthday?" he asked.

"Anger, regret..." I said, trailing off.

"Why regret?"

"Because it's my fault she had to leave him. He hated me, not her."

"Why do you think he hated you?"

I looked away, rubbing my hands together. "Maybe because I'm the rainbow child," I said. "He didn't love me enough to try again as a dad."

My grandma once told me Mom had a miscarriage years ago. Mom didn't know I knew. She was scared it would break me.

When our session was over, I waited in the lobby for Mom to pick me up. I sank into one of the stiff chairs, the kind that creaked with every shift, and picked up a magazine from the coffee table. The room was silent, except for the ticking clock and the soft clatter of the receptionist typing. I flipped through the glossy pages, barely registering the pictures of perfect homes and happy families. My mind still stuck on everything we'd talked about in the session.

Rain tapped on the windows, making the parking lot blurry. Cars passed by their headlights flashing across the room. I glanced at my phone to check the time.

A familiar voice reached my ears, one I recognized instantly. I walked over to her. "Lyra?" I said, tapping her shoulder.

She turned, surprised. "Acelin? What are you doing here?"

"Same reason you are," I said, trying to sound casual. "Unless ya want to tell me why you're here?"

She hesitated. "Uh—"

I realized I'd said too much and stuffed my hands in my pockets. "Sorry." I started awkwardly walking away.

"Bye?" she said, still frowning, like she couldn't figure me out.

The next morning at school, I stopped by the water fountain. As I bent down to drink, I noticed a boy at the far end of the hall. His eyes were locked on mine, holding a look that made my chest tighten. He wore loose black pants and a fitted navy shirt. I didn't recognize him; I'd never seen him before.

Later, near the lunchroom, I saw him again. He was following me, his head tilting as though waiting for me to react.

"Hello?" I called out, but the hallway stayed silent.

I ignored it and went to my locker. As I grabbed my books, I felt warmth on the back of my neck. I spun around quickly, almost losing my balance. "You scared me," I said, my heart racing.

The boy stepped back, his hands raised as if to show he meant no harm. "My name's Jackson. Do you remember me?" He pointed at his chest. "Jackson White? From middle school?" he added, "You know, with my curls and glasses?"

I blinked, then clapped my hands as recognition hit. "Oh, ya! You used to steal my food and take my art projects, pretending they were yours!" I grinned, the corners of my mouth pulling up a smile.

Jackson White was the boy I had heard people talking about in the library a while ago. His name seemed familiar, but I couldn't place it. He was someone I had always wondered about after all these years. We had grown up together as childhood friends, but high school pulled us in different directions. His dad was the one who sold Mom wine before she stopped drinking, but

CHAPTER 5

I never thought to ask about Jackson.

"I was the one with you when you passed out at the bar," he said.

"You were there?" I asked, closing my locker.

He shrugged, acting like it didn't matter. "Yeah," he said casually. "I hope you're doing better now, not addicted to whatever was in your drink." He chuckled. "And remember, never trust your drink around strangers," he winked.

"Huh?" I didn't think that was funny. It felt wrong for him to joke about something that hurt me. Plus, knowing he was from Burn Wood made things more complicated. Why would he come to Cherry Hill? "I'll see you around, Jackson."

The school bell rang. He stayed there, holding his book bag, watching me as I walked down the hallway. The connection we once had felt distant now, like a thread ready to snap. Trust wasn't something I gave away easily anymore. How did he know about the laced drink? I never saw him at the bar when I was with Moe, yet he was there, watching me.

The swim room was under construction, with diving boards stacked high, ready for the next game. The air smelled of burnt wood from the new sauna near the locker rooms. Warmth from the sauna mixed with the cool air coming through the old wooden windows. Fresh towels were neatly stacked on shelves, and the locker rooms had just been cleaned.

Drew's office door was open. On his desk was a piece of paper with strange symbols written in a language I didn't understand. New framed pictures of his sister decorated the walls. A cup of fresh coffee sat on the desk, showing Drew had just been there. I sat in his plush leather chair. My eyes were drawn to a half open drawer with a stack of *"get well soon"* cards. Who were they for?

Suddenly, a loud banging broke the silence, followed by a muffled scream. Someone was trapped under the pool cover, with only a little air left at the top. I froze, unsure of what to do. I rushed to the cover, trying to lift it, but it only moved mechanically. The banging grew weaker, like the person was drowning.

I dashed to the wall where the buttons for the cover were, but they were broken. None of them worked. I looked up and saw a sign: *"Do not use."*

My heart raced in sync with theirs. I couldn't let them die. Sweat beaded on my skin as adrenaline rushed through me. I tried the buttons again, finally hitting the right one to slowly open the pool cover. A girl floated on the surface, her hair trailing like seaweed. I grabbed the cleaning stick, pulling her towards me.

I laid her down on the cold stone floor, waiting for any sign of life. With trembling hands, I pressed on her chest, preparing to do CPR. She coughed before I could begin. Water spilled from her lips, and I breathed a sigh of relief.

Her eyes shot open, and she screamed, "Someone tried to kill me!"

"What?" I asked, stepping back to give her space. "Who?"

She choked, "It all started—" She pushed her wet hair behind her ears. "When I got these letters."

"What letters?" I asked, panic rising in my chest. "What do you mean?"

Her hands shook as she looked at me. "They're going to kill me." She pushed herself up and ran towards the exit doors.

I stormed through the doors of the library, feeling determined. I had been putting off the article, but it had to be rewritten and published. The truth about this school needed to get

CHAPTER 5

out. Students were falling apart, and the principal had no clue what to do next. He had to take responsibility for what was happening at Cherry Hill High. I knew the risks, but I was ready to expose the truth.

"Hey, I wanted to know about the publishing process," I said, standing over a girl with long black hair.

She looked up, her eyes wide. "Aren't you part of the book club?" she asked, typing on her computer.

Maxes Amaretto. She had a huge crush on me during our book club days. Her smile was perfect, she always smelled good, but she was annoyingly persistent. She cried when I didn't read her book recommendations, acting like it was the end of the world. One time, she made cookies for the club, and I threw mine away because they had nuts in them. She reported me to the principal for being *rude*.

"But—"

"But you stopped coming," she interrupted, tossing her long hair off her shoulder.

"And I'm glad I stopped," I replied, sarcastically. "Can you just help me publish this article, please?" I pulled the article from my bag, the title bold and clear: **"The Chilling Secrets of Cherry Hill High."**

Her eyes widened as she read the words. "This is about the school theories, the missing children, and the deaths that happened here?" She smiled at me. "Mr. Acelin, you're going to shock the town with this one." We both smirked at each other.

In lab class, I sat next to Moe. She twirled her hair while chewing on a piece of gum she'd been nursing since lunch. I stayed focused on the teacher's lecture, but I could feel her eyes on me.

The teacher noticed me zoning out. "You're late again, Mr.

Jones," she said, pulling me back to reality.

Moe leaned in, whispering, "You're late, just like in first hour," she teased. "Are you mad at me?" I didn't answer. "Acelin, please," she said, brushing her leg against mine. I hated when people touched me.

"What?" I snapped, losing my patience.

"Why aren't you talking to me?"

I shrugged, not looking at her.

The principal's voice came over the intercom, calling us to the auditorium. As the class filed out, I said to her, "You stole my homework and put your name on it. I got in trouble for it."

"I'm sorry," Moe said. "Jamie's been distracting me, and I needed a grade."

I rolled my eyes, running my hand through my hair. "Now we both failed the assignment."

We walked into the hallway. "I know," she said. "I won't do it again."

"Promise?" I asked.

"Promise." She locked her finger with mine.

The hallways were packed, students rushing to grab front row seats in the auditorium. Jackson and I bumped into each other as I scanned the crowd for Lyra, but she was nowhere in sight. Her scent lingered nearby, but it felt out of reach. I couldn't find her. Transitioning from class to assembly was always the worst—anything could happen, fights, hookups, students skipping.

I finally stepped into the auditorium.

As I walked, my foot hit a small teddy bear, one I recognized from a victim's locker. I picked it up, and my heart raced. Bloodstains dotted its fur. Panic ran through me, and everything seemed to blur. I glanced at Jackson. His face showed curiosity,

CHAPTER 5

unaware of what I saw. He watched me, copying my every movement, but slower. Without thinking, I threw the bear into the nearest trash bin.

When I looked up, I saw the same blonde-haired boy I always see in my dreams. He was facing me in the mirror, mirroring my every move. I closed my eyes, and suddenly, I was in a car at night. A girl sat next to me, and guilt flooded me as I watched her blow weed smoke in my face. Her scent was familiar, nostalgic.

I sat up quickly, gasping for air.

"Acelin, you okay?" Jackson asked, his voice reaching me.

"What's going on?" I looked around, noticing everyone was still focused on their tasks.

"Nick is just starting his speech."

"How long was I asleep?" I asked.

"Since you walked in. Are you sure you're, okay?"

I nodded, still feeling dizzy. "I'm fine."

"Good morning, everyone," Nick cleared his throat. "I am so proud of each and every one of you guys. The hard work and dedication you've poured into this school year have elevated you to some of the finest students here at Cherry Hill High." He cleared his throat again. "This year has been a roller coaster, marked by tragic losses. But let's honor their memory by spreading kindnesses, by living fully for those we've lost. Now, let's give a thunderous applause for the remarkable class of 2007!" The students erupted in cheers. Nick held his head high, medals glinting around his neck.

From the back corner, the football team unleashed playful dog noises, matching the volume of the cheers.

"I'll be back, I'm gonna go to the bathroom," I informed Jackson, rising from my seat.

Halfway to the auditorium doors, a burnt smell drifted through the cracks, and tendrils of smoke curled into the air. A chill crept over me—something was wrong. Just then, a janitor burst through the wide doors, locking eyes with me. His voice was hoarse as he shouted, "Fire in the school lab!" He bolted past me towards the exit, nearly knocking me off balance.

Nick, even the leader, was the first student to burst through the exit doors, shoving everyone out of his way. The fire alarm blared, and the sprinklers activated, drenching everyone in their seats. Their cries mixed into a loud, fearful noise. I stood there, frozen in the chaos, my mind racing. Students pushed past each other, scrambling for the exit.

Hesitant to leave, my eyes scanned the faces—searching for Lyra Barns. I stumbled over students and crashed to the ground. Footsteps pounded into my back as I instinctively shielded my head. Jackson's voice reached me, "Acelin!" he called, fading in and out like a distant radio signal. I strained to respond, my throat raw, but my body pinned to the floor.

His sweaty hands gripped me, yanking me upwards. The water coming down triggered memories—the locker room, Nick and his friends wielding water guns at me. The memory of being soaked, sprawled on the floor, resurfaced. I panicked as Jackson guided me towards the exit. I could tell by his concerned face that I officially lost my mind over a girl.

Outside, the sunlight hit my eyes. Cherry Hill, once dark and gloomy, was now bathed in warmth. Lyra stood by Nick, her hand wrapped around his wrist. She made him feel invincible, as if he'd scooped in to save her. He tenderly wiped away her tears, and she mouthed the words *"I love you"* to him. What a joke! He ran out the door without even trying to help anyone but himself.

CHAPTER 5

The ambulance arrived, sirens blaring, drowning out the frightened cries from the students. A paramedic took my hands, checking for injuries.

"Did you get hurt?" he asked, concerned.

"No, I'm fine," I replied, my voice hollow. My eyes remained fixed on Lyra and Nick.

"We heard it was a false alarm," the man said to his coworker. "The smoke came from the hot sauna. A student left the temperature too high."

The firefighters rushed past me, their heavy boots pounding to the ground. I wondered if it was just a mistake, a forgotten knob left on, or if there was more to it.

Which student tried to burn us alive?

6

Chapter 6

On Monday morning, I received the worst news of my life. Detectives pointed to a chair, silently motioning for me to sit. Fear gripped my chest, and I sat down, my mind racing of different things.

"They want to ask questions about some of the students you mentioned in your article. You might know things that others don't," Mom said, glancing at the detective for confirmation. "One of the students from your school actually reported your article to the police."

The man cleared his throat. "Have you heard anything unusual from any of the students? And can you provide the names of the people you got your information from?"

I was shocked to learn my article had made it into the newspaper. I hadn't expected it to get so much attention, especially since it started as just a few conspiracy theories written in my room. But this was a good start for me.

"Well," I swallowed hard, nervous under the detective's gaze. "I just hear the rumors around school."

"What made you want to write this story?" The detective

CHAPTER 6

raised his eyebrows.

"I'm a writer, sir," I replied, keeping my voice steady. "I worked on the article alone to bring peace to everyone who's lost someone at that school."

The detectives exchanged looks at each other. "Do you know anyone named Katie Waters?" he asked.

"No," I said, shaking my head as I looked at Mom, silently pleading for her to get me out of the conversation.

"I think it's best you guys leave," she said, her tone harsh. "My son doesn't seem to have any information."

The detective paused, caught off guard. "Alright... we'll be out of your hair. Have a good day, and here's my card," he said, slipping it into my jacket. But as he turned to go, he hesitated, one last look at me. There was something in his eyes; he suspected I knew more than I'd let on.

At midnight, the town was quiet, wrapped in silence. I stepped into the diner, comforted by the warm smell of freshly brewed coffee. A woman with tattoos peeking from her rolled up sleeves greeted me with a smile. "A regular coffee, please," I said. She nodded and poured the steaming drink into a mug. I took it black with a touch of honey and grabbed a blueberry muffin—the kind my dad used to bake when I was younger. He'd cut them into quarters, always saving a piece for the mice that scurried around our house.

The doors swung open, and a man stumbled in, barely able to stand. He leaned against the counter, slurring his request for a strawberry milkshake. The stale scent of cheap liquor clung to him, mixing with the aroma of coffee. He reminded me of my father, with shaky hands and hollow eyes. His greasy hair stuck to his forehead as he reached for the milkshake.

A mother with her baby stopped to pick up food. The baby's

cries filled the diner, making me want to leave. Yet, something about the man held my attention.

He suddenly began to sway, mumbling the words to a song I didn't recognize. His voice grew louder as he clumsily twirled, his feet shuffling to the song he could only hear. The other customers stared, some amused, others uncomfortable, but the man seemed lost in his own world, singing and dancing without a care.

Eventually, I slipped out, the cool night air brushing against my face as I stepped onto the sidewalk. My eyes scanned the parking rack where I had left my bike. Empty. My stomach sank—my bike was gone. Someone had taken it. I glanced around, but no one was in sight. The flicker of a streetlight broke the silence as I kept looking.

When I finally gave up, I called Moe. Our friendship was messy—one minute we were at odds, the next we were all each other had.

She stepped out of the car, smiling. "You're always in trouble, huh?"

I shrugged. "Feels like my worst nightmare."

She nodded. "I get it. I think I'll miss you and that bike." She looked at me. "It suits you."

"All you had to say was that I'm a weird nerd without a car, and—"

"What?" She laughed. "I didn't get a car until I made my first sale of those pills everyone's always after." She brushed small rocks from her smooth hands. "Let me cheer you up." She yanked me upwards. "Nick is throwing a party tonight, and we're totally going."

"Are ya crazy?" I ran my fingers through my hair. "I hate Nick."

CHAPTER 6

"It'll be fun. I don't want you to be sad tonight." She gave me puppy eyes. I couldn't say no to her.

I exhaled. "If I go to this party, I won't be touching a drop of alcohol."

After a forty-minute drive, we arrived at a house by the lake. Shouts and laughter echoed, drawing me towards the backyard. I followed the noise down a path lit by dim, warm lights, and spotted a girl and her friends. Their voices were loud with the edge of alcohol. Two guys struggled to keep her up, teetering as they moved. Her brown hair spilled over her face, her red lipstick smudged, and she wore a crop top with ripped sheer leggings. She brushed past me with a smirk.

I kept moving, nearly stumbling over the thick sand, when something else grabbed my attention. Nick burst out of the house, looking desperate, as Lyra chased after him.

Lyra's voice cut through the music filled with frustration. "I feel like I'm babysitting you!" She stormed across the lawn, her drink sloshing over her legs.

Nick tried to grab her hands to calm her. "I didn't invite her! I don't even know who she is," he said, his voice low but serious. "Let's just forget about it, okay?"

Lyra yanked her hands free and shoved him back, making him stumble. "I saw her hug you!"

"A hug?" His tone turned defensive, his face partially lit by the glow of string lights hanging from the trees. "You're overreacting."

"So... it's fine to flirt with other girls?" Her eyes flashed, anger sharpening her features as other people tried to pretend they weren't listening.

He smirked, rolling his eyes. "You're blowing this way out of proportion. It's not that serious."

"Pathetic," she said. "She looked at you like she knew you."

He crossed his arms, stepping back, his jaw tight. "If you want to break up, fine." He walked off back inside.

Quietly, I stepped up behind her, hearing the sniffles from her nose. "You okay?" I asked.

"Acelin?" She wiped her tears, using her sleeve to stem her runny nose.

"Crazy story on how I got here."

She settled onto a beach chair, fingers fumbling through her hair. She decided to tidy herself up using a small pocket mirror from her purse. She could barely keep her eyes open from too much liquor.

The mirror dropped from her hands, sinking into the sand. I picked it up, leaning on her. I felt the warmth of her breath on my lips. The smell of beer reminded me of her intoxication. Should I had kissed her? I hesitated. I didn't want it to be a mistake. I wanted it to mean something—to the both of us.

A loud crash interrupted us. Someone fell onto a table full of beer cans. Composing myself, just looking into her eyes I said, "I'll be in the house," I stuttered over my words. She remained silent, her eyes followed my every movement.

Moe and I met up at the beer pong table, and I threw down a challenge: whoever took the most shots by the end of the night would win, and the loser would face a dare.

I'd already knocked back five shots, but Moe hadn't touched her drink. She raised an eyebrow. "What happened to not drinking?"

I leaned in close, speaking just above the noise. "What's wrong, afraid you're going to lose?"

Moe grabbed my arm and pulled me to the center of the dance floor. She swayed on me, her back pressed against mine,

CHAPTER 6

and I wrapped my hands around her waist, pulling her closer. Suddenly, another girl slid between us, spinning me away from Moe. Her hands framed my face, and before I could react, she leaned in and kissed me. I didn't resist; I let it happen, savoring the moment.

Over the music, I shouted, "What's ya name?"

She smiled, her voice barely heard over the music. "Mandy."

Mandy led me outside, where I spotted Moe deep in a conversation with a guy wearing a Burn Wood jacket. Against the unspoken rules of our school, she was openly flirting with someone from the rival side of town. Mandy leaned in, kissed my cheek, and then hopped onto the guy's motorcycle. "Bye, Acelin," she called back, her smile lingering as they sped off. I wiped away her lip gloss, still feeling its trace on my skin.

"That girl was my first kiss," I muttered to Moe. "And it was supposed to be with Lyra, only Lyra Barns!"

Moe laughed, her drink spilling over the rim of her cup. Raindrops began to fall, and I turned to hurry towards Moe's car. But then I froze.

"Lyra!" I shouted. Our eyes locked. Nick trailed behind her, his smirk uneven.

Lyra swayed, barely able to keep her balance from the alcohol. "Worry about yourself!" She rolled her eyes, brushing past me.

I followed, determined to talk to her. "I just want to make sure you get home safe."

"Nick is taking me home. Just leave, okay?" she whispered as Nick came up beside her.

Nick's hand landed hard on my shoulder, giving it a shove before wrapping his arm around Lyra possessively. "Look who finally crawled out of the house," he sneered. "I'm taking my girl home. Got a problem with that?" His arm tightened around her shoulders.

"Nah," I said quickly. "Just wanted to make sure she had a ride—"

"You don't think I can handle that?" Nick leaned in close, his breath hot against my ear.

"Acelin, let's go!" Moe called from her car, her fingers twirling through her hair.

I smirked. "You two have a good night," I said with sarcasm, stepping away from them.

The next morning, I woke up to a glass of ginger ale and slices of bread neatly arranged on the living room table. It was a remedy for hangovers, a little ritual that reminded me of Mom—she'd do the same after a long night out. She left it there for me.

The scalding shower washed the sweat from my hair and scrubbed away last night's beer stains. Afterward, I headed into the kitchen, where I could hear voices through the open window. Nick's dad was outside, parked in a massive camper—another camping trip with Mom, which meant cozy cabins and daily rounds of golf.

She stood by the front door, picking up her bags. "Are you going to help, or what?"

I walked over, water dripping from my hair, a towel around my waist. "How long will you be gone?"

"Maybe a week," she said, glancing at me. "And shouldn't ya be at school?"

I hesitated. "I don't have a bike anymore. Some kids trashed it."

She paused, looking at me with concern. "Why didn't you tell me? How long have you been skipping?"

"Just today. I'll figure it out," I muttered, avoiding her eyes.

CHAPTER 6

She sighed, setting her bags down. "Oh, that reminds me. Your dad wants you to have his motorcycle. He was clearing out the garage and thought you could use it. Surprising, huh?"

I blinked. "A motorcycle?"

She rubbed her temple. "Yeah," she said. "I know you two don't talk much, but maybe this could help. Maybe it's his way of trying?" She kissed my forehead, her touch warm. "I'll see you in a few days."

An hour after waiting for the motorcycle to arrive, a truck rumbled to a stop in front of me. I waited as the driver stepped out—a woman handed me papers to sign. "Sign here," she grumbled, pointing to a dotted line. I took the pen, my name scrawling across the paper, leaving a small smudge.

The black motorcycle had yellow stripes along the front and back. An envelope was attached to the side. Inside, there was a note from my dad: *"My son, I'm giving you this to keep safe and to continue with my so—"* but the rain had smudged the rest. Anger burned in me as I crumpled the note and threw it away. Hearing him call me his son hurt, and for a moment, I thought about leaving the bike behind.

* * *

As I pulled into the school parking lot, I turned off the engine and slipped off my helmet. I ran a hand through my hair, trying to tame it, and slung my bag over one shoulder.

Students standing by the lockers had gone silent, their conversations put on hold. They stared at me like I was something out of place. I kept my face neutral, refusing to let their attention get to me.

Then I spotted Nick. He was leaning against the wall, but something in his posture had shifted. His eyes locked onto the bike through the window, his jaw tightening. He recognized it. He looked between the bike and me, and it made me feel weird.

I headed straight for the art room. It was empty, just the way I liked it. The quiet, the smell of paint—it felt like a safe place. Today's assignment was to draw a memory from our childhoods. On Fridays in art class were always intense; our teacher believed in using art as therapy. Students often walked out with tears or slammed their sketchbooks shut in frustration. For me, though, it was peaceful. Watching emotions pour out onto paper fascinated me.

I set up my sketchpad, but then Moe appeared at the door. She pressed her lips against the glass, leaving kiss marks smeared on the window. I tried to ignore her, but she wouldn't give up. Finally, I got up and opened the door.

She walked in, her book bag stuffed and bulging with work. Moe always had her ways—paying off the nerds in the library to do her assignments. But today, they were on a field trip, building talking toys or something.

"How did ya find me?" I asked, leaning against the door frame.

Her lips curled into a smile. "Because I—"

"Stalking me again?" I interrupted, raising an eyebrow.

"You wish," she shot back. Her grin widened. "I think you know what I'm here for."

I sighed and sat back down on the stool. "And what might that be?"

She dropped her bag on the desk beside me, her eyes locking onto mine. "Finish my work," she said, her voice all sweet.

I huffed. "I'll help, but only if you owe me my dare."

CHAPTER 6

Moe stepped closer to me. "A dare?" she asked, her voice teasing.

"Yes," I replied, my confidence fading. "You never finished ya drink at the party."

Her eyes narrowed, amusement dancing in them. "What kind of dare are we talking about?"

I hesitated, my thoughts scrambling for the right words. "I dare you," I said finally, my voice dropping, "to make out with Jamie."

Her brows furrowed. "Jamie? Why Jamie?"

I shrugged, avoiding her eyes. "Because," I said, my heart racing, "Why not?"

Moe studied me for a moment. Then, a smile came. "Fine," she replied simply, and with that, the conversation was settled.

When school let out, Moe didn't waste any time. She had a mission, and that mission was Jamie. She found him on his way to practice, his bag slung over one shoulder and a folded newspaper in his hand. He was scanning the headline: **Another Murder Mystery... A Student from Cherry Hill High Found Dead.**

Moe sat on a bench near the field, her legs crossed. She didn't even try to hide her intentions. When Jamie finally passed by, she rose to meet him.

"Moe?" he said, startled. His brows furrowed, his voice already impatient. "What do you want? I've got practice."

"Relax," she said, brushing off his tone like it was nothing. "Follow me."

He glanced at the paper in his hand, then back at her. "Listen... I've been clean, and I plan to stay that way."

Jamie had been off drugs for weeks, trying to get his life back together. They slowed him down, messed with his memory, and ruined too much he had going on for himself. But today, he felt himself slipping. What did he really have to lose?

She stepped closer, her tone softening just enough to sound inviting. "Oh, Jamie, you really think that's what this is about?" She held his hand, her smile as innocent as she played to be.

Moe was a girl he'd always cared about, but never someone he could picture as a girlfriend. She was wild, unpredictable, and impossible to pin down. She wasn't the settling down type, yet there was something about her that always pulled him in.

He rolled his eyes but didn't pull away. "Parking lot or locker room?"

"Parking lot," she said without hesitation. "Actually, the locker room!"

Jamie sighed, glancing towards the field where his teammates were waiting. "Can't this wait until after practice?"

"Fine."

By the time practice ended, Moe was still there. She sat on the bleachers, her eyes fixed on Jamie the entire time, her phone in hand like she was mentally recording every detail. When practice finally wrapped up, Jamie approached her, his face flushed from running drills.

He casually draped his arm over Moe's shoulders.

Nick's expression shifted as his eyes went to Moe. He motioned Jamie to come closer to him. "Seriously, Jamie? Moe?"

Jamie shrugged. "Relax. No one's gonna find out about us."

Nick raised an eyebrow, unimpressed. "Don't disappoint me," he smirked. "Let me know if it's tight or loose," he winked with a smile.

Jamie punched him lightly on the shoulder, grinning. "I'll tell you about it later." He walked back to Moe, his smile growing wider.

CHAPTER 6

Later, Moe showed me the video—a recording of the two of them. It wasn't just a kiss or playful teasing; she'd crossed a line, one I didn't think she would.

My stomach churned as I watched the clip on her phone. She'd done it—she'd gone through with the dare. But instead of feeling nonchalant, I felt a wave of something I couldn't quite name. Disgust? Jealousy? Guilt? Maybe all of it at once.

"Moe," I said, my voice tight. "I dared you to kiss him, not... all that."

She shrugged like it was no big deal. "You never said I couldn't have a little fun with it."

I sat up straight, trying to keep my frustration in check. She moved closer, wrapping her arms around me. "Wait... are you jealous?" she asked.

Our eyes met, and I stood quickly from the bed. "No!"

"Relax, you're still my favorite, Acelin."

Before I could react, she took my hand and pulled me back to sit. I froze, not knowing what to do or say. Her breath was warm against mine. My shirt was already off, and now she was wearing it. We called ourselves *"just friends"* but at that moment, it didn't feel like it.

She didn't kiss me. She didn't even cross that line. To her, I wasn't someone to love—I was someone to control, someone to boost her ego.

Chapter 7

Mom invited Turner over for dinner—Nick's father. I invited Jackson, the gentleman with flowers for my Mom. He believed showing up empty handed was rude.

The doorbell rang, and Mom rushed to answer it. I heard a voice that felt all too familiar. "Hey," Nick's voice echoed through the kitchen. My heart skipped a beat. I almost dropped the plates in my hands.

Jackson pulled me aside, his expression tense. "I think I got you into some trouble," he said, his frown deepening.

"What do ya mean?"

"Nick's here. I didn't know he would be," Jackson explained.

"Me neither. But what's the problem?" I asked.

"Bro, I invited Lyra too. She told me you didn't reply to her texts."

"I didn't reply for a reason!" I set the plates down on the counter, the tension in my chest growing.

When Lyra arrived, she slipped through my window, landing softly on the floor. My heart raced as I quickly closed the

CHAPTER 7

window behind her. Mom and Nick were so caught up in their conversation that they didn't notice a thing coming from upstairs.

"Get in the closet," I whispered, motioning towards it. "Just until Jackson comes up." Lyra hesitated for a moment, her eyes scanning the room, but then she slipped inside, pulling the door shut just enough to hide.

I took a deep breath and tried to act normal, before walking back into the kitchen.

Nick grinned as he settled into his seat. "So, this is where my dad hangs out at," he said, eyeing the room. "I should stop by more often. I can hang with Acelin." He took a bite of food, glancing at me.

I leaned towards Jackson. "Can you keep Lyra company in my room?" I whispered.

"Yup," he whispered back.

Meanwhile, Mom rambled on about needing more bug spray for their golfing trips. She always bought the same kind, the one I was allergic to. I never told her; she liked the idea of figuring it out herself, without asking her friends for bug spray recommendations.

Nick's phone buzzed non-stop.

"You gonna answer that?" I nudged him, helping myself to more corn.

He hesitated. "Yeah, it's probably my girlfriend. I'm seeing her later."

It wasn't Lyra who called—it was Jamie, asking Nick if I was with him.

"Do you remember when you *borrowed* my sketchbook from art class, Nick? My grade dropped because of that," I teased, saying it loud enough for Turner to hear.

Nick looked surprised. "I didn't do that," he protested, turning to his dad for backup.

Turner chuckled. "Nick's always been like that. He took Tommy's homework once and forgot to return it."

Nick shrugged it off. "Tommy was the smartest kid before Acelin was even known."

Mom cut in, "How are the piano lessons going, Nick?"

"Piano lessons?" he said, suddenly embarrassed.

I couldn't resist. "You're taking piano? Does the football team know?"

"Shut up, Acelin!" Nick snapped.

I had no idea who I was seeing more: Nick or his dad. I really hoped Mom wouldn't marry Turner. I'd be crushed if they did. The thought of Nick as my stepbrother was something I couldn't bear.

I stepped away from the table, Nick and Turner caught up in a debate about his secret piano lessons. I grabbed a plate of corn and mashed potatoes for Lyra, heading to my room.

I opened the window for fresh air. The sound of crickets filled the night; the scent of food lingered in the air. It was peaceful—especially with Lyra in my room. She admired the drawings I had done, even picking up my ninth-grade poetry book.

She traced the sketch I'd drawn on my desk. "Swans," she said, her fingers running across the drawing.

"You like them?" I asked.

"They're beautiful," she said. "Your room is incredible."

I smiled, feeling a bit nervous, but her presence made everything seem right. "Thanks. I spend a lot of time here."

She tucked her hair behind her ears and looked through the telescope by my window. "What else is interesting about you?"

CHAPTER 7

I hesitated, unsure. "I used to fence in freshman year."

"And the trophies?" she asked, intrigued.

"Down in the basement," I replied.

Fencing had been my escape. It was an easy way to forget everything else. Watching my Mom blend in with the other parents, handing out protein bars and snacks, made me feel like we belonged in Cherry Hill.

Lyra's attention shifted to the record player on my desk. She pulled out a few albums, excited to see the music I had collected.

"Go ahead, play something," I encouraged.

She found "Bennie and the Jets" by Elton John, and before I knew it, she was singing along with a lotion bottle as her microphone. I watched from the bed, hands in my pockets, amused.

Downstairs, the sound of music caught their attention. "Is that music?" Mom asked.

Jackson jumped in. "Uh, that's just Acelin's TV. I'll tell him to turn it down," he said, standing up.

"I'll check too," Nick said, grabbing Jackson's arm to stop him.

Jackson pulled away quickly. "No need. Acelin likes his privacy."

Back in my room, Lyra fell onto me, her hands resting on my shoulders. She leaned closer, her lips kissed a trail up my neck, leaving a warm feeling. My hand slid under her shirt, but we stopped there, both holding back. We didn't kiss.

A knock at the door pulled us back to reality. "They're leaving!" Jackson called.

Lyra's carefree attitude, hiding the fact that she wasn't single, unsettled me. If we ever became something real, would she cheat on me? Would she find someone else? Still, it felt good to be her secret.

I managed a polite nod as everyone got ready to leave. "Thanks for coming," I said, shooting Nick a brief look.

Turner clapped a hand on my shoulder. "Your Mom's got news she's been keeping from you, boy."

Mom interrupted before I could ask. "I wanted to surprise you, Acelin," she said, her voice full of excitement.

"What's the surprise?" I asked.

With a casual shrug, she revealed, "I won a golfing contest… seven thousand dollars. I'm planning our next camping trip as well."

Jackson saw an opportunity. "Could I go?"

Nick jumped in. "Lyra and I will be there too," he added, slapping me playfully on the back of the neck.

"We've got a cabin. Everyone can come," Turner said. "And then it's off to the golfing contest."

The idea of sharing a cabin with everyone didn't excite me. Jackson being there might make it bearable, but with Nick around, it would complicate things with Lyra and me.

That night, Jackson crashed on the couch while Lyra left quietly. I stayed up late, listening to podcasts about serial killers, trying to distract myself.

When I finally went downstairs, I saw Jackson in the living room with a girl sitting close to him—Mandy from Nick's party. The girl I'd kissed. She was wearing his oversize football shirt and looked surprised when our eyes met.

Jackson noticed me. "Acelin, meet Mandy Johnson," he said casually.

I kept my face calm, ignoring the twist in my stomach. "Hey," I said, acting like I didn't recognize her.

Mandy studied me for a moment. "Acelin, right? From the party?" her voice was raspy.

CHAPTER 7

I glanced at Jackson, who was watching me with an unreadable look. "Party?" I said, forcing a small smile like I didn't remember.

Jackson let out a quiet laugh and leaned back. Mandy looked between us like she was trying to figure something out but then shrugged. "Maybe I got you mixed up with some else," she said, brushing it off.

Jackson didn't say anything, but the way he looked at me made it clear he wasn't fooled.

I eventually drifted off to sleep but was quickly jolted awake by Jackson's urgent knocking on my door. His knocks were fast and hard, each one louder than the last.

I rubbed my eyes and got out of bed. When I opened the door, Jackson was standing there, looking worried.

"Acelin, your Mom knows," he said, glancing down the hallway before looking back at me.

Downstairs, Mom confronted me. "Is there something you need to tell me, or should I call that friend you're always arguing with?"

My heart raced. "What do you mean? There's nothing," I said, looking at Jackson for help, but he avoided my gaze.

"Why is Nick saying you were on drugs at some bar and that you fought with him?"

"Why he talkin bout me?" I shot back.

"Just tell me what happened!" Mom demanded.

Jackson finally spoke up. "Nick started that fight first. He's been causing trouble for Acelin his whole life."

I couldn't help but ask, "Isn't it weird you're dating Nick's dad, even though he's married?"

Jackson agreed, and we both looked at Mom for answers.

She glared at us. "That's none of your business!"

I could feel the anger building, but arguing wouldn't help. I knew trying to change the subject wouldn't work either. "I'm sorry, it was months ago. I'm fine now," I said, my voice heavy with the lie.

"Is that when you got the bruises?" she pressed.

"Ya," I said, my voice quiet. "But things are better with Nick now." Jackson's expression shifted—he was stunned by my lie.

"Does Nick still hurt you?" she asked, her voice filled with concern.

"No," I lied, feeling defeated. Jackson looked at me, disappointment clear on his face. He didn't say anything, but the silence between us spoke volumes.

I decided tonight was the night to steal his flash drive as revenge. But not just any flash drive—this one had something important on it, something that could ruin him. Nick was cleaning up after his party, celebrating his presentation speech about getting students to join a sport. All I had to do was grab the flash drive and erase his speech. He'd be left embarrassed, speechless in front of the whole school. It was the perfect plan.

I headed upstairs to find Nick's room. The hallway had five closed doors. I opened one and stepped in, but it wasn't Nick's room—it was his dad's office.

The room was filled with trophies in a glass case, secured with a key code lock. On the desk, there were photos. The picture of Nick and his mom was placed behind a newer one of Nick and my Mom. Seeing it made my stomach drop.

I left the office and found Nick's room. The walls were covered with football posters, car pictures, and even an ad for his dad's club, *The Phoenix*. There was a photo of Tommy in his football uniform next to a picture of Lyra. That surprised me. I didn't think he liked her enough to keep her picture up.

CHAPTER 7

His room was cleaner than I expected, not like how he usually was. On his desk, I spotted the flash drive, bright red, sitting on top of his laptop. Without thinking, I slipped it into my pocket.

Just as I was about to text Jackson, my phone buzzed. His message read: *"Hide ASAP, they're coming up!"*

Panic hit me as I scrambled around, looking for a place to hide. I spotted the closet and quickly ducked inside, pulling the door shut just as I heard footsteps approaching.

I crouched behind a pile of clothes shoved into the corner of Nick's closet. It was cramped, but there was just enough space to stay hidden. I stayed close to the door, peeking through a small gap.

There she was, Lyra Barns, sitting on Nick's bed, her eyes fixed on him like he was the most important thing in her world. But her expression didn't match. She looked more upset than happy, like being with him was the last place she wanted to be.

"Why can't you get hard for me anymore?" she said. "This has been the third time."

"Get over yourself, I just had a long day." Nick pulled up his pants.

"Who else are you seeing?" she asked. "Are you cheating or something again?"

"Stop asking me dumb question—" He froze, his eyes locked to the dresser. His face went pale. "Wait... where's the flash drive?"

"What are you talking about?"

He dropped to his knees, frantically scanning the floor as if the flash drive had magically fallen there. "Lyra, if someone finds it... if this gets out... I'm done."

Lyra's expression shifted to concern. "Done? What do you mean?"

He looked up at her, trying to stay calm. "Just... help me look for it, okay?" he said, nicely.

"I don't care about a fucking flash drive. Can we just fuck already?" Lyra fell back on the bed.

Nick barely spared her a glance, his movements becoming more frantic. "You wouldn't get it. If someone has it... I'm done. My life will be over."

I texted Jackson repeatedly, my fingers flying over the screen. *"Help me get the hell out of this house."* Panic tightened my chest as I moved further back into the closet, trying to stay as silent as possible.

As I shifted back, my hand hit something hard. It was a motorcycle helmet. Not just any helmet. It looked identical to my motorcycle at home. That helmet was part of a rare set, nearly impossible to find. How the hell did Nick have one?

I stared at it, my mind racing, piecing things together. Something about this didn't sit right. I remembered the way he looked when he first saw my motorcycle. My breath hitched as Nick's muffled voice grew louder, his frantic search intensifying.

The doorbell rang, echoing through the house.

Jackson stood outside, pacing back and forth, unsure of what to do. He was trying his best to keep Nick distracted, making sure he wouldn't catch me sneaking around. For a second, I thought I was going to get caught again and ended up beaten. But Jackson's plan worked. He managed to get Nick to let him in, then pushed his way down to the basement. That gave me just enough time to slip out of the house unnoticed. Of course, Lyra followed them, but it didn't matter. I had the flash drive. It was the best plan I'd ever come up with. The one that changed everything.

CHAPTER 7

* * *

The hallways were packed with students, all shoving and weaving their way towards the auditorium doors. It was chaos. Backpacks were being snatched, and a few unlucky nerds were having their lunch money taken. This was the perfect time for the people who sold condoms to make money.

Inside the auditorium, we waited ten minutes for Nick to start his speech. Behind the stage, he paced back and forth. I could see the curtains moving in the breeze. He looked unprepared.

Finally, he stepped up to the podium. He gripped the edges with shaky hands, struggling to find the right words to say.

"Good morning, students of Cherry Hill High," Nick began, his voice shaking slightly. "I've been waiting for this day all year, ever since I noticed a lack of participation in sports this season. I'm going to speak from the heart, and I hope you'll listen." He took a breath. "If you join a sport, we will provide extra safety for students who don't feel safe after school, starting today. So, join a sport, do it for the ones we've lost here. Do it for them," he said with no excitement.

He finished his speech with a forced smile and bumped into the principal as he rushed off the stage. I stood there, confused, watching him. Had I grabbed the right flash drive? It felt too easy—too smooth for him to say.

Walking into the gym, a tall coach with an intimidating presence caught my attention. She had always been a bit scary, her eyes low like she knew things others didn't. "Acelin Jones?" she asked.

I looked up, surprised. "Yes?"

"Why did you stop coming to practice?"

I shifted uncomfortably. "I was busy with schoolwork," I mumbled, wanting to move on and not talk about why I quit.

She grinned. "If you think about it again... you don't need to sign up. Just come to us after school, and we'll talk more. Can't wait to play with you this season!" I nodded as she brushed past me.

I walked over to the concession stand, grabbing a steaming cup of coffee and a muffin, the kind that tasted like the ones at the diner. I glanced at the kids signing up at the sports tables, one by one, committing to stay after school. They were all signing their lives away, knowing the risks but willing to ignore them. The promise of extra security felt hollow—there were barely enough staff to keep track of us, let alone protect us.

Crumbs from the muffin fell onto my white shirt, leaving a stain. I wiped at it with napkins, but all I did was smear it, making it worse. I threw everything away, but then something caught my eye.

Remy Glen, the girl who had been in the picture with Nick at a party—the one he had cheated on Lyra with. She looked even more beautiful now. Her hair had brown and blonde highlights, and her almond shaped eyes matched her face perfectly. Her figure was slim, more toned than when I'd last seen her.

I tried to look away, but our eyes met. From the corner of my eye, I saw her walking towards me. I didn't want to seem scared, but I wasn't sure how to handle talking to her.

"My coach wanted me to talk to you about fencing. I'm Remy, what's your name?" She extended her hand.

I stumbled over my words. "Ya... I know how things work." Ignoring her hand, I turned to walk away.

She quickly stepped in front of me, blocking my path. "Okay, meanie! See you at practice?"

CHAPTER 7

"No," I replied curtly, walking off without another glance.

Outside, Lyra ran up to me. We hadn't been on good terms since she agreed to go on the camping trip with Nick. I'd stopped answering her calls again.

"Acelin! Is everything good between us?" She picked at her nails.

"Sure," I said, adjusting my helmet.

"I'm sorry. I should've said no."

"Good. Now I have to listen to him fucking you in the next room." I started up my motorcycle.

She rolled her eyes. "Can you not leave? I want to talk." She grabbed the bike handles.

I nodded, my stomach sinking in as I turned off the bike. "Nick doesn't like ya," I shrugged my shoulders.

At that moment, Remy walked up to us, holding her gym bag and looking as calm as ever. I wasn't sure what she was going to say, but I had a feeling it wasn't going to be good.

"What are you two talking about?" Remy asked, looking between Lyra and me with a raised eyebrow.

I hesitated, but didn't want to hide anything. "About how Lyra agreed to go camping with me and her boyfriend, knowing I like her."

Lyra immediately snapped back, her voice defensive. "I didn't know he would invite me, okay!"

I turned to Remy, trying to keep things light. "Well, maybe Remy should come to keep me company?"

The silence stretched between us, both of us staring at Lyra. She gave a small, heated smile. "Okay," she said, clearly trying to sound like she didn't care.

"Great!" I replied, trying to hide the mix of emotions flooding through me.

I glanced at Remy, trying to understand why she'd agreed to come with a stranger. We didn't know each other well, so why had she said yes?

Ever since Remy's last boyfriend, she seemed to have changed into a slut. He was close with Johnny and the football team over in Burn Wood. After their breakup, her nudes were leaked all over school. At first, people shamed her, but then they started to admire her, even wanting to be her friend.

Remy had been a child model and was always known for her looks. She was on track to be in a Playboy magazine until her dad stepped in when he got out of jail. He pulled her away from all the drama her mom had gotten her into. After that, Remy started dressing provocatively, often getting suspended for it. She had a reputation for loving older men who bought her beers and gave her money. So, I figured she said yes because she was easy.

After grabbing a burger, I stayed after school to check out the fencing practice. I was surprised to see a lot of popular students playing this year. Remy was already geared up and sparring with someone. The coach called me over. "Let's get you suited up," she said.

I got dressed in the gear and stepped onto the floor. Remy was the person I was facing since she had won her match. I swallowed hard, feeling nervous. Everyone stopped to watch. I took my stance, my hands sweaty, trying not to embarrass myself. I started slow, but Remy got aggressive, throwing me off. I told myself not to let a girl beat me in front of everyone, especially the coaches who'd invited me to join the team again.

Points started going in my favor. I noticed Remy was getting tired, her breathing heavy. It was the perfect time to strike. I used the foil technique to hit her torso and legs. I won.

CHAPTER 7

Everyone seemed impressed. I didn't really expect to win, but I smiled and took off my mask, slicking my sweat drenched hair back.

"Welcome to the team," Remy said, walking off with an attitude. My smile faded as I could tell she was jealous; she'd never lost to anyone in practice before.

Chapter 8

On a chilly Monday morning, whispers spread like wildfire throughout town about Katie Waters. She was an academic star, with a bright future ahead of her, but now she is gone.

The night before, Jackson and Frances, a girl he'd recently started talking to, had gone down to the Frosty River. They found Katie's body, pale and lifeless, covered in deep stab wounds. The same girl I once saved in the school swim room from drowning. The same girl the detectives had questioned me about was gone.

Jackson stood outside talking with the police. His palms were sweaty, and he fidgeted with the hem of his shirt, avoiding eye contact. He felt a knot tighten in his stomach with every question the officer asked. His voice stayed calm, trembling with anxiety and confusion on what he saw that night. He glanced nervously at the officer's face, feeling a wave of fear hit him. The gloom outside didn't help the edge he was feeling.

Katie's locker became a shrine overnight, adorned with roses and somber tributes bidding her eternal peace. The town was

CHAPTER 8

shattered as local law enforcement took the stand, prompting an abrupt school day.

In the wake of the tragedy, new faces joined the staff at the school. Katie's parents launched a legal battle against the school, seeking justice for their daughter. But the school tends to get away with the deaths, again and again.

Peering out my window, I caught sight of a red car, unmistakably belonging to Jackson's father. It had been years since our paths crossed.

To my surprise, he was here to visit Mom and me. Time had changed him. His hair, once short, now fell in long locks. I remembered the nights spent in his basement, tasting wines. The walls were lined with bottles, each with its own story. He liked the darker wines, saying they made him feel powerful. Over time, his reputation grew, and the townspeople, once unsure, became regulars for buying his wine.

He wore a black suit with a pink tie, his polished black shoes reflecting his attire. He carried a bag, featuring the pink logo of his wine business. He set the heavy bottle of wine on the kitchen table; he seemed unaware of my Mom's changed habits—her days of wine tasting were behind her.

"Acelin?" he said, his surprise loud. "My, how you've shot up! You're the spitting image of your dad, and your—"

"Jim! What a pleasant surprise. Is that wine for me?" Mom interrupted before he could finish.

"Yes, indeed," he replied, his smile revealing his dimples.

Jim and Jackson's relationship was always the one I wanted with my father. Jim always used to bake cookies for Jackson and me. On Halloween, Jim would dress into costumes and act out as that character. When Christmas came, he would leave us gifts all around the house for us to find them. I always found the most gifts.

Jim looked back at me. "How tall have you grown?" he said.

"6'1," I answered.

"Nearly as tall as me!" He smiled again. "I was hoping Jackson might be here with you. We had a major fight at home about his mother. She's battling Alzheimer's, so it's been tough for him."

Mom cast a glance my way. "Oh... I'm not sure where he could be."

I echoed her sentiment. "Yeah, sorry, Jim. But we'll let you know if he turns up."

Jim's gaze wandered the kitchen, and he turned into a stillness, hoping to catch a hint of movement from upstairs.

"I'll show you out, and thank you for the wine," Mom offered.

His gaze shifted between Mom and me, a hint of suspicion in his eyes. "Sure," he said as he adjusted his belt for comfort. I gave Mom a subtle nod, silently offering to escort him out myself.

His voice dropped to a low, serious tone. "I'm aware he's here. And just so you know, I'm not just looking for Jackson out of concern. He owes me money." His smirk was big. "Enjoy your day, and don't forget to leave a good review on my wine site," he added, before slipping into his new vehicle.

"Will do!" I said, not fazed.

Later that day, the town was forced on lock down. Ever since more deaths started back up again, the news channels spiraled. Police cruisers stalked out every street corner, lurking for danger. Families swarmed stores, hoarding supplies.

Nick found himself in a scandal. Allegations of recordings, brought forth by a teammate, had been let out. His flash drive held the answers people were craving for. Desperate to know

CHAPTER 8

what was on the tapes. Cameras flashed in front of his house. News reporters stood on his lawn. He was placed in handcuffs, one of his eyes swollen, and dried blood stained his white tank top.

I stood witness at the end of his lawn, hearing the unfolding drama. His dad tried getting everyone off of his property. As I retreated to my motorcycle, Moe appeared. "What are you doing here?" she said, her voice as worn as her weathered lips.

"I swung by the store to pick up some things when I heard about the lock down," I said.

"Oh… you heard about those tapes too?"

"Ya, makes you wonder what's on them, right?" I thought out loud. "But why is he being arrested though?"

"Some people think he has something to do with Katie's death," she said. "I heard that the person who told on Nick was Katie's boyfriend."

Katie's boyfriend had been in the locker room with the boys when the tapes were made. He believed Nick was involved in Katie's death and the other students at Cherry Hill High. The boyfriend knew what Nick was capable of—insights that others weren't privy to.

Nick and I locked eyes as he slid into the back seat of the police car.

"Let's hit the diner. I'm starved," she continued.

I paused from getting on my motorcycle. "Have you seen the streets? It's crazy out there."

"And?" She dismissed my words.

We found the diner's lot deserted. What was left was overflowing trash bins and the echo of absent staff. I wasn't on shift, not a chance. I indulged in a strawberry milkshake and two burgers to sate my neglected appetite—peanut butter and crackers had been my substance for too long.

Moe's phone buzzed, snapping the silence. She stepped outside, her movements stiff, shoulders hunched. From the window, I watched her pace around, her grip was tight around her phone. When she returned, her face was composed, but her eyes—those told a different story. She sat down like nothing had changed.

"Everything okay?" I asked.

"Yeah," she said quickly. "They cleared Nick." She placed her phone flat down on the table. "People are calling her death another suicide." Her fingers tapped nervously on the table, making it clear there was more to it than that.

"How is it a suicide if she was found with stab wounds?" I asked. "Why do they say every death is a suicide?"

She shrugged. "Because no one has the real answers," she casually stolen a fry from my plate.

I had a sinking feeling that I was the one who saved Nick when they searched his house. The flash drive they were probably looking for was sitting right there in my closet, hidden under my dirty clothes. It was ironic. I'd taken it thinking I was one step ahead, but now it felt like I'd unknowingly kept him out of trouble.

"Acelin, you alright?" she continued.

I was stuck in a frown, my hands running anxiously through my hair. Frustration bubbled up inside me, and I felt my heart race as I tried to process what she said.

I came back to reality. "I think—"

"You think Nick is the school killer?" Moe asked, staring at me intensely.

"I think… he is."

"Shit," she laughed nervously, her voice shaky. She glanced

CHAPTER 8

around, biting her lip, as if trying to mask her unease with humor.

On the way home, rain poured down hard, blurring everything outside. Jackson had been gone since Katie's body was found. I needed someone to talk to about the truth I was hiding. The flash drive in my closet wasn't just my secret. It was Nick's. The guilt of having it was eating me alive.

Through the curtain, a figure staggered towards my yard, collapsing. It was Jackson, soaked to the bone, his shirt in tatters, blood staining his lips. He gasped for air as the relentless rain pounded down on him. "Help!" His plea sliced through the storm. I rushed to his side, carrying his weight as I ushered him inside.

"What happened to you?" I asked, panic edging my voice.

"Just… a moment," he panted, taking off his shredded shirt.

I gave him space to breathe. "What's going on? Is someone after you?"

"It was my dad," he confessed, the words heavy with pain.

I was stunned. "What do ya mean?"

"I stole money from him."

"How much? We can return it," I assured him, sitting close to him.

"Hundreds… thousands… I deserved this," he said, resignation in his voice.

I was at a loss for words. That wasn't the Jackson I knew. The brother who'd never do something like that. There was more to the story he wasn't sharing. I rummaged for a first aid kit to tend his wounds. That's when I found it, his jacket, crumpled on the floor. Unfolding it revealed a gun, trembling from my hands.

He searched through my dresser for a clean shirt while I

clutched the jacket. I threw it at him. "Who even are you?" I asked, narrowing my eyes.

I questioned my own understanding of Jackson. Was he still the friend I knew, or had he morphed into someone unrecognizable.

"Please, it's not what it seems," he pleaded.

"Then enlighten me," I said with sarcasm.

"It's about my mom. She's got Alzheimer's, and my dad… he wants to put her in a senior home so he can be with his new, younger girlfriend."

"He's seeing someone else?"

He took a deep breath in. "Yeah, my parents are still married. But you don't just abandon someone you love because they've changed. You're supposed to be by their side." Jackson held his chest before he spoke again. "He took her healthcare funds into his winery. I took the rest to save us, but she barely even recognizes me anymore," he confessed.

"I can talk to my Mom—"

"No, I handle my own problems. I'll figure it out," he said, tossing some bloody tissues into the trash. His voice was finally steady. "We've got bigger things to worry about, right? That flash drive you took, did you ever check what's on it?" He nodded towards the closet.

"No, I haven't yet."

"We need to see what's on it," he declared walking over to the desk, his fingers trembling as he connected it to the computer.

Nick's face filled the screen, his voice brimming with excitement. *"Hey there, blog, Nick Adonis here. Today I'm throwing one of the biggest parties in Cherry Hill. I'm making this a weekly thing, for every Friday or Saturday. Stay tuned folks."*

The video shifted to a scene in his backyard, his father in

CHAPTER 8

the background, busy with golf gear in his garage. The camera flipped to Nick again.

"Big day for us. It's the season's final football game," Nick announced. "And there's Tommy, my right hand man. Hey, Tommy! Swing by and say hi." The camera zoomed onto Tommy, his dirty blonde hair catching the sunlight.

"Hey, everyone," Tommy greeted with a casual charm. "I've got a good feeling about this game."

Nick's hand obscured the lens, promising more footage. "Catch you after we clutch this win," he said, the screen fading black.

In the next clip, the boys board the bus, after the win against Burn Wood. Tommy, seated at the back, seemed off. He was constantly clutching at his knee. That night, Johnny had broken his leg not by accident. Rumors swirled that Johnny targeted Tommy during the game. Despite the knee pain, Tommy kept it away from Nick, masking his discomfort with a towel draped over his head and a smile that didn't quite reach his watery brown eyes.

With a click, Jackson brought up another video, the one that Nick feared about the town seeing.

In the locker room, the boys had a wall full of tally marks, each name followed by marks for each person they'd slept with.

"Yo, Tommy did you ever fuck that one teacher?" Nick said as he slapped a wet towel to Tommy's back.

"Which one? The French one, the one who mocks about being in love?" Tommy Joked. "I already fucked that."

"Hell yeah?" Nick laughed, turning the camera to capture Tommy's sweaty face, his hair soaked. The boys engaged in playful antics around the locker room, chasing each other with water guns.

"That's another tally mark for me!" Tommy said.

He pushed Nick away from the wall to draw his tally.

"You want to know who I really want to sleep with?" Nick asked Tommy.

One of the boys in the background shouted, *"Katie waters."*

Nick had a summer fling with Katie Waters, even though she was much younger than him. People whispered about them secretly dating, keeping their relationship hidden from everyone. Her age was the problem.

"Hell no!" Nick said, pointing the camera towards the boy who called her name. *"I want Seulgi Sew. The one from Japan."*

Tommy interfered. *"Seulgi is all me. Nick, if you want to sleep with her you win. But she's my girl or I'm talking to Lyra."*

Nick showed the camera to his face. *"I will not let you talk to Lyra,"* he smiled.

"Come on, she's trying to smoke tonight with me," Tommy smiled.

The end of the video left Jackson, and I silenced. "We need to take this to the authorities!" I said as Jackson paced around the room. A storm of emotions played across his face. I waited until he came up with words. Still nothing from his mouth. After a moment, I suggested, "Maybe we should show this to Drew first. He deserves to know about his sister."

"Acelin, are you even listening?" Jackson asked. "We can't get tangled up in this mess. We technically broke into Nick's house."

"You're right," I conceded, shaking my head in disappointment. "But the tape doesn't prove anything. Maybe he didn't kill anyone."

He nodded in agreement. "But they still mention Katie and slept with a teacher."

The car lights outside died down; Mom was home. I dashed

CHAPTER 8

downstairs as I scanned for any signs of the earlier chaos. Jackson followed, pausing to double check the upstairs for any blood drops.

Mom entered, unfazed, she shifted through the mail. Jackson took a seat next to me on the couch.

Mom bit into an apple, her gaze fell on us. "Why the nerves? Is everything alright?" She waited for an answer, looking at me. "Acelin, I want the truth," she probed.

"It's nothing major," Jackson deflected, avoiding her stare. "We were just discussing prom shopping plans."

Her attention shifted to Jackson's bruised face. "What happened to you?" she asked, concern shown on her face.

"I'm fine Christina!" He moved away from her hand as she gripped his face.

"But how did this happen?" she asked. "Acelin what is going on?"

"I don't know," I frowned.

Jackson filled in. "I've been taking boxing lessons. Today's match just didn't go my way," Jackson fibbed, seeking my support to change the topic.

I cleared my throat. "Speaking of prom, I was hoping you would take me prom shopping soon," I redirected the conversation.

She smiled, "Of course! I'm excited for you both! Oh, and Acelin, there's a note for you on the porch."

"Okay!" I retrieved the note from the porch. Bold red letters spelled my name—a chilling warning left for me. My heart raced as I read the ominous warning: *"Stay out of people's business or you're next."*

Jackson's touch startled me. "What's wrong?" he asked.

"I think… I'm next… to die." I whispered, my mind racing.

Jackson looked confused as I walked briskly out the front door.

I remembered Katie Waters warning me that if I ever received a letter, I would be the next to die. I thought about Drew. I recalled him having a letter similar to mine. I wanted to know what was on the one he received.

As I headed to the school, I found the main doors locked. The side doors were propped open by a janitor taking out the trash. Inside, Drew's office was unlocked, and there was another red stamped letter that looked familiar to mine. I took the letter off his desk, but before slipping it into my back pocket, I saw it was addressed to Seulgi.

I considered planting the letter in Nick's locker. I thought that would've made Drew suspect Nick of being involved in his sister's death, if he ever went looking for his letter. A police search would've happened, and Nick would be accused of the crime after all.

My heart pounded as I touched Nick's locker, my fingers shaking. What I was about to do could have changed everything. Just one letter slipped inside. But then, the janitor caught sight of me. Panic took over. I threw up my hood and ran through the halls, heading towards the side doors. The letter stayed clutched in my hand. I should have slipped it in quickly, but I didn't.

* * *

Assigned by the book club, I was tasked with photographing the students around school. Entering the boy's locker room, I felt a mix of nerves and a lack of confidence. The halls were

CHAPTER 8

safe, filled with teachers busy decorating their doors.

"Nick, calm down!" Jamie pressed.

"Calm down? He blamed me for his girlfriend's death!" Nick retorted back to Jamie. After Nick's been released from jail people had been accusing him of killing her out of Jealousy, for dating her new boyfriend.

"We have a game soon. Do you wanna be benched?"

"Jamie, the fucking tapes are out. Someone took the flash drive from my place, I look guilty!" Nick paced around the locker room, throwing a white towel from his neck onto the floor. "Forget the party this weekend. It's done. When I find out who stole from me, I'll kill them."

The boys grumbled. The word *kill* made me tense up; he was talking about me, the thief. As they got dressed for gym, they speculated about who the person was that stole from Nick, even suspecting Lyra Barns.

Nick made eye contact with me. "Yo Acelin!" His gaze pinned me.

"I-uh," I stuttered.

"You what?" He questioned as he stepped closer to me.

I turned away from his face. "I don't know who took your stuff," I managed to say as I clenched onto my camera.

"Nick, fuck off," Jamie said, stepping in front of me. Them, being just as tall as I was, sometimes made me feel a twinge of fear.

"Let's go, boys. Let Jamie protect his new best friend," Nick said, his voice laced with jealousy.

For the first time, I felt empathy for Nick. I just wanted Nick to experience the same pain he'd caused me. But seeing the weight of his worries changed something in me. Instead of going through with it, I chose to keep the letter safe with me.

"You good bro?" Jamie asked, his lips pressed tightly. "Nick is fucking crazy," he laughed, placing his hands on my shoulders.

"I got used to it," I affirmed with a nod.

Changing the subject, Jamie asked, "Have you heard from Moe? She hasn't been answering my texts."

"I just saw her yesterday."

His brow furrowed. "Where?"

"She was over my house," I said. "She crashed on the couch last night."

He hesitated for a moment, packing his gym bag. "Hold on, are you two…?"

"No, absolutely not! That ain't happening," I asserted, shaking my head emphatically.

He nodded, sure of his thoughts. "Would you mind inviting me over, if she comes back to your place? She has been avoiding me again."

"Sure."

"Do you want to smoke?" he asked, holding up a bag of weed.

Without a second thought, we headed into the shower area of the locker room.

We settled on the floor, using our jackets against the damp ground.

He looked concerned. "Do you know how to hold it?" he spoke again, laughter punctuated by coughs of smoke.

"No," I chuckled. "How do I hold it?"

"You can hold it between your index finger and thumb. Just find whatever way feels comfortable," he advised.

"Shit! I think I inhale too much in," I coughed dramatically.

"You're fine, trust me," he assured me with a smirk. "I haven't gotten high in a minute."

"It should always be that way."

CHAPTER 8

He nodded. "Ever since Moe kissed me, I just wanted to change for her. She called me a bum, a druggie." I heard the sadness in his voice. Jamie did look more neater, his shirt tucked in, and a haircut every two weeks. I thought he was really changing.

"I didn't know you cared that much about her."

"Yeah, I want to get clean, leave the drugs behind. Moe's words, they cut deep." We exchanged a look. "You probably can't relate. Your life seems so put together."

"How do ya know?" I responded softly. "I wish I could say my life is perfect."

He put out the blunt, his expression shifting as he spoke. Jamie was the type of person who talked about his feelings when he felt a genuine connection with someone. "I hate my mom and dad," he said with a laugh, dusting ashes off his shirt.

"What did ya mom do?"

"She had me that's the fucking problem," he said, his weary eyes betrayed his emotions. "I remember, I had a cousin, more like a brother. I started doing heavy drugs after he was taken from me. He took the fall for me." He quickly wiped his eyes. "I, um, when we were kids, we tried to rob a store as a dare. He told me to run, and the cops chased after him instead. I haven't seen him since."

"Do you think he's out of jail now?"

"If he is, then fuck him. He doesn't even bother to reach out to me. He's labeled as a troubled teen, so it's likely he's at Dooms Institute."

I shook my head. "I hope I never go to a place like that. I swear, I would kill myself," I said.

He nudged me gently. "Be quiet, I can't imagine life without you," he joked.

After the school day ended, the drama involving Nick began to dissipate. The principal had a conversation with Nick, emphasizing the importance of keeping his videos private. The principal himself was only aware of the rumors circulating among the students, not the content of the tapes. The French teacher had been removed from her position at Cherry Hill High. She tried denying hooking up with students and Tommy Graves. Meanwhile, Katie's boyfriend was suspended for his disruptive behavior and instigating fights with Nick.

As I made my way to my motorcycle, Lyra approached me.

"Hey," she greeted.

"Hi," I replied quickly. "I was about to grab a bite." I offered her my hamlet.

"Could we stop by the diner? Their muffins are my favorite." She accepted the hamlet.

"Most people can't stand them. They are my favorite too."

"Let's go," she said, her smile stuck as she climbed on behind me.

I could sense her heartbeat against my back. She held onto me tightly. The motorcycle rumble seemed to startle her as we took off. She gripped my waist even tighter with each turn. She seemed overwhelmed with thoughts, worried about not holding on securely enough. Eager to earn her trust, I increased the speed. She rested her head against my back as she closed her eyes.

At a red light, I glanced back at her. To reassure her, I removed my hands from the handlebars and placed them on her thighs. As the light turned green, she once again wrapped her arms around my waist.

We finally arrived at the diner. My hand brushed against hers as I took the helmet. She looked away, a small smile tugging

CHAPTER 8

at her lips. "Are you cold?" I asked, noticing the way the wind made her hair whip across her face. "Yes," she said, pulling her arms around herself and glancing around. I shrugged off my school jacket and handed it to her. As she put it on, the oversize sleeves fell over her hands, and she bunched them up to fit her arms.

We sat down, and once again, our eyes met. Lyra was always good at flirting, and I couldn't help but wonder what she was really thinking. Whenever she got quiet, I couldn't shake the feeling that she might regret being with me.

"What can I get for you guys today?" the waitress asked with a smile, placing glasses of water on the table. I glanced at Lyra, waiting for her to order.

"I'll have a blueberry muffin and tea," she said, handing the menu back.

"The usual for me," I replied as the waitress walked away. "Are you excited about the camping trip later?"

"Yes, I am," she replied, her voice gentle.

I couldn't help but to smile. "Good."

She gathered her hair into a ponytail. "You know, you always make my days better when it's falling apart."

"I could say the same, but we're just friends. I don't think it's appropriate to state."

The waitress arrived with our order. I saw her daily on my shifts but still haven't learned her name.

Lyra sipped her tea. "Acelin, I don't want any awkwardness on the trip, especially with Remy around."

"Remy?" I paused mid bite of my muffin.

"Do you find her attractive?" A hint of jealousy hit her tone.

"Maybe focus on your tea while it's still warm."

She flicked straw paper at me. "You didn't answer!"

I couldn't help but to stare at her lips. Smooth and full, likely enchanted by a lip plumper. Being close to her felt like shooting fireworks, bursting into my stomach, and her scent of warm brown sugar vanilla, relaxed me.

"It's you I'm interested in—"

"Oh please! You wouldn't know how to handle me."

"Should we put that to the test?" I replied with a laugh. As I glanced outside the window, a gentle drizzle of rain began just as we were preparing to leave.

By the time we arrived home, the rain had intensified. "Hurry! I'm soaked!" she said with a laugh. I opened the door, Mom and Turner were seated on the living room couch, talking. She took a quick sip of his wine glass, thinking I wouldn't see. I resisted the urge to say anything about it.

In my room, Lyra was busy fixing her mascara and drying her hair. "I think I need a shower," she remarked, eyeing her attire.

"Okay," I responded. I handed her freshly warmed towels from the dryer.

As Mom and Nick loaded the truck, I checked the time, eagerly waiting for Remy's arrival. I fixed my hair in the mirror and picked out an outfit while Lyra finished her shower.

"Apologies for taking too long," she said, entering my room with a towel draped around her. She clutched the clothes I had handed to her earlier. I assumed she would have dressed in the bathroom.

"It's okay," I said, my voice faltering.

She extended the lotion bottle towards me. "Would you mind applying this on my back? I always miss spots."

"Um, sure," I said, taking the bottle from her hand.

"Wait, is this too much?" She turned towards me. "I don't want to make you uncomfortable."

CHAPTER 8

I raised my eyebrows. "No... not... at all."

I squirted a little amount of lotion onto my hands. I began to rub it down her back, making my way to her waist. She let out an excessive sigh, closing her eyes. I tried keeping my eyes only on her back, but her towel slipped from her hands. I saw her chest trying my hardest not to stare. She placed on her underwear and pants while sitting down as I continued rubbing lotion on her.

"Why did you stop?" Her breath hitched as she fixed her eyes on me.

My heart pounded through my chest. "I can continue if that's what you want—" Her lips met mine in a sudden kiss. Pulling back, I managed to ask, "But what about Nick?" My pulse raced with the question.

"I don't care about him right now," she said, climbing on top of me and kissing me intensely. Her chest pressed against my bare skin; my shirt already tossed aside. Anyone could have walked in and misunderstood the moment, but I didn't care. She stopped and smiled, her eyes locking with mine. I glanced at her chest which sat perfectly. I couldn't understand how someone could make me feel this way. So alive. So vulnerable. I was in love, truly, and for the first time. The harder I tried to deny it to myself, the stronger it grew.

Footsteps echoed up the stairs, causing Lyra and I to panic. I tossed her shirt, which she hastily put on. The cherry scent of her lip gloss lingered on my lips. "We should go downstairs," I suggested as laughter bubbled between us.

Jackson arrived first, followed by Remy, who was the last to show up. Nick had driven himself, clearly avoiding my company. As I loaded the final bag from Remy into the car, she turned to me and asked, "Acelin, would you mind sharing a room with me?"

I was unsure, I didn't want to stir any emotions in Lyra. Still, I forced a smile and said, "Ya, why not," as I secured the bag in place. Lyra's eyes stayed fixed on Remy and me.

Jackson approached me with a smirk. "So...?"

"What are you talking about?" I asked, pretending not to know.

"Nothing, man, it's all you!" he said, his tone full of teasing.

"Shut up, Jackson," I replied, shaking my head.

"And?" he pushed, stretching the word out like he was fishing for more.

"And what?" I shot back, trying to keep my annoyance in check.

"About you and Lyra upstairs. I'm not slow, like did you hit or what?"

"Don't be so loud!" I smiled, quieting him. "Not yet, and now with Nick in the picture, I can't."

"She's into you, bro. You've got to make a move. Plus, her friend's pretty cute." He glanced at Remy sitting in the truck. "Man, these girls are nothing but drama," he muttered.

Jackson climbed into the truck, and I followed, sitting next to Remy. We shared headphones, laughing about the time she wore an inappropriate shirt to school. She was known for skipping school on Fridays, which often got her suspended. Rumors said she had a new boyfriend she was sneaking off to see, but he supposedly never went to our school. Everyone knew she hated dating anyone from the same school to avoid drama.

While I talked to Remy, Lyra rested beside me, playing with my fingertips until she fell asleep. Her head leaned against the cold window, so I slid a pillow under it. She shifted slightly,

CHAPTER 8

grabbing my hand for comfort.

Remy noticed our hands, and her look made me nervous. It was a reminder that Lyra and I needed to be more careful. In that brief moment, I couldn't shake the fear that she might have already said something to Nick about it.

Chapter 9

We finally arrived at the cabins, nestled deep among the trees. After picking our rooms and settling in, I couldn't shake the eerie feeling the place gave me. The walls were covered with hunting trophies—mounted bears and other animals, their glossy eyes seeming to follow my every move. Turner lit the fireplace, its warmth filling the space as we tried to get comfortable.

Jackson, not wanting to be left in his own room, hauled his luggage into the room Remy and I had claimed. He made the couch his bed. He spent hours on the phone, having a conversation with his mother, hoping she would remember him again. Remy lingered by the doorway; she stared at me as I unpacked. A bottle of painkillers tumbled out, rolling at her feet. She handed them back without saying a word, and a wave of relief washed over me, she hadn't read the label.

I had been getting hooked on painkillers for a while. I didn't want to admit it to myself, but I was slowly becoming just another junkie from Cherry Hill High. The feeling was addicting. Every time I took them, it was like all the stress and

CHAPTER 9

pain just melted away. I knew it was a temporary escape, but I couldn't help but to want that feeling again.

I finished adding the last touches to a sketch I had started while we were in the car. I used the dim glow of my phone to see my work. Everyone was asleep, giving me the peace I needed to focus on my drawing.

"Whose titties are those?" Remy asked, catching sight of the drawing.

"Just a drawing," I replied quickly, closing the sketchbook.

She sighed, clearly impressed. "They're so well drawn," she said, settling down on the bed beside me. The subject of the drawing, though, was Lyra's chest.

I glanced at her as she slipped an oversize shirt over her swimsuit.

"Jackson can take the other bed," she spoke again. "The couch doesn't look very comfy."

Jackson shot me a grin, waiting for me to agree. I didn't really want to share a bed with Remy, but as her hopeful eyes met mine, I gave in. "Sure."

"I used to think you were a bad student," she frown, tucking her hair behind her ears. "When those rumors about you were going around, I didn't believe them. A school shooter?" She laughed, shaking her head.

"Good, I don't believe the rumors about you." Her rumors were the worst. People claimed she gave blow jobs in the school bathroom for five bucks or sent naked photos to the football team as a *"reward"* after every win. The truth was far from it. Remy was still a virgin. On top of that, she'd never done anything remotely sexual beyond a kiss.

She closed the gap between us, "I'm off for a swim. Care to join?"

I nodded in agreement. "Yeah."

In the kitchen, I found Mom and Turner, their relationship still a mystery to me, preparing salmon and salad—my dad's favorite. It seemed like a veiled attempt by her to mask her longing for him by claiming it was my preferred dish. Meanwhile, Nick and Lyra's argument escalated until Jackson stepped in, demanding silence.

Outside Remy was soaking in the hot tub, savoring a honey drizzled bowl of fruit. I sat next to her. "You took your time," she teased, playfully kicking her legs in the hot tub.

"Sorry, I got caught up eating the salmon my Mom made."

"I couldn't wait until dinner, so I whipped up this fruit bowl."

"It looks good."

"Do you want to taste?"

"Ya," I replied, accepting a spoonful from her. "I just couldn't stand listening to Nick and Lyra argue over the same issue," I wiped my mouth.

She gave me a knowing look. "I noticed something between you two in the car…"

"Yeah, I know," I admitted, embarrassed.

"Don't worry, your secret is safe with me," she assured me with a smile.

"Um, and what about you?" I tried getting the subject off me. "Who do you date?"

She hesitated, "I can't say…"

"Come on, tell me," I urged hoping she would confess her feelings.

"It's too risky." She stood up and walked over to the pool. With a dive she was in the water.

"Wait, come back!" I called, following her. Perched on the pool's edge, my feet submerged as I asked again, "Tell me if it's

CHAPTER 9

him."

"Who?" she inquired, swimming closer and grasping my legs.

"Stop it, let go," I laughed, splashing water at her as she attempted to pull me in.

"Do you really want to know?" she teased, coughing up a bit of pool water.

"Yes," I leaned in eager for her confession, but she seized the opportunity to pull me into the water. I plunge to the pool's bottom, holding my breath.

As I wiped the water from my face, she climbed onto my shoulders, laughing. I struggled to stay up top, with a push, I freed myself from her grip.

"Why would you do that?" I couldn't help but to raise my voice, though I tried to stay calm.

She looked at me, her eyes wide with concern. "I was just playing."

"I'm getting out," I said, my voice annoyed as I swam out.

"Acelin?" She followed me, her voice tinged with regret. "I'm really sorry," she said gently, her hand touching my arm. "I was just playing."

Her sad, pleading eyes melted my frustration. "No, it's me who should be apologizing. I didn't mean to snap at you."

Just then, Lyra and Jackson appeared. I quickly turned away, busying myself with drying my hair, while Remy wrapped herself in a towel.

"Ace, you're not leaving already, are you?" Jackson asked, dropping his towel and kicking off his swim shoes.

"I've been out here long enough," I replied. "My lips are turning purple."

"Same," Remy chimed in, standing by my side. Lyra's gaze flickered between us, suspicion written all over her face, but she remained silent.

Jackson gave a nervous chuckle. "Well, I'll catch you guys upstairs!"

I headed upstairs, with Remy following close behind. In the room, I reached for the painkillers, desperate for the relief they gave me from the thoughts hitting me down. I couldn't stop thinking about Lyra's concerned look when she saw me with Remy. I hated how angry she seemed. Then, my mind kept circling back to the problems at school and the letter I'd gotten. Taking the pills felt like the only thing that made sense at that moment.

After a shower, I found Remy dividing the bed with pillows between us. Then, in the stillness of 2 a.m., she woke up.

"Acelin, are you awake?" she whispered.

"Yeah," I said, turning to face her and shifting a pillow out of the way.

"It's Drew Lu. I'm seeing him," she confessed.

As shocked as I was, I tried to stay calm. "I won't tell a soul," I promised, linking my pinkie with hers. I already had a feeling it was him. The person she would link with on Friday nights seemed like that was Drew's idea.

She wrapped herself in the blanket, turning away towards the window.

The next morning, Jackson burst into the room, his voice booming as he tried to rouse Remy and me. Lyra was right behind him, searching for me, only to find Remy's head resting on my arm. The pillows that had been between us were gone. "Acelin!" Jackson's shout snapped me awake, just in time to see Lyra's disappointment. She ran down the stairs. "Oops! I didn't mean for her to see you guys," Jackson said. I glared at Remy, still asleep, oblivious to the drama.

CHAPTER 9

"Jackson, shut up," I said, tossing a pillow at him in frustration. I tried chasing after Lyra but Nick was by her side. Jackson always enjoyed stirring up trouble, knowing full well Remy wasn't even my type. I was just bored and lonely. He thrived on the awkwardness of my dating life, unlike me.

I gently woke Remy, placing the breakfast Mom had prepared on the bedside table for her. Then, I stepped outside to take in the view of Burn Wood. That's when Turner approached me.

"You like the view?" he asked, his smile revealing a perfect set of white teeth. I wasn't in the mood for small talk, especially with him. He had a wife at home, yet there he was, cozying up to my Mom.

"Ya, it's nice," I replied.

He offered me a cigarette, but I declined. "You really remind me of Nick's best pal."

"Who?" I asked.

"Tommy," he said, lighting his cigarette.

"What was Tommy like?"

Suddenly, my phone buzzed off with a jarring ring, drawing Turner's attention. A message from Moe brought my world crashing down. The problems I thought I'd left behind in Cherry Hill had followed me to Burn Wood. The article I'd written about the killings at our school was causing a stir again.

My classmates from the book club had been bombarding me with texts, asking me where I've been. They thought I was hiding. The first time it circulated, it merely raised eyebrows, but now, it's threatening to end everything for me.

A crime show interviewer wanted to discuss the article with me, to delve into how I was coping with the loss of students I was supposed to be friends with—students I never met.

Remy stood in the kitchen, scrolling through the comments

about me. I snatched her phone, I read each comment of being a *"Horrible liar,"* a *"Snitch,"* a *"Clown."* There were a few kind souls telling me to stay safe.

Nick's anger grew as he confronted my Mom, accusing me of ruining his life. Someone had tampered with my work; the version spreading wasn't mine.

Mom was disappointed, a tangible force read on her face as she read the twisted words on the phone. She must have been wondering why her son would frame someone who was practically family, *Nick*. My heart raced, my palms sweated, I feared Nick would've destroyed me. "Did you write this framing Nick?" she asked.

"No, I never said he killed anyone!" I reread the article.

Cherry Hill High Class of 2007' Darkest Secrets.

I never imagined I would be the one to say this, but the victims who've passed will forever hold a place in my heart. Deep down, I know Nick Adonis is responsible for the deaths of my friends, Seulgi Sew, Tommy Graves, Katie Waters, and the other lost souls. I wish these death's could stop. My friends were taken away from me so soon. Nick must be stopped, before it's too late.

—A.J

Mom was angry. "When we get back in town, you're doing that interview. You'll clear Nick's name, and you better pray the school doesn't expel you," she threatened, her hand raised as if to strike me.

"I swear I ain't write that!" I shrugged my shoulders.

CHAPTER 9

"Then who did?" she asked.

"I don't know?" I frowned.

"This is why our lives are ruined now because of you," she whispered.

"Wow," I squinted at her as I backed out of the kitchen. Slowly, I made my way to the room, with Remy trailing behind. I tugged at my hair on both sides, feeling overwhelmed. Remy reached out, holding my wrists to stop me. "You okay?" she asked softly. I gently pulled away from her.

Nick had his own threats to deliver. As Remy moved away, Nick walked up, trying to hit me. But no, I didn't let him get the chance to embarrass me. I threw a punch to his face. He held his cheek while Remy held her mouth in shock. Nick and I stood face to face. His fist balled as he was about to hit me, but Lyra came running over to stop the fight.

"Nick, chill out," Lyra stepped between us.

Nick and I held each other's gaze. "Hit me, come on," I said.

He left with a smirk as he continued down the stairs. "Let's see how long you last back in Cherry Hill," he said, Lyra following closely behind him.

Hours went by, I watched the others leave for the golfing contest, through the window, choosing to stay behind. The negative comments continued to pour in, and the familiar smell of dark roasted coffee hit a little comfort to me, coming from downstairs. It used to remind me of the diner, my haven from the world. I felt trapped in the cabin.

Downstairs, Jackson was cooking, wearing an old, dusty apron. "Shouldn't you be with the others?" I asked.

"No," he replied, not bothering to turn around.

"You mad at me too?" I ventured.

"Never. I stayed because I know how you get when people

are upset with you." He handed me a mug of coffee. "I saw the letter you took from Drew. It was in your jacket."

"Jackson, I—"

"You trying to get yourself killed?" he asked.

"It was so stupid, I wasn't thinking straight."

He sighed. "What will you do when you go back to school? If you didn't write that article, then who did?"

"It could've been anyone," I said, tugging at my hair in frustration.

"Well, there's something else you need to be worried about," Jackson said, leading me upstairs to Nick's belongings.

Jackson was focused on an article about Tommy Graves. It explained how Tommy's mother had sued his father, accusing him of hiding the truth about Tommy's death. A former maid had come forward, revealing the family's secrets, like an affair that had happened and a hidden sibling. The article also mentioned disturbing details from Tommy's autopsy.

The father, eager to protect his image as a famous lawyer in Cherry Hill, denied the allegations surrounding the case. He was embarrassed by the way his son had died and remarked on how *weak* Tommy was for getting laced so easily. News reporters seized on his comments, outraged that he would speak about his own son in such a way.

I placed the folded newsletter back into Nick's varsity jacket. "Why would Nick still have this?"

We exchanged a look. "He's still grieving."

"We need to talk to Tommy's mom," I spoke again. "The address is on the newspaper. We could go to that house, maybe it's Tommy's mom house?"

"Yeah, and she probably knows who was last with her son," Jackson nodded in agreement.

CHAPTER 9

We had to uncover the truth, no matter how deep we had to dig for more answers on Tommy Grave's death.

* * *

With shaky hands, I secured the stall door, straining to hear the conversations made me. I glanced through the narrow gap, I saw boys swaggering in, boasting about what they'd do if they found me. They were just trying to stir up trouble, seeking attention in the worst ways.

"Looks like Acelin is in deep shit," one of the students said. He sniffed a line of white powder off of his palm.

"I always knew Acelin was a weirdo but didn't think he had the guts to ruin Nick's life."

"Shut up, his life is not ruined. No one even believes that dumb article because it's from a school," he said, pushing his brunette hair back. He pulled his pants down to use the urinal.

"He's so fucking dead." The skinny boy laughed as he watched his friend urinate.

As they left, I thought I could slip out unnoticed, but the bell already rang, and all eyes were on me. *"You sure you didn't kill Tommy yourself!"* Someone yelled as I passed them, their laughter stinging.

Moe's grip on my arm was tight as she pulled me into the library.

"I warned you not to come today, you dummy!" Moe hissed.

I let out a weary sigh. "I ain't think people would still be talking about it."

"Right," her face relaxed, annoyed.

"Moe, that wasn't the version of the article I wrote," I said, holding her hand, seeking comfort.

Her eyes wavered. "I want to believe you, but I just don't know anymore." She withdrew her hand. "It's in your name, Acelin."

"I'll prove to everyone I didn't write it."

"Until then, stay away from me," she said.

The intercom crackled with my name, summoning me to the office. Mocking faces peered from the classroom doors, paper balls pelted at me, their taunts echoing the hallways.

The principal's tone was serious as he greeted me. "Acelin, we need to talk about the serious errors you've made—"

"I didn't spread that article. It was supposed to be school friendly," I defended myself.

"Our school's reputation is at stake, and Nick's parents expect you to clear his name on national TV," he stated flatly.

I felt a surge of anger. I was tired of being manipulated, of being told what to do—I didn't even feel a twinge of sympathy for Nick anymore.

"You have two choices," the principal continued, his finger jabbing the air towards me. "Get expelled or do the interview."

"I'll do the interview," I said, rising from my seat.

"And one more thing," he added. "If you dig any deeper into those killings, you'll face jail time or be sent to Dooms institution. And you're out of the book club."

I left the office, fists clenched, struggling to maintain control. I needed answers, and there was only one place I could think to look, the book club room.

I barged into the room, accidentally scattering papers from the desk's edge onto the floor.

"Um, Acelin, you're not supposed to be here," Julie, the school president, protested.

CHAPTER 9

"I need to talk to Maxes," I demanded, ignoring her. Maxes was responsible for publishing the article. I thought maybe she was the one who switched out the article.

Julie tried to block me, stretching her arm across the doorway, to the back room. "She's not here today," she lied, avoiding my gaze.

Maxes appeared, her thick eyebrows raised in surprise. "Look who decided to show up after leaving me with a mountain full of articles to publish."

"You've made things worse by altering my article."

She frowned. "I didn't even read your article. I just sent it off for publishing."

"Then who tempered with it?"

"I don't know!" she said, her voice trembling as she reapplied her lip gloss.

I slammed my hand down on the table. "That's bullshit! You do know."

She hesitated, then spoke. "Well... it's bullshit," she mocked me.

"I want to fix this. Please tell me who did this to me," I pleaded.

"Well... you could apologize to Tommy's mother for using his name for clout. Tommy's birthday is today, and his mom is having a party. You should come."

A wave of relief washed over me. This could be the chance for Jackson and me to uncover the truth about Tommy's death, and clear Nick's name.

"I promise to help you," she spoke again.

I nodded as I dialed Jackson's number. I paced around the library door. The hallways were filled with students sneakily reading the article at their lockers, risking suspension. Near the bathrooms, I heard police dogs and officers searching for any troubled students, dealing drugs. Then the principal announced a lock down, and panic set in me. I still had Drew's letter in my bag that I stole from his desk.

I ripped off my tie, sprinting down the hall, only to spot the two detectives who had questioned me about Katie Waters. They were standing by my locker.

I stumbled out of the school building, nearly colliding with Jackson.

"Whoa, take it easy!" he said.

"I can't," I panted, "We've got to get out of here."

He eyed me, concern etched across his face. "Why do you look so sweaty?"

"I've been holed up in the bathroom all day!"

Jackson's gaze shifted past me to the two detectives walking out towards us. "Are they here for you?"

I tugged at his backpack, urging him towards the parking lot. "I have the address of Tommy's mom's place. Maxes gave it to me."

"Maxes. The weird girl?"

"Just meet me at Tommy's house, okay?" I pleaded, slipping on my hamlet and revving up my bike.

As I rode away, worry crept on me. What if the mom rejected me, or worse, called the police. It felt like everyone was turning their back on me. Moe didn't listen, Lyra gave me the silent treatment, and Remy's with Drew—the one person I'm scared of who would destroy me for stealing his letter. Everything was happening too fast, and I couldn't keep up.

Arriving at Tommy's mother's house, I was greeted by a wild garden, tall, trimmed bushes, and a stone house. Nick's car was parked out front.

Nick emerged, his expression sour. "Acelin?"

CHAPTER 9

Jackson stepped forward, protective. "Don't start anything."

Nick scoffed, "Why would I? It's my boy's celebration." He held a piece of cake on his plate; underneath it, a letter peeked out—the same one I had received.

"What's that?" I asked, nodding towards the letter.

"None of your business," he snapped, trying to conceal it. "Don't forget that I'm still coming after you—"

"I got one just like it," I said, cutting him off. "Can I see?"

He handed it over, *"I'm watching you,"* it read.

"Keep it," he said, a smirk playing on his lips. "And good luck with your investigation."

We watched him drive away, our backs turned to the door, when a voice broke the silence. "Who are you boys?" It was Tommy's mom. Her hair was cut short to her shoulders, blonde, and she wore red lipstick that left a mark on her wine glass. Her pale, rosy face was streaked with tears. Dark circles under her eyes told a story of stress, but they weren't too noticeable.

"I came to help with the party," I said.

We followed her inside, surrounded by memories of Tommy. She offered us drinks, but I was there for answers.

She studied me, recognition dawning. "Acelin, right? I read your article."

I struggled to swallow, feeling as if the walls were closing in. Jackson's eyes were wide, mirroring my own panic. "It wasn't my intention to write—"

"I'm glad you wrote it." She moved some hair from her lips. "Nick was upset about the rumors, but I made sure he didn't hurt you."

Jackson finally spoke, breaking the tense silence as we sat down on a couch. "We used to go to school with your son. We were really close to him."

"Tommy never mentioned you guys," she said, her voice steady as she set down her wine glass. Her eyes locked onto mine. "I knew... I knew, I recognized you from somewhere, Acelin." She turned to Jackson. "Could you give Acelin and me a moment alone?"

"Of course," Jackson replied, glancing in my direction. I winked at him letting him know it was okay to leave.

The old radio player skipped off beat, making me feel unsettled. "His father was an alcoholic, more concerned with football than his son's wellbeing. I knew Tommy was suffering, I saw it."

Her tears began to fall, I felt an ache in my chest. She continued, her words a torrent of grief and frustration. "When I found out he was dead, I blamed those kids from Burn Wood. Tommy had called me one night. He told me what Johnny did to his knee."

Tommy thought that if he smoked, the pain would've gone away. The fact that he couldn't play football for next season didn't fit right with him. Football was his life.

"I have been trying to find the person who laced my son." She paused, her eyes narrowing. "I been losing sleep, taking my medication for a personality disorder they say I have. They call me crazy!"

"Mrs. Graves," I said, my hand instinctively reaching for my heart. "I am deeply sorry."

"My name is Susan," she corrected me. She walked over to a drawer. She retrieved a necklace from a small silver bag. "I want you to have this. It belonged to Tommy."

I hesitated, overwhelmed by the gesture. "Why give this to me?"

"You were a friend to him, right?" she said. "It's time for me

CHAPTER 9

to let go of some of his things."

Curiosity overcame me. "Who was with Tommy last?"

"He mentioned he was going to a party with Nick..." Her voice trailed off, her hand pressing to her forehead. "He was with—"

"You guys need to come see this!" Our conversation was abruptly interrupted by Jackson's return, his breaths were short and urgent.

Outside, a chilling scene waited for us. Pictures of Tommy, with knife stabs, and red X's through his face, adorned the garage. Susan broke down into tears, dropping to her knees crumbling the pictures out of anger. Jackson and I exchanged a glance, the moment of the situation settled in my bones.

The necklace, a symbol of a life lost too soon, felt heavy in my hand. It was not a cruel prank, it was a violation of a mother's mourning.

I couldn't help but wonder, where was Jackson when this happened?

10

Chapter 10

Dressed in the suit Jackson had handed me; I couldn't shake the anxiety I felt. Jackson, now living in my basement, always carried a key around his wrist. I had spent hours setting up the space to make it feel welcoming for him. He used to live with his grand mama, who had also taken in his mother. His grand mama didn't like Jackson staying out late for football because he never made it back in time for supper. So, she kicked him out.

"Let me help," Jackson offered, his hands steady as he took the tie from me.

"Thank you," I said, relaxing my hands. My eyes glued to the mirror.

"I want you to know that I was in the kitchen talking to Frances on the phone. I didn't see anyone outside until I heard a rock hit the window."

Tommy's mother's house still haunted me. The eerie silence, the shadows, the feeling of something hidden. With his necklace in my hands, it felt like a sign, a reminder not to give up on his case.

CHAPTER 10

"Well, it's over now." I smoothed out the wrinkles of the suit. "I have better things to worry about."

I didn't know what to expect, and Mom didn't make it any better by repeating how my life was over, again and again. She was wrong, though. People stopped talking about it. Some said it was just a school stunt to cover up other lies happening around town. The mean comments stopped, Nick's life was back to normal, so why couldn't mine?

The lights overhead dimmed slightly, and the host straightened his papers, signaling the show was nearing its end. The cameraman gave a subtle nod, and the buzz of the studio faded as the final segment approached. The host with blue hair turned towards me, then back to the papers in his lap.

"Thank you for tuning into *The Cherry Hill Crime Show*," he said to the audience. "We want to clarify that the information in his newspaper article was erroneous," he continued, thrusting the microphone towards me. "But before we go, Acelin, with the awareness you raised, do you believe the real killer will stop?"

I Scanned the audience for Mom. I found her eyes encouraging me to stay calm. Her silent instruction to breathe was my only support.

"Well…" I spoke.

"Just *well?*" The host prodded, amusement in his voice as laughter rippled through the crowd. His smudged eyeliner seemed to mirror the dark humor of his question. "Who do you admire more among serial killers? Ted Bundy, John Wayne, or perhaps Caril Ann Fugate?" His grin widened, anticipating my response.

Their laughter was a harsh reminder of my discomfort. I wanted nothing more than to escape. Then, a voice from the front row pierced the tension, *"I love you, Acelin!"* The audience inhaled in shock.

The host sprang from his seat. "Did you catch that, Acelin?" He gestured towards the woman. "You've got admires!"

The grinning faces were overwhelming. "I can't do this anymore," I said, retreating backstage.

The host regained control, concluding the show. A chorus of boos clamored for my return. "That's a wrap for *The Cherry Hill Crime Show!*"

Mom caught up with me backstage. She walked to the film producers, her voice loud. "You guys tried to humiliate my son on national television?"

"I'll speak with the host," one of the producers said, attempting to calm her.

I bypassed them, my mind racing with fear. My hands betrayed my composure as the crew offered water and a towel to calm me down. "I need to leave!" My outburst drew attention. I was having a panic attack.

You see what you've done?" Mom snapped at the crew. "My son isn't cut out for this." She steered me towards the front door.

On the drive home, my tie became a shelf for my face, hiding my sorrow. Mom sat beside me; her presence steady but silent. She didn't ask if I was okay—she didn't bother. She understood the pain I carried, a pain that had been growing for months. And still didn't do a thing about it. I had tried to stay strong, but everyone has their limits, and I reached mine.

On the front porch, another letter lay under the mailbox, held down by a rock. The letter was written in an old style, with the words in red ink. The letter said, *"Moe is next to die."*

I tried to contact her but got no response. As I tried calling

CHAPTER 10

her again, Remy's footsteps echoed up the driveway. She had come straight over after fencing practice, the very one I had missed due to the TV show demand.

"Sorry for showing up so late," she said.

"It's fine, I just got home myself."

"I saw the show," she began tentatively, "just wanted to make sure you were alright."

"I'm okay," I replied, the letter I had been clutching now crumpled in my pocket.

Her curiosity showed. "What were you holding?"

"Nothing, just a silly letter," I deflected, tucking the letter away from view.

"Drew got one too. I wish I could see what was on it."

"Believe me, you don't," I warned, the content too disturbing to share.

She walked up to me, taking a seat on the porch steps. "I've been trying to figure Drew out. He's so secretive, it's strange."

"He really is," I said, sitting beside her.

"I've only ever been with him at school," she confessed, biting her lip with nervous energy.

"You deserve better than Drew," I stared straight into the distance.

She sighed. "It doesn't matter anymore. My dad's moving us out of town tonight, away from the mountains."

My heart sank. "You're leaving?" I faced her. "You're leaving from Cherry Hill?"

With a bittersweet smile, she nodded. "I'll really miss you, Acelin Jones," her voice shook. She wiped her eyes from crying. "I just really didn't want to leave you," she held her hands on her face.

I frowned. "Hey, it's okay," I wiped her tears from coming

down. "I'll just be a call away."

Our eyes met, in a breathless moment, she kissed me. It was a kiss of closure, a bittersweet end to a chapter I haven't explored. It felt neither right nor wrong, just a final goodbye. I never saw Remy again, but I cling to hope that our paths cross once more in the future.

* * *

I held the gun, standing by the window, pointing it to my head. I saw my reflection in the moonlit glass and felt anger tense through my body. I thought about firing the gun, shattering the window, releasing my anger. I wanted others to feel my pain. But deep down, I knew, those letters, the article would all stop one day. I knew that hurting, or anyone else, wouldn't have solved anything.

I was high on painkillers as Mom called for me. I quickly stashed the gun under my bed. Today was a masquerade party at Nick's dad's hall. The thought of seeing Lyra with someone else made it unbearable to even think about attending.

"Can you help me with this necklace?" she asked, breaking into my thoughts.

"Sure," I replied, fastening the necklace around her neck.

She glanced back, "Aren't you coming?"

I shook my head. "Got too much homework. And Jackson, my date, isn't here."

She beamed with excitement. "I'm going out for dinner after the ball. I'm finally a nurse!"

"Really? Congratulations!" I said, surprised. "Why didn't ya say something sooner?"

CHAPTER 10

"I did, during the camping trip. You stayed behind," she said, her smiling fading.

"Sorry."

"Well, I'll see you later." She continued down the stairs, her dress trailing behind her. I watched her leave, regretting that I didn't give her a severe apology.

When it hit midnight, the masquerade party had ended, but there was still Mom's celebration to attend. Without many suits of my own, I ventured into her closet and found one of my dad's old suits. It was an all-black suit he'd worn to his prom with Mom.

Before heading to the dinner, I stopped by a flower shop and brought beers, my first drink in months. As I drove Mom's car, I sipped on my third beer, the nerves settled in. I caught a glimpse of the cheerful gathering inside the restaurant. Mom was chatting with Nick as if he were her own. It felt like I was on the outside looking in at a family that I never met before.

I entered the five-star restaurant, my name promptly checked off the front desk before being led to a table. I had made an effort to look sharp, my hair slicked back and a fresh haircut in place. Mom's face lit up when she saw me, the suit clearly making an impression. She kissed my cheek, and I handed her the flowers. Her smile waned as she asked if I had been drinking. I denied it, and she turned back to the others, her smile returning.

Sitting at the end of the table, I felt disconnected from the celebration around me. I checked my phone for a message from Jackson, the one person who never judged me, but there was nothing. He was probably with Frances, his new girl, leaving me to ponder alone.

Lyra sat across from me, her laughter mingling with Nick's,

a fake performance. I caught her eye, hoping she would speak more of her passions—baking, her cherished plants— but her eyes stayed on me, halting her words. She resumed, her voice soft, "My plants are like children," she said as I finished her last word in my head, *children*. She always called her plants her children. I continued looking down at the menu.

Our eyes met again, and she gestured towards the outdoors. I waited until she left first, then followed her lead.

Side by side, we sat in silence. Her beauty was undeniable, her eyes a deep, warm amber, her skin glowing. Her shoulders bare and her body adorned with glittering sparkles. In her presence, I found a sense of peace.

"You okay?" she asked.

"Do I look that bad?" I joked, my eyes drifting from focusing on her.

She smiled, a knowing look in her eyes. "Just checking on you. I'm sorry for acting mean to you."

"I need you Lyra Barns," I said, resting my head against the cool glass window. "You can't keep doing this to me."

She nodded. "I'm thinking of leaving Nick for good."

I shifted up. "What changed ya mind about him?"

"You."

She leaned in close, her hands cradling my face, and kissed me. A kiss that felt like a promise, even if it wasn't real. We were in full view of the window, the world watching, but at that moment, it was just us.

Nick shouted at Lyra from the doorway, urging her to return inside. I remained silent as she listened to the boy who repeatedly mistreated her. "It's best you head home, Acelin," he suggested mockingly. "You don't want to ruin your Mom's big day, right?" he said with sarcasm. "You're drunk."

CHAPTER 10

I struggled to my feet, I confronted him. "Oh, I apologize, brother, didn't mean to upset you by kissing our girlfriend."

He dismissed me with a smack of his lips. "If your Mom ever marries my dad, just know, I'll always be the better son," he smiled. "Your Mom loves me. She already mistaken me for her own, I think I won."

"Aren't your parents still together? Should I expose that truth inside, shatter everyone's day?" I challenged myself.

Adjusting his suit, he was nonchalant. "They're divorcing, so say what you will. My mother's likely fucking someone else at this moment." He stepped forward. "This thing between you and Lyra? It's over."

Retreating to my car, I shouted. "Fuck you!"

"Leave, Acelin. This isn't your place," he said, hands in pockets, as he returned inside, shoving his hands through his blonde hair.

* * *

When the sun rose, school began. After days of avoiding Drew Lu, I finally had my first conversation with him.

In the stillness of Drew's office, I waited for him to break the silence. He glanced at me, then at his watch. His usual attire was replaced with a suit.

"So, how did you find the, uh, the fans?" he asked.

I was puzzled. "What do ya mean?"

"That interview where you detailed the tragedies here. I was your biggest supporter," his tone dripped with insincerity.

"You tampered with my article?" I confronted him, though I

wasn't surprised; he was a likely suspect.

"Didn't you want the fame?" He rose, circling me like a predator.

"No, you made my life harder."

He spun the chair I was seated in to face him. "I saved you!" he said. "I gave you fame. It's what you wanted."

I locked eyes with him. Trying to read his secrets on his face. "Not like this," I said with deep breaths, hoping he would release his grip on the chair. "I just wanted the bullying to stop at school."

"It will stop," he stepped back, smirking. "Just wait and see."

"Can I leave?"

"I'll see you soon. Acelin." He lingered by his office door, watching me exit.

As school ended, I felt compelled to reach out to Moe. Finally making contact, I braved the biting cold outside. My ears stung, my hands stiffened, and my eyes watered. She approached, breathing warmth into her cupped hands. Fidgeting with her hair, wiping her mouth from a plastic bottle of liquor she clutched.

"I wanted to show you this letter." I handed it over to her. Her sniffles were the only sound in the frigid air.

Her eyes widened in alarm as she read it. "This isn't a joke. Where did you find this?" she asked, crumpling the note in frustration. "Me dying next?"

"I know, it's serious," I reassured her.

"Ever since that new swim coach came, everything has felt off," she said, her voice cracking.

Without thinking, I confessed, "I've been stalking Drew." If I faced consequences, I didn't want to be alone. Jackson was untouchable, too important to me. "I know Drew's routines, his

CHAPTER 10

habits, even his diet." She bit her nails anxiously, her knuckles red, her face flushed with fear. She wasn't alone in her terror now; I shared it. "He tampered with my article, twisted its words, it was all him." We locked eyes. "I think it's him writing these letters."

"We're going to the authorities!" She declared, gripping my arm tight, like she always did when something serious was happening.

I pulled away quickly. "No, we can't!"

A frown creased her brow. "Why not?" she asked, her voice quivering. "Why this fixation on his life?"

"Because…" I hesitated, my voice low. Admitting my fascination with Drew's life wasn't easy. There was something about him that resonated with me, a sense of shared pain and loss. He seemed to understand the ache of unanswered questions, much like the ones I had about my father's absence.

Her face relaxed. "Then let's go see him," her voice low. "You're always watching him. Show me what he's up to today," she said.

We spent an hour on the road. Her plan was to blame me if things went wrong, but I didn't care about her feelings right then. I glanced at her and saw tears running down her face. Her hands shook as she gripped the steering wheel, barely able to focus on the road.

As we got closer to his penthouse, the energy of the city shifted. A line of black trucks followed us, their presence impossible to ignore. Outside his penthouse, people in suits stood like statues, their eyes watchful. The trucks ahead of us had license plates marked with a bold *"M"* making the situation serious.

My eyes widened. "Moe," I said, grabbing her arm to halt the car. "We need to get out of this line!"

Panic flashed in her eyes. "Damn it!" She hit the brakes hard and swerved out of the line. I shut my eyes, hoping we'd escape the closing gates.

But we were intercepted by a towering figure clad in black, a red *"M"* emblazoned on his suit jacket. He signaled for us to stop, ensuring we couldn't leave. "Names?" he demanded, peering at Moe. "Step out of the car," he ordered, a smile played on his lips as he tucked away his glasses. Moe looked petrified, her eyes wide with fear. I had to be the strong one for the both of us, even as my own fear threatened to overwhelm me.

The fog swirled around us as another figure approached, his voice booming through the mist. "Look who we have here," Drew called out. "My, boy," his smile failing to mask the chill of his touch as he patted my cheek.

I stammered an excuse. "This is not what u think—"

"Right… let's have a chat in the backyard," he suggested with a head nod.

A group of stern-faced young men escorted us. Moe was beside me with worry, her gaze downward as she contemplated our fate. Had I led her to her own death? If Drew was really behind the threatening letters, I feared the worst for her.

Marco, Drew's imposing father, lounged by the pool. He held a cigarette in hand, the rising fog added an eerie touch to the scene. He remained unfazed until Moe's sob broke the silence. Her face hidden behind her shaky hands.

Drew introduced me to Marco as the boy who had been stalking him. The realization hit me, the cameras. Drew knew about my surveillance all along. He knew I had been following him after school most of the time.

Marco, inked with tattoos, questioned me with a deceptive

CHAPTER 10

calmness. "Acelin is this your girlfriend?" he asked, his attention turning to Moe. Her tears soaked her shirt as he ran his fingers through her hair.

We were ushered to sit across from him, and I discreetly held Moe's hand under the table, offering silent reassurance. "No, she is not."

Marco continued, "My daughter will be turning eighteen in a couple of weeks." He took another puff of his cigarette. "I wish I could've found out who tried to kill her sooner, as a birthday gift, but I failed."

"I've been seeking the truth as well," I said, trying to steer the conversation.

"Ah, the articles," he flicked his lighter, his accent thick. "Drew's been watching Nick, but there's no evidence linking him to any crime. Still, I want him killed." He put out his cigarette, the smoke curling in the air. "My daughter used to date his best friend. Drew went to work at your school to see what kind of person Nick was. But we found you, Acelin Jones."

"Please, don't kill me," I begged, clutching my hands together.

"Not only did you write an article, but you made a deal with the devil. You wanted fame?"

I shook my head yes. "I just wanted the bullying to stop, that's all."

He stood up from his chair. "From now on, you and your friend are under my control. I own you both." He stood up over us. "Acelin, you will work for me," Marco finished.

Drew chimed in, "Training starts this week. I'll pick him up tonight," he bowed.

Moe's gaze fixed on me as the men forced me down onto the table. My cheek pressed against the cold glass, leaving a mark on my face. The men that held me down were young, their stories untold. The urge to fight back was strong, but Drew's grip on the situation was tighter. Any attempt to run would be met with a consequence or death.

They branded us both, marking us invisibly, only delectable under a special light. The gravity of the danger I had brought upon us was crushing. Moe's knees were bruised from begging. She wasn't required to endure the training that waited for me, but she would be next if I failed as a Member. I sat, paralyzed with fear and regret, unable to make an apology to Moe.

They made the stakes clear: silence was our only lifeline. Speaking out would mean death for us and our families.

Moe's slap was a remainder of her pain and my guilt. With Marco returning to Japan, Drew resumed control, leaving me anxious about the unknown training that laid ahead.

Jackson's arrival sparked a serious conversation. I confessed everything about Moe and me, and how I needed to fabricate stories for my absence at school and to Mom. His disappointment stare cut deep, marking the first time he seemed to judge me, hard. He called me *selfish*, and I couldn't disagree. I'm a product of this harsh town, and the burden of my choices weighed on me all night. I paced, packing my bags, while Jackson sat silently, his red eyes speaking volumes in a corner.

As the clock struck midnight, my world turned upside down. Black trucks circled my home. Drew, a grin on his face, sheltered me from the rain with an umbrella while I collapsed, too burdened to even carry my luggage.

Drew's men lifted me, offering empty reassurances. "You're going to be fine Mr. Jones," the man said. I dared not to look back at my home, wishing for more time to make things right with the ones I hurt.

Behind the curtains, Jackson, now the keeper of a secret too

CHAPTER 10

heavy for me to bear alone, now saw me as a Member.

11

Three Months Later

The training wasn't as I anticipated, yet I had adapted. Mom believed I was at a fencing camp. The school principal was under the impression that I was taking time to concentrate on my mental health after the ordeal with the article going through town. In truth, I had been honing my skills to become an assassin within an organization called the Members.

Classes were held every Friday. The instructor preferred to stand by the chalkboard, pacing with a cane that he would slam onto a desk to jolt our attention. His real name was unknown to me, and I had no desire to learn it. He was named Tooth Fairy by some, for his habit of collecting the belongings of those who failed to become a Member. He would take wallets, shoes, watches, money, even rings. He would go through their possessions and claim his spoils.

"The confusion among you all is worrying," the instructor had adjusted his tie. "You are all here because you have been selected." He scanned everyone with his eyes. "Our mission is to take over one of the most potent drugs out there. The drug

THREE MONTHS LATER

that causes people to hallucinate, erases identities, lives and births anew."

I often thought about the creator of the drug, the one that claimed Tommy Graves. The same drug I had been laced with, to why he made this drug in the first place. The drug came in various strains, affecting each person differently. Some, like me, managed to survive.

My hand rose, then hesitantly lowered as all eyes fixed on me. "What will we do with the drug, once we take it back?"

"Do you really wish to know?" He had challenged me.

"I believe others here share my curiosity," I said.

"Alright, four eyed boy," he glanced at my glasses as I adjusted them on my face. "We'll approach this one step at a time, agreed?"

I nodded. "I ain't intend any disrespect."

"Embrace the harshness." The instructor had dismissed the interruption. A bell broke into the silence. "Class is dismissed. I expect to see you all next Friday."

I didn't make any close friends among the Members. The few I called friends never stayed long enough to maintain the bond. Most people kept to themselves, avoiding the risk of betrayal. I did the same and was eventually promoted to a larger bedroom. At first, I had been assigned to a bunk bed in a cramped, crowded room. Apparently, I had made a good impression on Drew.

Drew handed me a set of fresh towels as we stepped into my new room. "You're moving in ranks, that's why you're getting a Member's room," he said, clapping his hands together. "Once the mission is complete, we're heading to Japan."

My heart skipped a beat. "Japan?" I had echoed.

"You'll also get a tattoo to secure your spot here." He showed me his wrist, with a symbol of the square's.

I had frowned. "What about the mark on the back of my neck?"

"That's not visible," he assured me. "I'll be downstairs if you need anything."

After he left, I took a long, hot shower, resting my head against the stone walls. The bathroom mirror was much bigger than the one at home, reflecting my full figure. The scars on my back, remnants of childhood abuse, were my deepest insecurity. My dad also punished me by making me sit outside in the freezing cold or burning my skin with cigarettes. I knew it wasn't truly him; it was the liquor's doing.

Now, I contemplated cutting my hair, changing my appearance to match the transformation I felt within as a new Member. I wanted to shed the image of my father who I looked like. I opened the closet doors. I searched for something to wear, but all I found were black garments and various shades of nude. I chose an all-black outfit. As I descended to the living room, I was greeted by the sight of a celebration.

"Hey, Acelin, get over here!" Drew shouted. "Everybody, meet one of our newest Members!" He raised his glass, and the men cheered in my honor.

"I'm happy you decided to stay," a Member had whispered to me. Yet in my mind, I was thinking about leaving this place. I wasn't a killer, and the sight of their joy in such deeds was unbearable. I didn't want to become like them, nor did I wish to understand their desperation for a drug.

Drew breath reeked of scotch. "We need to fix you up. Follow me," he said. We took an elevator underground. Down there were training rooms, undercover medics, and injured people. Most were hurt from gunshots or brutal training fights.

THREE MONTHS LATER

A chair waited for me. As I gazed into the mirror, I thought of Mom's reaction. A drastic change like cutting off my hair might have led her to think I was having a mental breakdown. The stylist presented a digital catalog of hairstyles. I perused the options, settling on a low cut similar to the other boys.

With each snip, strands of my past fell away, memories I yearned to shed. Hair blanketed my lap and the floor. I closed my eyes, allowing the transformation to unfold. "You look almost like me," Drew remarked with a smile. I brushed some of the hairs from my neck and felt the unfamiliar smoothness of my scalp.

After the haircut was done, I stepped into the living room, where a boy around my age stood in the center. His wrists were tied, and a cloth muffled his cries. One of the men yanked the cloth from his mouth, and the boy's desperate voice broke through. "Please, sir," he begged, his voice trembling.

Drew stepped forward, scotch in hand, disdain darkening his expression. Without a word, he splashed the liquor across the boy's face. "You betrayed me," he said, his tone cold.

I lingered in the shadows, my grip tightening around the necklace that once belonged to Tommy Graves. The small hairs from my recent haircut still clung to my neck, itching like the guilt crawling under my skin.

Drew eyes landed on me. "Acelin, do the honors."

Silence hung heavy in the air. I tried to mask the fear in my eyes with a hollow laugh, but it was obvious. "What should I do to him?" I asked, standing beside Drew. The boy's eyes still were begging for mercy. How could I save him when I was just as lost? Taking that boy's life would mean giving up the last shred of my own innocence.

The table beside me held different weapons. It was a torture table, and off to the side, a gun rested, carefully wrapped in a silk cloth.

Drew watched as I hesitated to pick one. "What's the appropriate consequence for his betrayal? He attempted to expose all of us, Acelin."

I acknowledged with a nod, feeling uncertain. "Um," I said. The boy's screams grew louder.

He leaned in, whispering intently. "Reflect on those who inflicted pain upon you. Those who diminished your worth as a human being."

With trembling hands, I grasped the firearm and pressed the cold metal against his temple, my face averted. "Brother! Brother! Please, save me," the boy begged. I clenched my teeth, fighting the surge of unwanted empathy, my eyes squeezing shut.

Before I had the chance to fully regain my senses, one of the Members shot the boy. A precise shot, and the boy's form crumpled to the ground. His blood pooled around him. The crowd around me didn't flinch. They sipped their drinks, laughed, and carried on as if nothing had happened. Another Member approached, carefully retrieving the weapon from my hands with gloves. Drew's voice broke through my thoughts, his touch on my shoulder a heavy weight. "Acelin, you're dismissed for the night," he said, his tone tingled with disappointment.

As I walked back to my room, bloody footprints from the boy stained the dark marble floor. The death of a child, a specter, haunted my every step. I tore off my shoes and clothes, throwing them against the wall in frustration. Desperation clawed at me; I needed to hear Mom's voice, to find some comfort. But when I called, silence was my only answer.

I slept to escape the pain of almost committing a sin. When I

THREE MONTHS LATER

woke up, I watched the sunset from my window. I was grateful for the light of another day, finally free from the gloom.

A knock on my door made me flinch. I opened it to find a tall man, bald and silent, picking up the clothes I had thrown over my room.

"Mr. Jones, did you forget about your appointment today?" he asked, his voice proper.

"What appointment?" I asked.

"To get your suit tailored?"

I stood there, confused. He placed my clothes on the nearest chair and walked out the room. I followed him until we reached the kitchen.

Drew was slumped over the table, a shot glass in his hand. "Drew?" I nudged his arm, but he didn't react. I called his name again.

Slowly, he struggled to stand. "You gave me a fright," he mumbled, finishing the last of his drink. "Suit up, we're heading out," he said, gripping the railing for support as he made his way to his bedroom. I continued following the bald man into a room where men were being measured for their suits.

"Mr. Jones, it's a pleasure to tailor your suits. Meeting you is quite the honor," one of the Members greeted, his nerdy charm accentuated by a neat Afro. His glasses were perched on his nose.

"Nice to meet you as well," I replied, shaking his hand. Standing in the mirror, I watched their skilled hands take my measurements.

"How's your experience so far as a Member?"

"It's been…"

"Feel free to not respond if you're uncomfortable."

I felt a lump in my throat. "Being here is like being at home."

He looked me in the eyes. "Have you found your purpose in life?" He paused his adjustments on my suit sleeves.

"No," I said, meeting my gaze in the mirror. I grapple with guilt for considering this my second home. "I haven't."

Later that night, Drew and I drove through the city, passing party venues. Women in festive attire mingled with men stumbling out of clubs, propped up by their friends. A grin spread across my face. We entered one of the buildings, where a man at the door scanned the mark on the back of my neck, a symbol of my connection to the Members. He then scanned Drew's wrist.

I followed Drew to the bar counter. He loosened his suit jacket. "Care for a drink?" he asked.

"No, I'm fine," I declined. My eyes drifted to the half-dressed women and the cascade of money falling from above. I eyed the cash carpeting the floor, tempted to take some. Drew's watchful eyes stopped me. We exchanged a look, and I took the shot glass from him. The memory of being drugged at the bar in Cherry Hill came rushing back. I hesitated as I swallowed the shot.

"Do you miss Cherry Hill?" he spoke.

"I don't," I smiled as we cheered. "Can't ya tell I like being here?" My face looked guilty in a lie.

Drew handed me another shot. "The burden will be yours to bear, Mr. Jones," he warned. His words sat heavily; my existence felt forfeit already.

I had downed ten shots by then. I tried to stand, but I was too tipsy to keep my balance.

"Where are you going, Acelin?" Drew's grip halted me from leaving the seat.

I smiled. "Just need some water."

"The water is here at the bar, Acelin," he shouted over the loud music. "I've got something that'll make your day!" he laughed.

Drew guided me to a room, my arm draped over his shoulder for support. They called it a private show. A dancer entered, performing topless as I struggled to focus through the haze of the drunkenness. Soft touches brushed against my chest, and I leaned my head back on the couch. I closed my eyes, wishing for the moment to end. When Drew came back for me, he grabbed my face, lifting my head up. "You got bored that fast?" he made fun of me.

The dancer left as Drew led a few of the Members to help drag me out of the club. They put me in a vehicle, and one of the Members wiped my face with a cloth from his suit. I laid in the back seat, using my shoes as a pillow. I'd been drunk before, but this level of intoxication was new to me.

When morning came, I woke to find my clothes scattered on the floor. I had no memory of taking them off, though my underwear was still on. Beside me was a tray with green mints, a glass of chilled water, and a pill to ease the pounding headache. Underneath the mints, a letter from Drew caught my eye:

My Dearest Member,

Acelin Jones.

To think you would grow to be like a brother astonishes me. Your humor, your lessons, and the joy you bring are treasures. I long for the day you understand my actions. Once, I was like you, yearning for escape, and I found it. In time, you too shall rise as a leader, one of wisdom and discernment. My loyalty to you is unwavering. Embrace your new identity, command it, embody it. Make me proud! Let's meet at five for dinner.

—*D.S*

In the kitchen, the house was silent except for the television's chatter. Above the fireplace, a projector cast names, a leader broad celebrating *achievements*. My name was in third place. I didn't know how I had ascended the list without committing any horrible acts. I have only been through training—learning how to shoot guns and carry out small missions, like trafficking drugs and collecting money from those who bought from us.

A jittery man approached me, his movements tense. "Mr. Jones?" he asked, summoning me for training. His movements were cautious, he betrayed me as a menace. I followed him, sensing his heightened anxiety. He slouched while walking and gestured towards my destination, tucked behind an angled wall. His fear was loud but remained a mystery to me.

As I entered the door, a scanner circled me. A mist of smoke enveloped my body and seeped into my lungs. I settled onto a rigid metal chair, beneath the number that marked my rank: *Third place.* A boy emerged, his form in terrible condition, gasping for breath. He was supported by two Members, while another grasped his legs. They escorted him out of the training doors. "Mr. Jones, you're up," beckoned a voice. My heart thundered, weakening my breath. "Today's lesson is self defense. Drew intimated you've had prior training?" asked a woman. Recalling my first day, ambushed by Members, I had to fight four men. I learned the harsh lesson of no mercy. "Yes," I replied confidently.

She guided me through another door to a space where a mat laid at the center. From the opposite side, a girl approached. She had a pocketknife glinting in her grip. She looked strikingly like Lyra, with the same skin tone and tawny strands of hair.

THREE MONTHS LATER

"Victory is your ticket out. The countdown begins now. Best of luck," a robotic voice announced, emotionless.

Five minutes were on the clock. That was the only sound flooding my mind. I raised my hands, ready to fight, but thoughts of Lyra kept intruding. I couldn't bring myself to hurt her; all I saw was the face of the one I loved. My eyes flicked from the clock to the Members seated upstairs, watching through a glass window. She slashed my arm, blood dripping onto the mat. I glanced at the cut, then back at her. Her face was filled with fear, but I knew I had to do my job.

I grabbed her by the hair, pulling her closer to me. I twisted the knife out of her hand. She struck the back of my knee twice with her other, causing me to fall face first onto the sweaty mat. She grabbed my shirt and pressed the knife to my throat, leaving a shallow cut. I yanked her down as I managed to get back on my feet. The knife laid beside her. I picked it up and drove it into her leg, the sound of her scream filled the air.

With one minute left on the clock, the girl struck my jaw, and blood dripped from my mouth. She could barely stand; her blood smeared across the mat from her leg wound. I charged at her, slamming her into a table, and she crawled away from me. Overcome with guilt, I knew I had no choice but to end her suffering. "Please! Don't kill me," she whispered, blood and tears mingling on her face. Silently, I apologized in my mind, locking eyes with her. I watched her take deep, shaky breaths as I delivered a kick that knocked her unconscious.

The Members from upstairs clapped and placed bets on the victor—me. They had expected my victory, questioning why they would invest hope in a girl perceived as fragile, weak. I had been mistaken; she wasn't easy to beat, but I couldn't afford to be embarrassed. The Members came through the doors, lifting the girl. The woman who had spoken to me earlier led me to the doctor. My jaw ached, and blood seeped from the cut on my arm as we made our way to the doctor's room.

I had sat on the bed, pressing tissues against my mouth. "Is that girl going to be okay?" I asked, driven by curiosity. "She's not dead, right?"

"Focus on getting yourself patched up," the doctor had replied, beginning to stitch up my arm.

Embarrassment had washed over me for asking. "I'm just concerned about her," I had admitted.

A small smirk formed on her face. "Why do you care so much?" Her long black hair framed her face perfectly.

"She reminds me of someone from back home."

"Who?" she asked, gently placing a silk cloth around the cut.

"Lyra… her name is Lyra Barns—"

"Young love never lasts," she interrupted, tightening the cloth around my arm. "Now that you're here, you can forget about her."

As I made my way back upstairs. The living room was crowded with people watching replay videos of fights. They were debating who deserved the first-place rank. I then recalled the dinner Drew had scheduled with me at five. I hurried to my room for a shower.

After the shower, I wore an all black turtleneck to conceal some of the scars from the fight. I paired it with black-fitted pants.

On the living room screen, a clip of me kicking the life out of that poor girl played on repeat. The Members had cheered for me as they noticed my presence. My eyes met Drew's, his mouth full of half cooked steak. "I told you all, he's the one!" he shouted, pointing at me.

THREE MONTHS LATER

A smile crept across my face, followed by a burst of laughter. Hurting that girl gave my self-esteem a twisted boost, knowing I had done something brutal and gotten away with it. We sat around the table, discussing our mission again. The plan was to steal the drug the creators were producing, take down their business, and make millions in the process. Even if it meant killing every last one of them.

With every conversation, I nodded along, blending in effortlessly. Rounds of liquor were passed around the table. For the first time in years, I felt safe, included, like I mattered. My mind shifted, and I realized I didn't want to go home. I didn't want to see Cherry Hill again. I loved being one of the Members.

I was destined to live in Japan with Drew and the rest.

12

Chapter 12

I saw Drew sitting on the couch with a shot glass in hand, staring at his sister's portrait above the fireplace as the flames flickered below. She had pale skin, dark almond shaped eyes, and straight black hair, with a soft pink tint on her cheeks and lips. I stood behind him for a moment.

"Acelin, join me," he said, his eyes still fixed forward. I walked over and sat next to him; my eyes drawn to the fire. "Would you ever sacrifice someone you love the most?"

I laughed, caught off guard. "What do ya mean by that?" I asked.

He paused, lost in thought. "When I was young, to get where I am now, I sacrificed the person I love most, my sister."

"You killed her?" My voice cracked with disbelief.

"It felt like I did," he replied, finishing the last of his drink. "If only I had taken her to Japan sooner, she would still be okay."

I nodded; my eyes fixed on him.

"Who would you sacrifice, Acelin?" he continued, still facing forward.

I didn't hesitate. "My Mom."

CHAPTER 12

"Every villain has a story," he said with a smile, rubbing the rim of his shot glass.

I entered the classroom, and the Tooth Fairy sat at his desk, watching his pocket watch tick. I waited for the other Members to arrive, then pulled out my glasses and wiped the lenses with a cloth.

Next to me, a boy sat motionless. I watched him closely, studying his every move.

He glanced over at me. "Can I help you?" he asked.

"Sorry," I muttered, quickly looking away.

"Wait," he paused, meeting my eyes again. "I saw you in the newspapers."

I turned to him. "About Cherry Hill High?"

"Yeah," he said, raising an eyebrow. "I remember we voted you in as a Member a while back."

I frowned. "What do you mean, you voted me in?"

Just then, the Tooth Fairy tapped his desk with his cane, commanding our attention. "Today's lesson is what to do when held at gunpoint." He stepped away from his desk, eyes scanning the room. "If our enemy had you at gunpoint, would you snitch us out?"

The door to the classroom opened, and one of the Members called for the boy next to me. His name was Zero. He glanced at me, subtly hinting for me to follow him out. Once the Tooth Fairy turned to the board, I slipped behind them. In the hallway, Zero was guided by a Member into a lab room.

The floors were marble, the walls made of cement. Rows of chairs lined up next to lab computers, its wires snaking to the bottom. I followed them deeper into the lab. I spotted a teenage boy asleep in a chair, wires attached to his head. His feet and hands were chained.

A doctor injected something into the boy's arm, causing him to twitch. Nearby, another doctor measured precise amounts of chemicals, while another carefully documented each step. The liquid in the flask began to swirl, transforming into a small green substance. After a moment, the doctor added a white compound, watching the reaction closely.

Drew stood behind the doctor, arms crossed, waiting for the substance to take effect in the boy. Suddenly, the boy woke up, panic setting in as foam bubbled from his mouth. He screamed, thrashing against the restraints as the drug took hold.

"Do you think we should inject more?" Drew asked.

The doctor shook his head. "There's a risk he could die from an overdose. Precisely, we will monitor the effects, record his reactions, and ensure compliance."

On the computer, the boy's information filled the screen. His name, age, and address were neatly displayed alongside a photo that looked like it had been taken at school. Below it was noted details about his habits, routines, and even the places he visited most often. It felt invasive, like staring into a life that wasn't mine to see.

The cursor hovered over a folder labeled *"Activities"*, and with a hesitant click, more files opened. There were schedules, lists of people he had interacted with, and a map with pins marking his movements.

Name: Henry Cane Day

Age: 17

Day: 3 of testing

CHAPTER 12

Below, there were rows for symptoms, vitals, and results.

Increased heart rate. Muscle spasms. Sweating. Dilated pupils. Black veins appearing.

Henry's voice broke weak and strained. "Don't kill me," he gasped, his words struggling to escape as his chest heaved with each shallow breath.

"We're not here to kill you," Drew said coldly. "We just need to know how far you can go."

Henry's eyes widened in panic as his veins began to turn black, creeping up his arms like a sinister stain. His voice strained, "What's happening to me—" His body jerked violently, his head thrown back, and his hands curled into fists.

Drew leaned in closer, observing Henry intently. A spark of excitement lit up on his face. "Fascinating," he muttered.

I couldn't help but question the motives behind the Members' actions. If we were truly criminals, why go through all this trouble to create a drug that might help others from hallucinations? Was it all about the money? The profits? The power? Or was there something darker at play, something none of us fully understood?

Zero finally chimed in. "This is the second time we've tried to cure ourselves. If we just take down the creators and steal their drug—"

Drew interrupted. "That's the plan but it's too many creators—"

"So, we need to look for new Members?" Zero pressed.

"Our newest Member is Acelin. Let's see how he does first."

More doctors rushed in to help the boy, trying to manage his overdose. Zero's eyes scanned the distance, searching for me as everything unfolded. In the back of my head, I wondered why he wanted me to see this. Was it a warning?

A doctor approached and tapped my shoulder. "Acelin?" she asked, curious. "What are you doing here?"

I recognized her immediately—the same doctor who always patched me up after training. She had a motherly presence, and a gentle demeanor. But no matter how kind she seemed, I couldn't bring myself to trust her.

The shock in my eyes mirrored hers. "I got lost," I said, tugging on my suit jacket.

"Wait." She gripped my arm tightly. "Whatever you saw, you can't tell anyone about it."

"Or what?" I spoke. "Ya think I don't know what really goes on in this place?"

"Then see for yourself." She released my arm, her eyes fixed on me with a challenge.

The lab sank into an uneasy silence, interrupted only by the steady beep of the heart monitor as I walked away.

* * *

When Monday arrived, I met Moe. After all this time, I finally saw the way she looked at me—the same way she had when we were caught by the Members. She fidgeted with her fingertips, biting her lips until they bled. Neither of us spoke, just walked around the park in silence.

"Do you ever think you're coming back home?" she finally asked.

"I decided to go to Japan with the Members."

CHAPTER 12

"So, what will you do in Japan?" she asked, her foot kicking small rocks along the path.

"Become a leader and start my own business," we exchanged a look.

"Business of what, Acelin? You can't just jump up and say that."

"How can I not?" I asked, frowning. "Maybe this was supposed to happen to me."

As I walked back to the trucks, my mind raced, unable to shake the storm of thoughts. Her words echoed in my head, cutting deeper than I cared to admit. Was she right? Could that not happen?

"You're selfish," she rolled her eyes.

I paused before getting into the truck, a smirk on my face. "Then I'll be selfish," I said, watching her face frown. I took a painkiller, glancing back at her being escorted away.

One of the Members received a call. We were assigned to meet with a man hosting a celebration party with Drew. When we arrived, I entered through a gate leading to a mansion. Two trucks followed us, with Drew in the one behind me. As I stepped out of the car, a lady fixed my hair and used a makeup palette to cover any scars on my face. Drew pulled me in for a picture as the camera flashed in my eyes.

I buttoned up my suit and followed the Members, my nerves tightening with every step. Drew took off his thick glasses, smiling like everything was perfectly normal. "Are you ready?" he asked.

"What is this place?" I replied.

"Where the creators are," he led the way.

As we entered inside, the flashing lights and music hit me. Fireworks exploded outside, and the air was thick with laughter and celebration. Most of the people wore face masks, their identities hidden. A lady handed me a tiger mask, but I just held it awkwardly while Drew ignored it entirely. I couldn't shake the feeling that something terrible was lurking behind all the loud music.

A man with an eye patch over his left eye approached us. His dark blue suit looked sharp, but it was the black glove covering his hand that caught my attention. He removed it as he got closer, revealing his burn marks. He reached out to shake my hand.

"It's nice doing business with you," he said. "I'm Scar Face."

I paused briefly before shaking his hand. The act of grasping his scarred hand seemed like making a deal with the devil. I compelled myself to proceed. "I'm Jones," I said, concealing my discomfort.

Drew whispered to me as we reached a quieter room, "How about you go to the backyard? I need to have a talk with him first."

I felt a lump in my throat as the reality of our mission hit me. The true purpose of being here wasn't to celebrate—it was to earn the creators' trust only to betray them. I told myself it was for survival, that it had to be done, to save others. The creators held the key, the stain we needed to set things right. To finally stop the hallucinations.

In the backyard, a tea party seemed oddly out of place under the gloomy sky. Dark clouds hung low, and the air smelled like rain was coming. Bright balloons were tied to the tall gates, their colors standing out. Fairy lights flickered above the table, glowing softly.

The table was covered with a white cloth. It was loaded with snacks—cupcakes, cookies, sandwiches, and small pastries.

CHAPTER 12

There were teapots, cups, and saucers neatly arranged. The wind made the balloons sway, and the tablecloth fluttered slightly.

A little girl in a frilly dress walked up to me, clutching a tiny teacup in her small hands. Her wide eyes studied me as she held out the cup, offering me tea with a shy smile.

I took the teacup from her hand. She plopped down on one of the small chairs at the table. "Sit!" she chirped, motioning to the seat across from her.

I sat, feeling out of place at the whimsical setup.

"What's your name?" she continued, kicking her legs under the table.

"Acelin," I replied, keeping my voice steady. "What's yours?"

"Scarlet," she said, grinning as she reached for a sugar cube and dropped it into her empty teacup. "Daddy calls me Scar for short."

My stomach twisted, and the cupcake in my hand suddenly felt heavy. "Scar Face… he's your dad?"

She nodded enthusiastically. "Yep! He's the best dad ever," she nodded. "He always tells me one day this whole place will be mine. The house, the business, everything! Isn't that cool?"

I forced a tight smile, my thoughts racing. The man we were planning to betray, to destroy, wasn't just some untouchable figure of power—he was a father. And here she was, innocent and carefree, offering me cupcakes.

"Nanny, you don't talk much, do you?" she tilted her head.

"Nanny?" I raised my brow. "That's funny."

She giggled, raising her empty teacup like it was a toast. "I always wanted a Nanny like you."

I nodded slowly. The mission was starting to feel a lot more complicated than it already had. For the first time, I found myself questioning not just the plan, but everything I'd been doing with the Members to *people*. The people we've hurt could have had families who depended on them, loved ones who cherished them.

Drew's voice cut through the moment. He stood by the tall doors, his arms crossed, watching us with a smirk. "I see you've met my niece, Scarlet."

Scarlet groaned and rolled her eyes dramatically at him. "Lulu, you're such a mood killer."

Drew laughed. "Don't let her fool you, Acelin. She's more trouble than she looks."

I stood, brushing imaginary crumbs off my suit. "Well, it was nice to meet ya, Scarlet," I said, giving her a little bow.

She waved me off, pretending to be annoyed but unable to hide her grin. "Yeah, yeah. Don't get all formal on me. Come back and have tea with me again sometime."

"I'll hold ya to that," I said, smiling.

As I walked towards Drew, I glanced back at Scarlet, already playing with the balloons. The door clicked shut behind us. "She likes you. That's rare," Drew said.

"She's... different." I struggled to put my thoughts into words.

"She's family," Drew replied. "And family is the only thing worth protecting in this world."

Drew and I walked into a big dining room. The walls were gold, and silver lights hung from the ceiling. Long tables were covered with white cloth and neat decorations. Guests sat down as Drew went to a small stage and took the microphone. Servers moved around, handing out fancy dishes. I took a plate of shrimp to eat.

"Let's start the bidding contest, ladies and gentlemen!" Drew announced, waiting for the crowd to settle down. "Our first

CHAPTER 12

bid goes on Henry Cane Day."

A boy with thick blonde hair and blue eyes appeared on a screen, wearing an all-gray jumper with the number *#007* on it. I watched as the crowd glanced around, then a lady in a cat mask placed a bid of ten thousand dollars on him.

The thing about Henry was that he was very special to the Members. Unlike the others, he could endure far more tests in a single day, making him invaluable to their experiments.

Scarlet sat down beside me. "Are you bidding tonight?"

I was startled by her appearance. "What do ya mean?"

"They're bidding on children to see who survives the drugs they test on them. It's like a game these people play," she said, slouching.

Drew continued. "What we inject in them helps us figure out how to make better drugs for our community. We all remember what happened to the last child," Drew laughed, and the crowd joined in. "After we run tests on them, they'll be given a pill to make them forget what we did. It's mandatory for every one of those kids to take it."

The little girl tugged on my hand. I leaned over to hear her clearly. "They've been doing this for so long," she said. "I have no idea where those kids come from."

"Well..." I hesitated, choosing my words carefully. "What we're doing is for the best."

"That's what they all say Nanny," she stole a piece of shrimp from my plate.

He clicked a button, and the screen flickered to life, showing a video of a small child chained to a cold, metal chair. The child's body jerked violently; their face contorted in agony as they struggled against the effects of the drugs. Low whispers spread through the crowd, some laughing, others discussing the horrific scene as if it were just another piece of entertainment.

Drew's voice grew colder, his eyes scanning the room. "This is what we don't need. We don't want to turn them into monsters here, do we?"

The crowd responded. *"No!"* eager to show their support. There had been twenty-five kids who were bid on through the day.

At midnight, I was still sitting at the table, dozing off to the sound of clinking glasses and chatter. Scarlet was no longer at the table. Her teacup sat abandoned. I glanced around the room, but she was nowhere to be seen. Drew was surrounded by some of the Members. Their attention focused on something unfolding.

Drew and I locked eyes, and he gestured for me to come to him. "There's been a problem, our mission is going left."

"What's going on?" I asked, concerned flaring in my throat.

"Don't ask, just find Scarlet!" he shouted, already disappearing into the hallway.

I bumped into one of the Members, who shoved a gun into my hand. Without hesitation, I tucked it into my waistband. The house felt eerily quiet, the only sound coming from the faint creak of the floorboards beneath me. I moved upstairs, my eyes scanning every corner, searching for any sign of her.

A trail of crumbs caught my attention—muffins, scattered on the carpet. I crouched down, picking up a few pieces, my mind started to race. "Scarlet, are you there?" I called, my voice echoing down the long hallway.

Before I could take another step, a bullet whizzed past my ear. My heart jumped as I dropped to the ground. Scar Face pressed himself against the wall at the far end of the hallway, his arm extended with the barrel of his gun aimed in my direction. He

CHAPTER 12

didn't even look at me.

I ducked behind a table, gripping the gun tightly against my chest. My breaths came fast and uneven as I tried to steady myself. My pulse pounded in my ears, drowning out every other sound.

"Did you really think I'd fall for your trap?" Scar Face's voice slithered through the hall, taunting. But I still couldn't see him. I could hear his boots on the carpet. He was getting closer.

When I caught a glimpse of him, he turned his back. I pushed myself off the table and crouched low. Ahead, a marble statue offered a small cover. I ran for it, my muscles burned as I pressed my back against the cold stone, trying to steady my breath again.

Then, Scarlet appeared, walking behind him.

"Drew, you've always wanted what I had, my family, my success, everything!" He spun around, searching. "Don't forget how you got here!" he growled. "I made you what you are! And now you think you can take the money and leave me behind?" he laughed. "We had a deal!"

A gunshot rang out, one of the Members fired, the sound deafening. Scar Face staggered, clutching his arm as blood soaked his hand. A black bag dropped from his grasp, hitting the floor with a thump. He cried out.

Before I could react, Scarlet grabbed the bag and ran past me, holding it close as if it was everything. "Grab her!" one of the Members shouted.

"Scarlet, stop!" I said, but she didn't look back.

I chased her, rushing through the kitchen door. I ran too fast, not paying attention, and slammed into a table. A tray of food flew, plates smashing on the floor, but I didn't stop.

I followed her up more stairs as she pushed open the emergency exit doors.

The cold wind hit me as I rushed onto the roof. Scarlet stood near the edge, her hair whipping in the breeze. The bag was still pressed tightly to her chest.

"Scarlet," I called, my voice cracking. "Please, just hand it over. You don't understand what's happening here."

Her eyes, filled with hurt and anger, met mine. "You hurt my daddy!" she cried.

I stepped closer, reaching for the bag. "It wasn't supposed to be like this. Just give it to me, and we can fix this."

She shook her head, clutching the bag even tighter. "No, Nanny!" She took another step back.

The roof creaked under each step I took, the tiles uneven and cracked from years of neglect. The cold air made the roof feel fragile beneath me, like it could give away at any moment. My feet slid slightly with each movement.

I lunged, my hand brushing the strap of the bag. In my rush, my hand bumped into her shoulder.

It happened so quickly.

Her footing slipped, and she teetered dangerously on the edge. My heart stopped as I reached out to save her, but it was too late. She fell, her body disappearing over the side with a scream that faded.

I stood froze, the cold biting into my skin, but it was nothing compared to the numbness in my chest. The world felt like it was crashing down around me as I looked over the edge. She had fallen into the bouncy house below, where the tea party had been earlier. I still couldn't get myself to move. All I could think about was whether she was alive or not.

I had to cover this up, and there was only one person who could help me.

13

Chapter 13

I met with Zero at a coffee shop. The night was foggy, and the streets outside were quiet except for the occasional car passing by. Inside, the scent of freshly brewed coffee and pastries filled the air. The quiet conversations and the soft clinking of mugs created a comfort for me. But, not for long.

He sat across from me, his back straight and tense, stress radiating off him. "Hey," he said, his fingers tapping against the table, as if trying to distract himself.

His cheeks had that constant rosy hue, a detail that always made him look younger and strangely innocent, despite the things we both knew he was capable of.

"Did you do it yet?" I leaned in.

"Yeah, it's done." He glanced around, hoping no one had seen him. "You're lucky she fell into that bouncy house. It made it easier for me to slip the pill into her mouth."

"And the bag she was holding?"

"It was full of cash," he said, then tapped his hand against the table again, a nervous pattern I was starting to recognize. "But there's more." He leaned closer, lowering his voice like we were sharing a secret. "Drew knows. He figured out who took his letter." He looked around one more time. "You know, the one he wrote for his sister?"

I froze; the mention of that letter hit me with worry. Drew wasn't the kind of person to let something like that slide. My thoughts raced, trying to piece together how much trouble that might have brought me. Zero's eyes stayed on me, waiting for my reaction.

"Acelin, I'm telling you this because I think you should leave tonight. That night at his penthouse, I heard him talking to a girl."

Drew went back to town last night to finish packing up the last of his things from his Cherry Hill loft. He was preparing to leave for Japan, determined to start fresh with the Members. But just as he was finishing up, someone showed up unannounced. Their visit changed everything.

"I have something to tell you," Moe said, standing at Drew's front door, her hands clenched tightly at her sides.

"What is it?" Drew asked, cracking the door open just enough to see her face.

"I know who took your letter." Moe hesitated. "It was Acelin. I saw it on his desk at home."

Drew's brows furrowed, and his grip on the door tightened. "Acelin? My Acelin?" he asked, pushing the door open fully.

Moe's composure broke. She fell to her knees, her desperation spilling over. "Please," she begged, her voice cracked. "Release me from the Members control. I'll do anything for my freedom, just name it."

His accent grew thicker, his words sharper as he tried to keep his emotions in check. He knew he had to act quickly. "Come inside, let's talk."

CHAPTER 13

I exchanged a look with Zero. My heart sank, and my vision blurred for a moment. My thoughts went blank.

"Acelin, are you even listening to me—" Zero's words trailed off as his eyes shifted. I followed his gaze and saw a group of boys in suits nearby, their presence seemed of trouble.

Zero gave me the signal Members use when danger was near. I stood up slowly, buttoned my suit, and avoided eye contact with the boys. Zero slipped away in the other direction, making sure not to be seen with me.

In the parking lot, my hand rested on my gun, ready for whatever came next. I wasn't nervous, just prepared to kill if I needed to. Sliding into the driver's seat, I gripped the steering wheel. I noticed the scent of another boy lingering in the car. Before I could react, I felt the cold press of a gun against the back of my head.

I raised my hands. The boy leaned closer and pulled off his mask. His messy, wavy hair framed his face that looked torn between fear and desperation. "I need the money, okay?" His voice cracked, with a weak laugh and sob. "I'm not a bad person."

"I don't know what ya talkin about," I said, keeping my voice calm.

The gun pressed harder. He gritted his teeth. "You're wanted dead or alive. If you just cooperate, maybe you'll live."

My eyes stayed locked on him through the rear-view mirror. "Let's just talk this out—" With a sudden move, I grabbed my gun and fired, hitting him in the shoulder. He screamed as I pushed open the car door and dropped to the ground.

I ran through the parking lot, heading for the steps. My foot caught on the edge of something, and I tumbled down the hard concrete. Pain shot through my body, but I didn't have time to feel it.

A cry echoed behind me, followed by the crack of a bullet cutting past my ear. I didn't look back. I didn't know if it was him or someone else chasing me. My heart pounded in my chest, every beat pushing me forward. I dashed across the lower parking lot, my hands sweaty. Every sound felt louder, every shadow like a threat, but I kept running.

I burst into the nearest club, pushing past security and squeezing through the crowd. Flashing lights and the pounding bass made everything feel like I was stuck in slow motion. It felt like my whole life was flashing before my eyes. I didn't know where to run. I didn't know what to do. I was lost.

As I scanned the room, my eyes locked on a group of boys in suits standing by the bar. They weren't drinking or dancing. They were watching. Watching *me*. I needed to move—*now*. I ducked my head and headed for the back, loading my gun as I walked. I kept my eyes forward. My fingers shook slightly. People brushed past me, unaware of the danger lurking just feet away.

I turned a corner and ran straight into one of the boys hunting me. The gun slipped from my hand, clattering onto the floor. Panic hit me like a punch to the gut. I had dived onto my stomach, eyes locked on the gun, my fingers stretching out to grab it. *Almost there. Almost—* The boy grabbed my legs and yanked me back hard, dragging me across the floor.

I gripped the hidden knife from my pocket and swung it upward, jamming it into his thigh. His eyes shot wide open, and he howled in pain, stumbling back. I didn't wait. I sprang to my feet.

Another boy charged at me with a knife. I ducked the first swing and kicked a loose chair into his legs. He stumbled forward, losing balance.

CHAPTER 13

I started running down the hall. People screamed and scattered, running in every direction. The moment worked in my favor, making it easy to disappear back into the crowd. I pushed my way through the people on the dance floor, my breath short. The flashing lights stung my eyes, making it hard to spot the exit door. Just as I thought I was in the clear, a taser shot my side.

My muscles locked up, and I crashed to the floor. Pain hit through me like fire. *A taser.* My body twitched uncontrollably, and no matter how hard I tried to move, I couldn't.

* * *

My eyes fluttered open, but my vision was blurry. I blinked a few times, and slowly, the room came into focus.

My suit was torn, and dried blood stained my shirt. I glanced around, taking in my surroundings. The walls were cold and gray. An underground facility. A place where criminals went when they were no longer useful for the Members.

I sat up, my head pounding harder with every movement. My hands pressed against the glass window, fingers leaving streaks on the clean surface. *Where am I? How did I get here?*

Then I saw him.

Drew.

He walked with a smirk on his face. His black suit looked fresh, not a single wrinkle in sight. His eyes, usually calm, now carried something colder—something final. He stopped in front of the glass and pressed the button on the wall, activating the speaker. His voice crackled through.

"Welcome back, Mr. Jones," he said, his face blank.

"Drew..." My voice was rough, like I'd been screaming for hours. I coughed, clearing my throat. "Why am I here?"

He tilted his head, his eyes narrowing just a little. "I always admired you, Acelin. You're brave, smart, strong..." He paused, letting his words hang in the air. "But you're also a liar."

My heart skipped a beat. "Is this about the letter I took?" I asked, my voice still hoarse. "How did you find out?"

"I have eyes everywhere," he said. His gaze didn't shift, he didn't blink. He held the letter up in his hand.

My jaw clenched, anger hitting with a little bit of fear. "Did Jackson tell you?" I snapped, my voice louder now, more desperate. "Tell me!"

Drew let out a short, cold laugh. "Jackson?" He shook his head. "No, Acelin. I didn't need Jackson to tell me anything." He stepped closer, his face just inches from the glass. "You've been with us for four months. Four months of me teaching you everything I know. I treated you like a brother." He pressed his hand against the glass, fingers spread. "But you broke that trust."

"Ya gonna kill me, aren't you?" I asked. I wasn't sure if it was acceptance or pure exhaustion.

His face didn't change. "No," he said softly, almost like he didn't want to say it. "I'm not going to kill you." He stepped back, his eyes never leaving mine.

My stomach twisted into knots, my breathing unsteady. "Why do ya care so much about the letter, Drew?" I pressed, trying to get him to break. "Ya sister's dead. That letter won't change anything."

Drew's face hardened like stone. For a moment, I thought he would punch the glass. "She's not dead," he said, his voice

CHAPTER 13

strained. "She's in a coma, Acelin. She's still alive." His voice cracked, the smallest crack. "And when she wakes up, she's going to need the letter."

I froze. *Alive?* My breath hitched, and I felt my throat tighten. "She's alive?" I whispered, disbelief flooding every part of me. My eyes locked to Drew's face, searching for a lie, but there wasn't one. *She's alive.*

"Goodbye, Acelin Jones," he said, his eyes sad for just a second—just one second— before his face turned cold again.

I opened my mouth to speak, but no words came out. My hands pressed against the glass, my eyes pleading with him. "Drew…" I tried to say something, anything. An apology, maybe. A promise to make it right. But my lips wouldn't move.

Then I heard it.

Hsssssss.

A soft hiss came from the vents above me. I looked up, and I saw mist spilling into the room. *No, no, no, no, no.* I pound my fists against the glass. "Drew!" I yelled, my voice shaky. "Drew, don't do this! Please!" My hands slammed against the glass again, harder this time. My palms burned; my knuckles raw.

But he didn't look back. He didn't even flinch. He just walked away, his hands in his pockets, his figure shrinking as he disappeared into the hallway. The gas filled the room faster than I expected. My breaths got shorter. I tried to hold my breath, but it didn't matter. The mist crept into my lungs anyway. My body felt heavy. My hands slid down the glass, leaving smudged prints behind. I blinked slowly, my vision dimming.

Not like this. Please, not like this.

My knees gave out, and I crumpled to the floor, my cheek pressed against the cold, smooth tile. My chest rose and fell slower with each second. The room faded around me. I could hear my own heartbeat in my ears, thumping slower and slower.

Then, everything went quiet.

Black.

My arms were tied, and my mouth was sealed with tape. I sat in the back of a truck, feeling every bump and turn on the road. When the truck finally stopped, the sound of doors opening startled me. Three Members grabbed my arms, pulling me outside.

I stumbled as they pushed me forward. We entered through the back doors of a building. My ears picked up the distant sound of voices. I couldn't see anything with the blindfold covering my eyes, but I felt every turn, every step down the metal stairs.

When we stopped, I felt a soft carpet under my feet. They shoved me forward, and I landed face first on a bed. The thick, silky sheets smelled faintly of perfume. I kicked and squirmed, but the weight of one of them pressed me down hard. I screamed, but it came out muffled, the tape still sealed tightly over my mouth.

The air shifted, and I felt someone close by. A man's voice broke the silence.

"Calm down," he said. His tone was nonchalant, but there was something more underneath it. "There's no need to yell." I heard the Members leave. It was just me and an unknown man.

I stopped struggling, breathing heavily through my nose. The blindfold was pulled from my eyes, and my vision blurred for a second before clearing. The man stood in front of me. He looked normal, like someone you'd see on the street. He wore black pants and a white button up shirt with the sleeves rolled to his elbows. His eyes were framed by glasses that he slowly

CHAPTER 13

pulled off and wiped with a small cloth.

He crouched in front of me, tilting his head like he was studying me. His eyes were calm but far too focused. "Calm down," he repeated, his voice smooth like he'd said it a thousand times before. "I'm a doctor."

He reached towards my face, and I flinched, trying to pull away, but I had nowhere to go. He peeled the tape from my mouth, tearing it off in one quick motion. I gasped for air, my lips stinging. "What are you going to do to me?" I asked, my voice raw.

He didn't answer right away. He sat a suitcase right on top of the table. He unlocked it with two clicks, lifting the lid slowly. "I'm going to run a few tests on you," he finally said, his back to me. A cloth unfolded to reveal knives of all shapes and sizes, each one neatly arranged. Beside them were needles and small glass vials filled with a white powder. My breathing got faster, like I couldn't get enough air.

He slipped on a pair of blue gloves, snapping them over his wrists. He adjusted his glasses, pushing them up the bridge of his nose. He smiled to himself like he found something funny. I watched him closely, my heart thudding against my ribs. He reached down, his fingers hovered over the knives. He didn't pick one up right away. He just... stared at them. His eyes closed for a second as he took a deep, slow breath in and out. *He's enjoying this.*

I moved before I could think. I threw my body to the side, rolling off the bed with a loud thud. Pain shot through my shoulder as I hit the floor. I struggled, trying to stand, but my arms and legs were still tied. "HELP!" I screamed at the top of my lungs, my voice desperate. My voice echoed off the walls, but nobody came. Nobody would.

He crouched at the edge of the bed, looking down at me like I was a child throwing a tantrum. "There's no need to yell," he said. "This will all be over soon."

He grabbed me by the back of my shirt and lifted me like I weighed nothing. I fought harder, moving and twisting, but he didn't flinch. *He's too strong.*

His eyes had changed. Before, they were calm. Now, they looked hollow. Empty. He tilted his head, just a little, and said softly, "Stop struggling."

I saw him grab one of the needles from the table. My breath caught in my throat. My heart felt like it was going to explode. "No, no, no!" I yelled, shaking my head violently. "You don't have to do this!"

He didn't respond. He flicked the needle, tapping it with his finger. A tiny bubble of liquid slid down the metal tip.

My eyes looked around the room, looking for anything I could use to free myself.

Sweat dripped down my forehead, stinging my eyes. "Please," I whispered, my voice cracking. "Please, don't." The needle hovered over my arm. His gloved fingers were steady. Not a single shake. "Please," I begged again, feeling the tears burn hot down my face. "Don't do this."

I shut my eyes tight, heart pounding so loud it drowned everything else out.

A loud gunshot echoed through the room. The man in front of me fell to the floor, his body lifeless. Blood pooled around him; the metallic smell made my stomach twist. My breathing came fast and shaky as I stared down at him. *He's dead. He's really dead.* I felt myself laughing.

Footsteps rushed towards me. Zero and another boy appeared, moving fast. Zero's eyes were full of urgency. The boy

CHAPTER 13

with him had pale, dry lips, and he pressed a finger to his mouth, signaling me to stay quiet.

"I'm getting you out of here, Acelin," Zero said.

"I brought your stuff from the Members," said the boy with the chapped lips. "The Tooth Fairy was gonna steal your money and take your things." His eyes looked around like he expected someone to appear any second.

"Please, let me make it out alive," I begged as they untied me.

"We don't have much time," chapped lips said, glancing down the hall. "If they catch us, we're dead."

We moved quickly, running through the dim, narrow hallways. My legs felt weak, but fear kept me moving. Our footsteps sounded loud, and I could hear other footsteps behind us. Voices shouted from somewhere close. They were coming for us.

"Run faster!" Zero called out, glancing back at us as he sprinted ahead.

I pushed myself harder, legs burning, lungs aching. We turned a corner, then another. It felt like a maze, every hall looking the same. My heart thumped so hard it hurt.

We reached a metal back door. Zero shoved it open, and cold night air hit my face like a slap. Outside, a pickup truck sat running. Without a second thought, I jumped onto the back. My arms ached, but I pulled myself up, throwing my body onto the bed of the truck. Zero jumped in next to me. The chapped lip boy went after us.

"Go, go, GO!" Zero shouted, banging on the roof of the truck.

The driver hit the gas, and the truck shot forward. I grabbed the side to keep from flying out. The wind hit my face even harder, stinging my skin. I turned to see the hotel shrinking in the distance. For a moment, I let myself breathe. My heart was still racing, but I was alive. I could still hear the doctor's voice in my head. *"This will all be over soon."* I squeezed my eyes shut, trying to block it out, but it stayed with me.

We drove for what felt like forever. My muscles were sore, my clothes still stained with blood. *What do I do now? Where do I go?*

The truck pulled into a small, run-down motel near the train tracks. The neon *"VACANCY"* sign flickered like it was about to go out. The place looked abandoned, with cracked windows and walls covered in old graffiti. But it was quiet. And right now, quiet was all I needed.

Zero jumped down first, landing with a thump. He reached up to help me down, his eyes scanning the street for anyone who might be watching. "Come on," he said, his voice softer now. "We'll be safe here for a little while." We moved quickly towards the lobby. It smelled like old carpet and stale cigarettes. The wallpaper was peeling at the edges, and a flickering light buzzed overhead. No one was behind the counter, so Zero tapped the old bell a few times. "Here," Zero said to the man behind the counter, pulling out a few crumpled bills from his pocket. He looked at me. "We're staying here tonight."

I nodded, still too shaken to speak. I followed them down a hall, every step too loud in my ears. Room 12. Zero unlocked the door, and we all filed in. The room was small, just two beds and a tiny TV mounted to the wall. The bed closest to me had a faded red blanket that smelled faintly of bleach. I sat on the edge of it, my hands shaking.

The second I sat down, I felt all the pain hit me at once. My body felt heavy, my eyes stinging from lack of sleep. My head throbbed from where I'd been hit earlier.

Zero sat next to me. "You're safe now," he said quietly,

CHAPTER 13

glancing at me.

I didn't answer. I just stared at the wall, my mind spinning with everything that had happened. *I almost died. They were going to kill me. They still might.* I rubbed my face with both hands, trying to push the thoughts away, but they stayed. *Do I go home? Do I run? Do I hide?* I didn't have answers to any of it.

Zero leaned forward, resting his elbows on his knees. "I know what you're thinking," he said, his eyes fixed on the ground. "You think you're still trapped. You think they're gonna find you no matter where you go." He looked at me. "But you're wrong, Acelin. You're out now. They don't own you anymore."

I stared at him, my throat tight with everything I wanted to say. But no words came out. I didn't believe him. Not yet. "What do I do now?"

"There's this man I work for. He's been laying low for months, maybe even years. If he can do it, you can too, okay?" Zero said. He rubbed his fingers through his scalp.

I glanced at the ground, my chest feeling tight. "I think... I'm ready to go home." My eyes started to water for the first time in months. I blinked hard, trying to stop the tears, but they came anyway.

He nodded, his eyes steady on me. "I can cover this all up, okay? When you go home, don't ever think about what's happening up here. Forget it all."

Forget it? I wanted to believe it was that simple, but everything I'd seen, everything I'd done, sat heavy. My hands trembled at my sides, and I squeezed them into fists. *Can I really go back to normal? Will it ever feel normal again?*

"Okay," I said. We finally stood up and I hugged him tightly. For a moment, it felt like everything I'd been holding inside—all the fear, anger, and regret—spilled out in that hug. I didn't say anything else. I didn't have to.

In the middle of the night, rain poured down heavily in the streets, drumming against the roof of Zero's old car, he stashed. The windshield wipers squeak with every pass, barely keeping up with the water blurring the view ahead.

I sat in the passenger seat, silent, with my head leaning against the cold window. Water trails slid down the glass like tiny rivers. My suit jacket clung to me, damp. My bag was on my lap, arms wrapped around it like it was all I had left.

"You good?" Zero asked, keeping one hand on the wheel, the other tapping a slow rhythm on the gear shift. His eyes stayed on the road, focused.

"They'll find me," I replied, staring at the slick streets ahead. "They always do."

Zero didn't say anything after that. Just nodded like he understood. The rain filled the silence, tapping on the roof like it had something to say. I watched his hands on the wheel—steady, calm, like he'd done this a hundred times. He always acted like nothing could scare him. But I could tell he was tense.

The car slowed as we pulled up to the Cherry Hill train station. The parking lot was nearly empty, just a few cars lined up by the curb. The glow of the station lights cut through the rain, making the pavement shimmer like black glass. Zero parked but didn't turn off the engine. He leaned forward, letting out a deep breath. "If I never hear from you again, just know it was nice being a Member with you," he said, not looking at me this time.

"Same," I said, gripping my bag tighter. "Ain't no turning back now." I pulled the door handle. The cold hit me like a punch, rain soaking my clothes instantly.

"Be safe, man," Zero said through the crack of his window.

CHAPTER 13

His voice was serious, not like his usual laid-back tone. "Don't do nothing stupid."

I nodded, rain running down my face like tears. I jogged towards the train, shoulders hunched against the cold rain. My bag thudded against my side with every step. The automatic doors slid open to let me in. I didn't look back. I knew Zero was still watching, but I couldn't face him again.

Inside, it was quiet except for the noise of the overhead lights and the soft crackle of an old intercom announcing train times. I found a seat towards the back and sat down. My clothes clung to me, rainwater dripping from my hair. I shook out my jacket, my fingers trembling from the cold.

When I woke up, the train had stopped, and people were shuffling out. My neck was stiff from leaning against the window. I rubbed it, blinking the sleep from my eyes. The lights inside the train flickered once, and I knew it was my stop. I got up, my legs shaky, my body still sore.

I stepped off the train, taking a slow breath as I looked up at the sign: ***A welcome back to Cherry Hill.*** It felt like I was in a dream. I walked through the quiet streets, passing familiar places that once felt normal. The corner store with its flickering *"Open"* sign, the playground with the same old rusty swings, the alley where I used to cut through on my way home. Nothing had changed, but the energy felt different.

It was late, and the streets were mostly empty, but I still glanced over my shoulder every few minutes. Old habits. My feet dragged like I was carrying the whole world on my back. *Almost there,* I told myself. *Just a few more blocks.*

When I reached my house, I stopped at the edge of the front yard. The porch light was on, I stared at it, my breath coming out in short puffs of steam. *I should knock. No, I should just walk in. No... what if she doesn't want me back?* My head spun with doubt, but I forced myself to move. Step by step, I climbed the porch stairs. Each one creaked like it was calling out my return.

I raised my fist and knocked softly at first, then a little louder. *Please open the door. Please.*

Inside, I heard movement. Light footsteps shuffled towards the door. It opened slowly, and there she was. My Mom. Her eyes widened, and she gasped so hard it sounded like she'd lost all her breath at once.

14

Chapter 14

I sat across from Mom in silence at the kitchen table. She watched me eat, her hand covering her mouth like she was holding something back. Worry, relief, or maybe both?

I didn't know what to say. I didn't know how to explain everything that happened. So, I kept eating and pretended the food didn't taste like nothing.

I told her about the money I had earned, revealing only half the amount. The full sum was my secret to keep. I spun a story of poker games won at the fencing camps. She believed me. I hoped.

Days passed as I stayed home, consumed by depression and missing school.

"You okay, honey?"

"Yeah, just daydreaming," I replied. We soaked our feet in a bowl of warm water, wrapped in our white robes. We had a spy day. I couldn't shake the thoughts of being with the Members and that strange man again, so I needed to leave the house.

"Your friend Moe was pretty worried about you while you were gone," she said, looking at me over a magazine. "Your face is starting to clear up. I can't believe they watched you get beat up because you won some poker game?"

"I know, it's crazy, it was more like ah boot camp than anything. At least we're making it to the finals this year for fencing."

"I'm very proud of you, Acelin," she said with a smile. Guilt washed over me. Proud because I'm a good liar?

"About Moe, what did she say, exactly?" I adjusted my robe. "About me?"

She frowned. "Hm," the sound of her phone went off. "Sorry, I gotta take this call!" She took out her phone and answered. The whole day with her felt like we had a stronger connection for once. I got to know her all over again. My Mom, who had felt like a stranger, finally felt familiar.

The next morning, I felt like I was going to puke. All night, I couldn't sleep unless I exhausted myself from staying up. I was afraid Drew would break through my window and kidnap Mom. Sometimes, in the middle of the night, she slept in the library room, right by the window. I couldn't imagine what I would have done if she was kidnapped by the Members.

I was drenched in sweat, my hair plastered to my forehead. Jackson slipped into my door, a glass of orange juice in his hand.

He shook his head. "I don't know what they did to you, but you need to get up. You haven't showered in days," he said, his voice soothing yet filled with concern. Silence had stretched between us since my return home. Disappointment stuck on his face; he barely met my eyes. "Your hair, why did you cut it?" he asked.

"I didn't have a choice, Jackson," I replied, accepting the glass. "Do people at school still talk about me?" He had on his school uniform reminding me of the school memories.

CHAPTER 14

"People asked about you, but not in a negative way. Drew's no longer coaching, so they're looking for a new swim coach."

I rose from the bed. "Jackson, just tell me what they're saying about me."

He huffed. "Some think you killed yourself because of the bullying, others believe you transferred schools."

I stood up as I searched for a clean uniform. "I have to return to school. I can't let them see me as a coward."

"Why be bothered about their opinions?" He shrugged.

"Because I am," I said, our eyes locking. "Did you ever tell Drew about the letter I took from his desk?"

"Acelin, when you left, there was peace in this house. The Members never hurt me in any way." He shook his head in disappointment. "I have to go now, I'll see you at school."

After a long shower, I went into the kitchen to prepare breakfast. Jackson's words hit me, but he was justified in his feelings. Making breakfast brought back memories of oatmeal mornings at the Members' penthouse, surrounded by boys my age and men. Now, eating alone, I found myself missing their company—a thought I knew was horrible to think.

The school had the same old smell, flooding back memories. The hallways were crowded, classrooms filled with students skipping. The usual hookups still happened. Everything was still the same.

I sat in the office, waiting for the principal to meet with me.

"Welcome back, Acelin. I'm happy you chose to take some time for yourself," he said.

"Yeah, I needed it," I replied coolly, sticking to the lie that I had taken time off for my mental health.

"I've placed your grades on hold, so now that you're back, you can resume from where you left off. Does that sound good?"

"Yes, that's perfect. Thank you so much!" I stood up to shake his hand.

"Now, get going. You don't want to miss the second hour."

As I walked through the hallways, girls turned their heads, and boys stopped to ask about the scent of my cologne—a new fragrance no other boy could afford if it wasn't their daddy's money. Rumors circulated that I had a better car than Nick, the student who was considered better than anyone else.

Voices echoed through the halls.

"Who is he?"

"I need him so bad!"

"Can we please be friends?"

"Let me ride in your car!"

Searching for my sketchbook in my locker, I noticed Nick standing beside me with his friends, talking loudly, trying to gain my attention.

Nick faced towards me. "Yo Acelin, why haven't you been at school?" he asked.

I ignored him, shoving the last book into my bag. One of his friends slammed my locker shut. "Didn't you hear him talking to you?" the boy said.

I grabbed him by the shirt, pushing him against the lockers. "Did ya hear me not answer?" I spoke. The boy gasped for air, reaching out for Nick's hand.

Nick stepped back from the boy. "Just let him go, Acelin."

I shouldered past Nick. The boy wheezed, hitting Nick's arm in panic. "Why didn't you help me? He could've killed me," the boy said to Nick. Nick smacked the back of his head.

In the library, a food stand was set up, laden with snacks. I grabbed a coffee and some sandwiches, my first coffee in months. Settling next to a bookshelf, I began to sketch Lyra's

CHAPTER 14

eyes, drawing the freckles across her brows. I chose a colored pencil that matched her smooth brown skin and drew the white birthmark on the back of her neck. I hadn't seen her all day, and the thought of facing her again filled me with anxiety.

"You can really draw," a quiet voice said from behind me. It was Maxes Amaretto, the girl I had accused of publishing my article around town and ruining my life. I still found her utterly annoying.

I nodded sarcastically. "Thanks!"

"I can draw too, look," she said, pulling out her sketchbook. She ran her small hands over the artwork to smooth out the drawing, leaving pencil smudges on her palm. "I think you're almost better than me, actually." She flicked one of her pigtails behind her head. Her art was better, but since I didn't like her, I hated it. "I'm going to an art show tonight, not saying you have to come or anything—"

"Do ya ever shut up, completely?" We exchanged a look. "You been trying to get me to one for ages. My answer is still no."

Her eyes frowned, and her smile dropped. "I swear, I didn't publish your article around town, it wasn't me!"

"I don't believe you. You lie to me just like everyone else." I fed into her truth.

"I would never lie to you. Believe me—"

I gestured with my hand for her to be quiet.

"Fine," she said. We fell silent for two seconds. "Here's an art show flier," she slid it under my hand. "I'll be attending later, hopefully you can come. I'll have a surprise for you!" she whispered.

"Great!" I said, waiting for her to walk away. "But I'm not coming!"

She popped her gum and gathered her things to leave. A smile was plastered on her face as she walked out the door. I needed no distractions and couldn't afford to make any new friends.

When I arrived home, Maxes art show preoccupied my thoughts. I stared at my closet, searching for clothes that would help me blend in with the affluent crowd at the art show. The doorbell rang. I peeked through the curtains, but no one was there. "Hello?" I called out. No response. Paranoia had gripped me since my return; I had to be alert at all times. I grabbed a knife from the kitchen drawer, hiding it behind my back. The door knocked again. This time, it was Jackson. I opened the door.

"Are you going to stab me with that or are you going to put it down?" he asked.

"Oh! Sorry!" I placed the knife by the flowerpot as I chuckled. Frances was right behind him, applying lip gloss. Jackson had been talking with Frances a lot ever since I'd been gone. Their voices used to be low and secretive around me, but now they didn't even try to hide it.

"Just because I said something to you doesn't mean we're cool, got it?"

"Got it," I replied, closing the door, still yearning for a real conversation with him.

"And go put on a shirt, bro, my girl is here," Jackson called out from the living room.

"That's what I was doing!"

I dressed in black pants and a white turtleneck, aiming for a decent look. I used Mom's makeup palette to conceal the scars on my face, just a touch to cover the bruised eye. The remnants of my time with the Members still marked me. I slicked back what little hair I had left, needing to look and feel normal again. I drove to the address on the flier, arriving ten minutes late due

CHAPTER 14

to traffic. She didn't know I was coming. My attendance wasn't for her; it was to distract myself from the recent negativity.

A line had formed at the entrance. Parking lots were full, cameras flashed, and warm lights bathed the brick walls. People passed by in their fancy cars heading for the VIP entrance. It seemed I had arrived at a wealthy party, a gathering of adults, with no high school students in sight for once.

I was spotted by a man nearly drunk, trying to bypass the line to get inside. He waved his hands in the air, calling out to me. "Hey! You! I know you!" he shouted. "You're in the art contest, right?" He grabbed my arm and ushered me to the door. "I'm his assistant manager. His name is Ace—"

"Acelin Jones," I corrected. I played along with the lie to get us through the door. The man at the door checked the list, letting us in.

"My name is Greek," he said, his voice carrying a Russian accent. The name sounded familiar. I remembered seeing him on a wanted poster back with the Members, hearing rumors about how he was lying low and hiding. "I forgot my badge to get in but follow me."

"I'm here for Maxes," I told him, trying to match his pace.

"Yes! I know, how else would I recognize you?" he deflected. "Maxes always talks about you. She shows me pictures of you in her yearbook."

I frowned. "What?"

"There she is! If you need me, I'll be upstairs at the party," he said, grabbing a wine glass from a tray before staggering towards the stairs. The more I stared at him, the more his face started to click. His tattoo and buzz cut confirmed it—he was the one on the wanted poster.

"Hey, Acelin, you made it!" Maxes greeted me, pushing her

bangs aside.

I approached her slowly. "Yeah," I said, fiddling with a string in my pocket.

"Here, take this champagne," she offered, stopping a server to hand me a glass.

"Thanks," I said, accepting it. "How did my name get on the list?"

She hesitated, then confessed. "I might have taken your artwork from school without you noticing. It's being showcased today," she pleaded with sad eyes.

My heart raced. "Why, Maxes?" I demanded, keeping my composure as people passed by.

She looked down, troubled. "You would've said no if I had asked."

"Of course, I would've. Which piece was it?"

"The one with the girl's body. I had it turned into a sculpture."

I couldn't believe it. My grip on the glass tightened before I set it down, afraid I might shatter it. She had chosen *that* piece—the drawing of Lyra's body. The one I sketched during the camping trip a while back.

If Lyra found out, she'd been furious. Worse, she'd think I was obsessed with her. The thought made my heart pound in my ears. Everything I'd worked so hard to keep under control was unraveling right in front of me.

Maxes wore a look of regret as she continued, "Let's just see it. You'll get the credit," she assured me.

I forced a smile, but inside, I wanted to destroy every piece of art in sight.

As I entered the room, a hush fell over the crowd, their attention drawn to the lights illuminating my artwork. It wasn't meant for public display, yet there it was, an anonymous curved

CHAPTER 14

upper body that could belong to anyone. Who would ever guess it's Lyra Barns. People gathered around, snapping photos. The artwork stood alone in the white room, a red rope barring anyone from getting too close.

A man approached me from behind. "Acelin, right?" I shook his hand. "My name is—"

"Thomas Matt," I interrupted, letting go of his hand. "I know who you are. I'm your biggest fan." Although, in truth, I wasn't. He was well known in town for his art. Mom used to watch him on television when Sunday's hit.

He smiled. "Actually, I think I'm a big fan of you now. Here's my card," he placed the card in my hand. "I teach at Sunny Side Hill."

Sunny Side Hill College was tough to get into. It was the dream school for a lot of students at Cherry Hill High.

"It's an honor to meet you," I said, shaking his hand again.

"Call me after you graduate. I can get you into college by pulling some strings."

Jackson had once confessed that Sunny Side Hill was his dream school. I hadn't been sure about college until I started taking my life and art seriously. I wanted to share this opportunity with Jackson, but I was torn. I knew we both couldn't get in with the limited spots available. Yet, I had to prioritize my own path and follow my heart.

* * *

After all this time, I finally saw her again. She was laughing, braiding her friend's hair into a French braid, biting her lip in concentration. Her skirt seemed shorter than I remembered. I yearned for her touch, for the taste of her lip gloss that I secretly wore at home just to remember her. My Lyra Barns.

"Yo, cmon! Be ready to catch the ball," Jamie yelled.

The ball smacked my face. "If I wasn't looking, then don't pass the damn ball!"

"It's not my fault you're daydreaming about Lyra Barns," he teased, stretching out her name. "Where are you going?"

I began to walk over to the bleachers. "I'm leaving, fuck this," I snapped.

"Next point wins!" Jamie walked in front of me.

"I don't give a damn about basketball." I clumsily dressed over my gym clothes, struggling with my tie.

Jamie placed the ball onto the floor. He placed his hands over my shoulders. "Just talk to her. Tell her you miss her, it's simple," he said, his lips pouted.

"What could go wrong, right?" I spoke. I approached Lyra, interrupting her conversation. Her friends gawked at me as if I were royalty. Four months away, and I returned to school as a celebrity.

"Acelin?" Lyra looked stunned by my presence, her eyes devouring me.

I didn't want to waste any second with her. "I miss you, Lyra. I can't stop thinking about you. I dream about you... I can smell you through the halls—"

She silenced me with her hand. She walked me into the boys' locker room, the only quiet place nearby. "What's gotten into you?" she asked, her brow furrowed.

"I miss you," I confessed, holding her arms tenderly.

"How? You've been gone, I thought something happened to you Acelin," she observed me.

CHAPTER 14

"I'm sorry," I whispered, comforted by her hand on my cheek. "Please, go on a date with me."

"Acelin, I can't—"

"Don't say that as if I'm begging you."

She sighed. "I have to go, I have class," she had said, kissing my hand before she returned to her friends. Everything she did made me feel small, as if I were at fault for not reaching out while I was away.

I received a call from Mom. The bills I had paid off worried her. She asked if I was selling drugs, which I denied, though she was right. I reassured her that I had saved the money from work and that poker game to alleviate her stress. However, the truth was that it's still the money I made with the Members. When she questioned me about the car I bought, I avoided the subject.

Distracted by the phone, I bumped into Maxes in the hallway. She was rushing to a meeting. "Oh sorry, I didn't mean to bump into ya," I apologized, steadying her papers.

"It's fine!" She brushed her hair out of her face, rearranging the papers.

"More newspaper articles?" I asked as I walked with her pace.

"Yes, the principal is meeting us in the library."

"I'll go as well, I just left the gym, so I'm kind of sweaty."

We stopped at the library door. "I like you sweaty," she said.

"What?" I frowned.

"I said, I think you're sweaty too!" She tried to shift the conversation.

I grinned, then quickly straightened my face. I couldn't believe she made me smile, even a little. I was supposed to dislike her, not be friendly.

I was banned from all book club meetings after the article that went viral, disrupting my chances of all after school activities. I tried to stay inconspicuous as I entered the library behind her, pretending to check out books to avoid the principal. He was lecturing about not writing reports on school drama anymore, only reminders of school events. His anger was aggressive, and I knew I was partly to blame. Through the bookshelf, I flicked a piece of paper at the back of Maxes neck. She was sitting at the back table, easy to reach. She turned around, trying to catch me, then faced forward with a smirk. I threw another piece. She responded with a middle finger.

She left her seat, approached me, and playfully hit my arm. Maxes collected the papers I had thrown at her and hurled them back towards me. Our giggles disrupted the principal's reading. "What's that noise? Who's laughing?" he demanded. We quickly hid behind a shelf, out of sight.

"Do you want to skip school?" Maxes whispered.

"Yeah," I replied.

Maxes suggested we headed to Frosty River, her usual escape for drawing or silence away from her family. Her family was strict, and her younger sister had already moved out to avoid their rules. Maxes stayed to pursue her art, funded by her parents. She never had a long-lasting relationship due to her parents' interference. Her grades were all A's, as anything lower would jeopardize her art dream. She couldn't cut her hair, shave, get piercings, wear makeup, or even wear lip gloss and perfume. Every morning, she took advantage of the school bathroom to do what wasn't possible at home like getting herself ready. Our uniform policy certainly helped with her image. Otherwise, she would've faced bullying for her attire.

The day was smokey out, the fog filled the air with unexpectedly warm weather. She came prepared with her sketchbook,

CHAPTER 14

and I brought mine. She laid out a cover for the grass and arranged snacks—apple slices with caramel and buttered popcorn, each bag marked with our names in black sharpie. She also brought an empty glass jar, which she filled halfway with river water.

"Be careful at the edge," I said. The river's bed was strewn with heavy rocks.

She tucked her hair behind her ears. "I've been collecting jars to create little ecosystems for as long as I can remember," she said with a smile.

I arched an eyebrow. My fondness for her had never been strong, merely because she was different, but at that moment, I recognized our similarities. With Maxes, it all felt so natural to be myself.

"So, I'm guessing you have a collection of jars in ya room?" I asked, stepping closer to her.

"No, they're in my backyard. You could see it sometime when my parents are out of town," she offered, glancing up at me.

I hesitated, unsure.

She sighed. "Do you have a girlfriend or something?"

I stood in silence, staring into the distance, shifting on my heels. I scrunched up my face, pondering what to say.

* * *

I grabbed my stuff from my locker and made my way to the main doors. That's when I noticed a crowd of students gathered around my car. The football players were leaning on it, laughing and showing off like they'd just taken it for a joyride.

"Jackson, what's up!" I called out to him. The crowd around

my car began to thin out.

He grinned, biting his lip. "I'm thinking about asking Frances to be my girlfriend before prom. She's having a party tonight. You coming?"

"I can't, got prom shopping plans with Mom," I replied.

He was disappointed. "I thought we would go prom shopping together."

"You can go with me after my shift is over at work."

Maxes approached, her pigtails a giveaway. "Hope we can skip school again soon," she said, nudging my arm.

I found myself smiling. "Of course!"

Jackson watched her leave, then turned to me with disbelief. "Maxes? The girl you can't stand," he frowned. "What about Lyra?"

"I know, I don't know... ya making it worse, Jackson."

He shook his head. "You're officially crazy!" He opened my car door for me to get in. "Can I get a lift to yo job? I need something like a snack."

"Yeah, only because I finally have my Jackson talking to me again."

"Whatever," he said as he got into the car and fastened his seat belt.

My shift was nearly over, and cleaning the tables was the last task before I could leave. Jackson spent half the time on the phone with Frances, keeping himself occupied. My manager noticed how he was tidying up, straightening ketchup bottles and refilling napkin holders. So, the manager suggested he apply for a job where I worked. I nudged him to fill out an application. He was thrilled at the fact of us working together.

Outside, a group of high school students who often hung out after school were gathered. Jackson seized the opportunity

CHAPTER 14

to introduce himself and promote Frances's upcoming party. The job seemed like a perfect fit for him, given his love for socializing. A trait that made the diner a popular spot for students to skip class.

I was supposed to meet Mom after work to shop for a suit. Despite calling her three times, I hadn't received a response. I made a stop at the store to grab a few of her favorite things for movie night: Twizzlers, a new blanket for her bed, and some fresh flowers to replace the old ones from Turner. After waiting in the car for twenty minutes, Jackson and I decided to check out a nearby suit shop. I had my eye on a Gray and black suit, while Jackson liked an all-white suit. Lyra was likely going to prom with Nick, I resigned myself to being the third wheel alongside Jackson and his potential girlfriend.

Jackson looked at the suit prices. "When do I start that job? I might need to start like tomorrow," he said.

"Don't worry about the prices, I've got it covered," I reassured him.

He joked, "Thanks, dad Acelin."

"Anything for you, son," I played along, continuing to browse the suits.

"I'll be back, just gonna go to the bathroom," he said, heading off.

Jackson's phone buzzed, the name flashing on the screen like a warning sign. It was *her* —the girl from Burn Wood. She was the one who cheated on him, used him, and sneaked around with some of the football players on his team.

He stared at the screen for a moment, his jaw clenched in frustration. He'd been dodging her calls for days, but this time, for some reason, he answered.

"What do you want?" he said, his voice colder than usual.

"It's Mandy," the girl said. "Prom's coming up, and I was wondering if you would go with me?"

"No, you tried to set me up," Jackson said, his voice low. "You even stole from me, got me beat up, I can't talk to you anymore."

"I'm sorry, I didn't know they would come after you," she replied, sounding remorseful.

"Goodbye," Jackson ended the call abruptly, cutting off her plea.

Jackson looked sad coming back from the bathroom. I could tell something was on his mind, but I didn't want to snoop for answers. "There's nothing here," he said.

Sensing his mood, I suggested, "There's another store down the street. Let's check it out and get you ready for the party!" I smiled, hoping to lift his spirits.

The next suit shop down the street was smaller, but something told me it might be the right place. As I approached, I saw a woman with brunette hair sitting inside, her back to the window, her posture strikingly familiar. Jackson pointed out a boy who resembled Nick. My heart sank as I realized it was Mom with Nick, her affectionate gestures towards him remembering she used to be like that with me. She was spending her day off with him, not me, even paying for his suit.

Jackson sensed my pain and stopped me from going inside, insisting it wasn't worth the confrontation. I knew my Mom wouldn't care that I saw her. In a fit of hurt, I threw away the flowers and candy I had bought. I didn't bother looking for another suit after that.

When we got home, Jackson headed to the party, while I was still torn about attending. Then, a knock at the door happened. It was Lyra, looking as if she had a rough day, her anxiety through the roof. She confessed that she was done with Nick.

CHAPTER 14

She explained how she was sad without a prom date, her tears reflecting her disappointment.

I shared in her sadness. "Would ya like to come in? I'm on my way to a party, but it can wait."

She hesitated, wiping away her tears. "No, it's okay if you're leaving, I'll go back home."

"No, really, come in," I insisted, opening the door wider.

She twirled her hair walking inside. She pulled up her long socks to her knees. Her gaze drifted to the refrigerator, where she saw baby photos of me with my Mom. The ring of my phone broke the silence. It was Jackson checking if I was still coming to that party. As I reached into my pocket to answer, she softly tugged me towards the counter.

She began to play with my underwear band. I smiled, turning away from her as I waited for his words on the phone. The only sounds were the background music and Jackson's heavy breaths as he struggled to speak from being too drunk. She unzipped my pants and rubbed her hands into my underwear. Tripping over my words, I found it impossible to communicate effectively with Jackson. He was so intoxicated that he couldn't even complete a sentence himself. Clutching the edge of the counter with one hand, I pressed the phone against my ear with the other.

"How close are you?" Jackson's sluggish voice came through. *"Lyra and Nick just had a big fight, like twenty minutes ago. This could be your chance to get with her."*

My body stiffened as I felt the warmness of her mouth. My head slowly fell back in enjoyment, and I moved the phone away whenever I felt the need.

I tried not to moan into the speaker. *"Why did they argue?"*

"What you talking about?"

I moaned again, my throat tightening as I tried to keep my voice steady. My chest rose and fell in shaky breaths.

"I'm finna cum," I whimpered to Lyra.

"Are you coming right?" Jackson asked. *"You need to come now. I don't want to be here alone."*

I took the phone away from my ear. "Why did you stop? Keep going," I urged her as I ended the call with Jackson. She rose to her feet, her mascara smeared across her preppy face. I had oral for the first time in my Mom's kitchen. What was I doing with my life?

She wiped her mouth. "I saw you in the library one day with Maxes. What could you have said to make her smile like that?" I didn't have anything to say except stare at her. "You might not realize how much she likes you. Everyone knows it."

"I don't like her, really. She means nothing to me," I said as I gently held her face. Then, I fixed my pants. "Believe what you want then."

She looked deep into my eyes. "No! I want us to be together, Acelin. I want to be your girlfriend," she said.

I made a face. "I had to do all this just to get you to notice me?"

She kissed me quickly. I pulled back when she tried again. After all she did to me, this is how I got her. I wasn't sure she was worth it anymore. "Please, Acelin, I need you," she begged, hugging me tight. "We need to be together."

I stepped back. "No, I decide if I want to be with you."

"Don't do this," she cried, laying her head on my chest. "Please."

The lights in my driveway got my attention. An unfamiliar car was parked there on the curb. "Stay here, I'll be back," I said, disregarding her tears. Fear gripped me, suspecting a Member

CHAPTER 14

might be on my trail. But it was a false alarm. A lady was wearing an oval hat that shadowed her eyes. She approached my front door. It was Nick's mom; Lyra recognized her.

She entered, giving me a frosty look, silent as she sat across from Lyra and me. Her gaze stayed on me filled with raw hurt. She glanced at Lyra, and for a moment, the resemblance was striking. Like mother, like son. After all, I was dating Nick's girlfriend.

"Is your Mom here?" she eventually asked, breaking the silence.

"No, she's working late today," I answered.

"I need to understand where I stand in all this. Nick and his father seem to be moving on without me." She took a breath. "Turner and I, we're in the same house but not the same bed, and your Mom is the reason."

Lyra and I looked at each other. She nudged my leg, making me say something. I pretended to be sorry, but I really didn't care about Nick's mom. "I'm terribly sorry for what you're going through," I said.

Removing her hat, she rearranged her blonde hair. "I've seen the signs, especially when she's been around us," she frowned. "She took my son prom shopping. Who does she think she is?" her tone raised.

"Alright, that's enough," I said, standing tall. "Let's head to the door. I'll see you out." We both stood up.

The yelling outside made me twitch. I went to the door and saw Frances struggling to help Jackson inside while Moe carried his stuff.

"Are we disturbing y'all?" Moe asked as she approached us. My heart dropped at the sight of her. I had this nagging suspicion that she was behind telling Drew about the letter I had taken. It was the way she looked at me.

I pushed aside those thoughts; I didn't want to stir up trouble. With Jackson speaking to me again, I couldn't afford to get worked up over the past issues with things from the Members.

The lady was shocked to see drunk teens coming in late. "I was just leaving," she said, heading out, adjusting her hat. "Great, no supervision," she added, walking to her car.

"I'm sorry ya family hates you!" I shouted from the porch, laughing.

"You're just like your mother!" she shouted back.

I rolled my eyes. "Glad I could help," I said sarcastically, watching her drive away.

In the middle of the night, I couldn't sleep. I sat up, thinking about Lyra and me. I hoped I was following my heart and making the right choice by dating her.

"What's wrong?" she asked, waking up.

"I'm trying to figure us out."

"What can I do?" she replied. "Isn't this what you wanted, me?"

"Yeah?" I hadn't anticipated that dating Lyra would be so challenging if Maxes hadn't been a part of my life. But I followed my instincts. "I want us to be together," I confessed.

She smiled and said, "Us, forever," as she settled back into my arms. I stared at the ceiling, waiting for my thoughts about the discussion to quiet.

"Yeah us."

The day had been nerve wracking arriving at school. It was my first time being seen with Lyra Barns in the halls. The best part about it was that I was officially popular. First the hair, then the car, and now Lyra Barns. Being a part of Lyra's life completed mine. The doubts about us being together still got

CHAPTER 14

to me, but I liked the way I was treated at school because of her. She made sure I was included in everything. I sat with her at lunch, watched her practice, and skipped classes with her. I was living Nick's dream.

Lyra and I sat into the library room waiting for our next classes to start. "Why do you write your letters with a curve? Is that like a fancy thing you do?" I asked.

"It makes me feel elegant. Like I'm a mystery," she smiled. "I'm going to class," she kissed me on the cheek. "Don't forget about our senior dinner tonight. All of my friends will be there."

"I think everyone will be attending tonight."

"I can't wait!" she whined.

"I care about you, so I'll be there." My hand glided through her ponytail. "I'm gonna get to class as well."

My writing class was the worst. I always got bored and started to doze off reading Latin words. If it wasn't Latin, then I would read up on the news that was happening around town. We had a sub who wanted to go over an essay packet that was six pages long. The teacher always gave us the same prompt from last year. I didn't think anyone ever noticed. It was just worded differently.

In the corner of the classroom, I was left with a book covering my face. My legs were prompted up on a chair in front of me causing my legs to weaken. If my teacher was here, she would've thrown a fit about me sleeping in her class. Or she would make me stay after school to grade other people's papers without using a correction book.

Maxes walked in with her loud annoying voice, interrupting my sleep along with the cramp hallway bell.

"Wake up sleepy head," she removed the book from my face. She had her hair curled and wore lip gloss that was bright pink evening out her tan skin tone.

"I'm up," I said as I took a stretch.

"It seems we have an essay to write, which is just wonderful. Now I really need to focus. Did you know, I spent the entire night wondering—"

"Stop talking." I placed my finger to my lips. I started to pack all my things inside my bag. I just couldn't entertain Maxes like I used to. I was way too loyal for that.

She waved a piece of paper in my face. "Hello, does Acelin speak?"

I tried my hardest not to smile. "Can't you see I'm busy?" I tried to intimidate her.

"Did I do something wrong?" her voice cracked.

I felt bad about how I was mean to her. I just didn't know how to tell her I had a girlfriend. Why was it so hard? "Can you excuse me?" I waited until she moved out of my face to walk away.

She pressed her teeth together. "Can I go to lunch with you?"

"How do ya know I have lunch next?" I said, annoyed.

She looked down to the floor. "I was skipping this class and wanted to spend time with you in the art room."

How could I say no to someone who just wanted to be my friend? She was nice and not controlling like Lyra. But everyone knew that I dated Lyra. If they notice I talked to Maxes, the rumors would've said I was cheating.

"Wait." I grabbed her arm from walking away. "I'll meet you down there."

"We can just walk together?" she asked.

"I have to pee first!" That was the only thing that came to my mind. But then, I finally came to my senses to tell her about Lyra. "The thing is I have a—"

CHAPTER 14

She looked interested in what I was going to say next. She smiled hard, showing her white teeth slightly slanting her head. I couldn't do it. That look, she knew what she was doing to me. "You have a what?" she asked.

I mumbled. "Nothing."

The art room was silent, the scent of aged paint hung in the air. Freshly sharpened pencil shavings laid scattered on a desk beside a gnawed eraser. Maxes was drawing a sunset. Some of the colors were orange, red and with a light tone of bright yellow. The sun dipped below the horizon and the birds flew into the sunset. I wished we had more sunny days like what she drew. Her legs were crossed together, her posture was straight, she was delicate. The art Bannister was almost as tall as her. She kept her small hand gripping one edge of the broad to get a good angle.

"I didn't think you would come," she said.

"I said I would." I glanced around the room.

"Do you like it?" She turned around facing me to see my reaction.

I shrugged my shoulders. "I guess, how long have you been working on this?"

"Um, about three months."

I got closer to the art board admiring the details, but my hand slapped the wet paint that sat underneath us. "I'm sorry! I didn't mean to get that on you."

"Yes, you did!" She flicked more paint onto my uniform using a paint brush.

I looked down at my ruined uniform. "Maxes... this isn't funny!" Red specks lived on my shirt.

She looked around intensely. "Calm down before someone hears us," she laughed.

I grabbed another paintbrush, dipped it into a bowl of water, and playfully flicked it on her. Her mouth opened wide in surprise as some of the water found its way in.

"Why would you do that!" she said. She picked up the bowl of water and started to chase me around with it. I hid behind one of the art boards and ducked down. I was facing the opposite direction from where she approached. She dumped the water all over me.

I took her hands and held both of them in the air to shove more paint onto her face.

She stomped over to the cracked mirror and wiped it off. "You're such an idiot, Acelin!"

"That's not gonna come out ya know," I said.

The school bell rang. Students moved to their next classes. If her parents found out she was skipping with a boy, her art career would've been over. I'd get suspended, and Lyra would've broken up with me.

"What are we doing to do?" she asked, frightened.

I peeked outside the classroom door window. "We can make it to the laundry room once the bell is over."

She paced around the room nibbling on her clear polished nails. "It's my fault, it's my fault. I'm sorry, I didn't mean for this to go this far," she said.

"Trust me, I'll get Jackson to help us." I placed my hands on her shoulders to calm her.

Jackson had taken a key from a janitor's cart, slipping it into his pocket without anyone noticing. He glanced over his shoulder, making sure no one was watching, before he headed to unlock the laundry room doors.

Maxes and I carefully made our way through the halls, avoiding anyone. We ran past open doors, bent corners, and

CHAPTER 14

peeked down halls, leaving paint scuff marks behind. Our clothes were still soaked.

Jackson stood in the hallway leaning against the wall cleaning his nails waiting for us. He swung his arm out with the key holding it in front of him hoping we would congratulate him for saving us. "You guys look like shit," he said.

"Shut up," I mumbled towards him. I was still paranoid hoping not to run into Lyra roaming around the halls.

"I risked my life getting this key. That means food is on you today!"

"We can go to ya favorite restaurant," I said.

"Bro yes!" He balled his fist up with excitement. "See you guys after school," he winked.

Maxes and I started to undress inside of the laundry room. I faced the wall to give her privacy. I unbuttoned my shirt with dried paint hands wondering what she thought of me. She didn't say a word to me. I thought maybe she was nervous.

"You can turn around, you know," she said.

"Are you sure?"

"I'm not completely naked. I have on a bra and underwear. Get over yourself."

I grabbed her hand, pulling her closer to me. "Come here." I took a towel to clean some of the leftover paint in her hair. The paint was washable, easy to slip right out with water. Her doe eyes followed my every movement. I tried my hardest not to make eye contact with her, just to make things less awkward.

"Thanks," she said. "Are you going to the senior dinner tonight?"

"Yeah, I should be."

"I was thinking maybe we could—"

"No, we cannot." I slammed the towel down into a dirty

laundry basket.

She laughed, frustrated. "Sorry for even asking." She went to throw her clothes into the washer.

I bit my lip and shut my eyes, upset that I had to dismiss our conversation about the senior dinner. During the time we were together, we didn't speak. She didn't even look my way despite the looks I gave her. She had my attention every day more than anyone else. I thought about her a lot. I often wondered about what her room looked like or what kind of underwear she wore most of the time, cotton or lingerie. Today, she wore cotton with *"Wednesday"* written on them.

At nine, dinner began. Jackson and I were matching with our suits, while Lyra's black dress mirrored my attire. The senior dinner was a ball theme. Lyra and I captured our first night out in a photo booth. Nick, once hidden, now faced the past with his former love. Silent, he avoided Lyra, his actions spoke volumes of denial. I remained seated, observing him, as Lyra welcomed her peers. The event wasn't to my taste, yet I still went for the sake of popularity, a shield against the bullying that stopped.

Maxes finally walked through the door. She wore a short red dress. Who did she think she was, wearing a dress that showed that much skin? Her hair was in a bun, her nails polished red. Her legs were shaved, and her arms were as well, for the first time! Something wasn't right. Her parents must have been on vacation.

Jackson sat down next to me. "I see Lyra and Maxes became good friends," he said, handing me a cup of red punch with a splash of liquor.

Maxes complimented Lyra on her dress, smiling and hugging her like they were best friends. This was why I should've kept

CHAPTER 14

quiet about having a girlfriend. "I know I'm not the only one who notices what Maxes is doing."

"Then why did you tell her about Lyra?"

"I had no choice but to tell her. She overheard Jamie's big mouth asking about what colors Lyra and I were going to wear tonight."

"Man, sorry about that. I know how much you hate Maxes anyway." Jackson understood how I felt about her, so I knew a hundred percent I felt nothing for Maxes deep down inside.

Maxes walked into the hallway, and I couldn't help but to wonder what trouble she might have caused next. My curiosity got the better of me, and I followed after her. I knew I shouldn't have. I should have been with Lyra and her friends, pretending to be the happiest boyfriend ever. But instead, I peeked out in the hall, watching Maxes every move.

"Why are you following me, Acelin?" she shouted towards me.

"I'm not!" I revealed myself from behind a door. I should've known this was her trap to get me to follow her in the first place.

She raised her eyebrows, crossing her arms. "Then... why are you in this hall with me?"

"Okay, cut the shit." I walked over to her. "Talking to my girlfriend, laughing with her, hugging? You're jealous," I smiled.

She laughed. "You are a waste of time. You could've told me you had a girlfriend, I would've left you alone."

"Why should I have to say anything if I don't like ya? You're just mad that I don't want you and never will." I stepped closer to her, holding my hands in my pocket. "So, when I get back home, I will fuck the shit out of my girlfriend, who will never be you."

Her eyes widened, and a pang of regret hit me. Maybe I had gone too far? I could see the hurt in her eyes. "Okay, Acelin," she said, her voice lower.

She brushed past me, but I gently grabbed her arm. "Where are you going?"

"Let me go, now," she demanded as she snatched away.

"I'm sorry, I didn't mean it," I said, my heart aching. "Let's just talk this out."

"Kiss me if you're sorry," she challenged, her eyes filled with anger now.

I felt a lump in my throat. "Maxes, you know—"

"That your girlfriend is in there, so leave me alone," she interrupted, her voice breaking.

I wished she understood that I was just confused about my feelings. She came into my life too late and, I didn't know how to communicate it to her.

"You are making this hard for me," I said slowly.

She turned around, walking back to me. "How do you think I feel?" She pointed to her chest.

"Why didn't you just tell me that ya liked me, or whatever crazy, sick fantasy you have of me? From the beginning ya first saw me."

"I thought you knew."

Jackson came out the dinner doors. Drawing his eyes between Maxes and me. He shouted, "Acelin, come on! We're gonna make a toast."

The whole time, I felt trapped by guilt, knowing that she liked me while I sat next to my girlfriend. I thought maybe it was a sign to tell Lyra Barns about how I felt about Maxes.

Should I have?

15

Chapter 15

I could still feel the sting in my wrist from the last point, the one where I hesitated just a fraction too long. My opponent's blade had clipped my guard, sending me off balance. That split second delay cost me the final touch. The silver trophy sat in my lap, cool against my hands. It felt heavier than it should have, like it was mocking me. Second place. Not bad, but not enough. Across the gym, the winning team cheered, some looking at me like they were jealous.

I walked to the car, sweaty and breathless, pushing my damp hair back from my face. I glanced over as they loaded onto their bus, laughing. I didn't hate them for winning. Not really. But it still stung.

Jackson wrapped his arm around my shoulders. "Acelin… you did fine, bro. Second place is still top rank."

I wanted to argue, but I knew he was right. I had done my best, even if my head had been all over the place today focusing on the wrong things, second guessing myself when I should've been in the moment.

"Yeah, I… I understand." Part of me wanted to throw the

trophy away, to forget the whole thing ever happened, but I knew it wasn't that simple. I couldn't just erase a moment like this.

Jackson wasn't the type to linger, but he stayed with me, letting the silence stretch between us. He finally said, "Let's get home."

When I got home, I found a letter behind a flowerpot. It had a picture of Jackson and me in the school parking lot, taken on the day Mom was supposed to take me prom shopping. I thought those notes were done, but they still haunted me. I shut my eyes, clenching my jaw, and went inside.

Mom was home, and I still hadn't said a word about seeing her shopping for a suit with Nick. Every glance at her felt like a reminder to speak up, but I didn't know how to bring it up.

She started drinking again. I noticed it but was too afraid to accept it. She would come into the house around one in the morning, stumbling around the kitchen. She took off her heels so I wouldn't hear her, but I always did. She kept empty wine bottles underneath the sink in her bathroom. The wine was all from Jackson's dad; his logo was on every last bottle. I should've taken the first bottle he gave her that one time he visited us.

Later in the afternoon, I received a text from Maxes. After what happened at the senior dinner, I thought she would've hated me. She reminded me that the man Greek, who I met at the art gallery, wanted to meet with me again.

I brought a pocketknife just in case I needed it. I kept it inside my suit, tucking it into a small zipper. I walked around the silent art gallery. No one was in sight except for the lady at the front desk. My artwork was still in place with the lights surrounding it. It still had the thick red rope blocking the area to prevent anyone from getting too close. The lady at the front

CHAPTER 15

desk called me over, using her long nails to grab my attention. She looked down at a sheet of paper and glanced at me, as if comparing me to a picture. I awkwardly looked around until she spoke.

"Mr. Jones, right?" the lady said, fluffing out her long Afro.

"Yes!"

She smiled. "He's in room 302. Take the long hall down," she pointed towards a door.

302? How was I supposed to know where that was? I wanted to ask, but if I did, I would seem like a rookie. I walked upstairs towards the club doors that I remembered Greek running up to when he was drunk. Many tables were set up with dinner placed on the plates. Some of the food was half eaten, with numbers on the chairs in bold red. I left through a red door and went downstairs, which led to many different rooms. The rooms looked like hotel rooms. I followed the numbers on the doors until I reached 302. I knocked but got no answer. I opened the door and yelled out, "Hello?" There was another door inside the room where I could hear laughter coming from. I entered.

"Acelin!" Greek rushed from his seat and kissed me on the cheek. "I had to say I was his assistant manager to enter the gallery, how crazy is that?" he said to his friends. They responded with laughter.

The room was filled with other young men in fancy clothes and suits. It looked like they were in the middle of a poker game. It all felt familiar, like how I used to be with the Members back when I stayed with them.

He continued, "I usually have security walk you down here. I hope you didn't get lost?" he asked, lighting a cigarette.

"No," I said. "Is there something you wanted to meet about?"

I questioned aggressively.

He paused, caught off guard by my tone. "Drew has really messed you up, my boy," he said with a smile. The other young men sat around me, their eyes fixed intently on the scene. I slowly slid my hand inside my suit, feeling the tension in the air. A heavy silence fell over us, filled with unbroken eye contact. "Check him!" he suddenly barked.

I quickly pulled out my knife as one of the men held a gun to my head. I froze with my hands in the air.

"Hand it ova," said Greek. I placed the knife slowly into his hand as the man moved the gun away from my head. "I know you work for Drew. My two boys work for him."

"I no longer exist to the Members," my face frowned.

"You really think Drew is dumb, that you're dead? Give me a break," he laughed silently. "He's coming for you, my friend. He took my whole life away and ruined it."

"How?" I asked, my heart beating fast. "How do ya know he will come for me?" I knew the answer but just wanted to be delusional and ask.

"Him and I went to school together in Russia. He trained me to be a drug dealer, to live a criminal's life," Greek said, rubbing his fingernails. "I needed money badly, so I did whatever it took and became a Member." He stood up from his seat and buttoned his leather suit. "We were best friends until I wanted out. His dad killed my whole family, so I killed as many Members as I could."

For some reason, deep down, I knew Drew wouldn't hurt me. Around Drew, it felt like he forgave me for anything I did wrong during the Members training. So why couldn't Drew understand that I acted out of fear when I stole his letter?

"What do I do?" I asked.

CHAPTER 15

"We are going tuh kill him," he said confidently.

"I can't," I mumbled, looking down in embarrassment. I knew I'd regret it if I ever hurt Drew.

He shook his head, disappointment clear on his face. "Do you know why I called you? Your life is already over." Greek poured himself a glass of vodka. "I won't hurt you, don't worry." He patted my cheek. "When his sister wakes up, all hell will break loose."

"When the first time I saw you, why didn't you have this talk with me?"

"In front of Maxes?" He raised an eyebrow. "Of course not. She's been through enough already."

We exchanged numbers. He promised to keep me updated on Drew's every move with the help of the two boys who saved my life. I felt a growing attachment to Drew. If I could just talk things out with him, maybe he'd forgive me. It was my fault he didn't trust me. I stole from him. If I hadn't taken that letter, I could've been a leader in the Members' house, as powerful as Drew. I knew I could redeem myself, but time was ticking. I was running out of time to prove it to him.

"How much time do I have left before he notices me?"

"Lay low for now. Trust me, I have your back," he said.

When I made it back home, the front door was unlocked. The kitchen light was still on, and the smell of a fully cooked meal was ready to be served. Steak, rice, and potatoes. Steak gave me memories of the Members' house. That's all we used to eat most of the time. They thought it made them seem richer. But I didn't have an appetite to eat anymore.

"Hey bud." Mom tried to conceal pouring a half glass of wine down the drain in the sink. "Where were you?"

"At Lyra's house." Living a secret life was more complicated than ever. But the lie came out smoothly.

I sat down at the table and looked at the graduation colors she was picking out for me.

"Ya like that color? I'm thinking of doing the school theme colors, blue and red."

"How did ya know that my favorite color was blue?" I smiled. For the first time Mom saw me.

Her smile widened. "Because that's Nick's favorite color. I think you guys would have a good time at this graduation party I'm throwing for you two."

My smile faded and anger washed over me. I had to stay calm. "What do you mean, Nick?"

"Nick said that he would love to have a party with you." She walked over to the table with a plate full of food.

"He's a liar. He's just trying to please you and make me mad."

"What is your problem with him?" She rolled her eyes.

"With him? Or what is his problem with me?"

"I think it's just you. He's a nice boy."

I smiled out of anger. "Says the Mom who stood me up to go suit shopping with someone son." My throat tightened as I tried to speak again. "I even planned a movie night with you," I said, quieting down my tone.

"I don't have time for this. You're acting like your father."

"Really?" I walked over to her. "Really... my dad?" I could feel my heart shatter into a million pieces. I never thought she would ever say that to me. I could never be him and never wanted to be compared to him. "You are just a horrible Mom!"

"Watch your mouth," she said as she slapped me. Her ring printed into my face. I gasped and stood with my hand covering my face. After that, I never spoke to her again.

During the first hour of class, I couldn't focus. The night I had

CHAPTER 15

with my mother left me feeling drained, and I didn't think I had it in me to stay on track today. I went into the bathroom and pulled out some painkillers. I only had four left, and I hesitated to take them. I needed to save them for emergencies. What if I found out some other crazy news from Greek about Drew? I didn't know where I could refill them. Jamie didn't sell drugs anymore; he got clean for Moe. I didn't want to do hard drugs; I just needed something to straighten me out during hard times.

I struggled to get the cap open and banged it against the bathroom sink, causing all of them to spill over the floor.

"No, no, no, no," I said, trying to scrape them off the ground.

"Acelin?" Jackson said. He walked out of the stall, zipping up his pants.

"What are you doing here?" I frowned.

"I can't use the bathroom?" He walked over to the sink and noticed the pills on the floor. "What are you holding?" He looked at my hand and saw the pill bottle.

"Nothing," I said, hiding the bottle behind my back with a guilty look.

I saw a thought wash over his face as his eyebrows raised. He had figured out that the bathroom I was in was used to sell drugs. He snatched the pill bottle from my hand. "What the fuck," he had shouted, pushing me into the wall.

"Just relax!" I said, holding both of my hands up.

"How long have you been—" He turned towards the sinks and placed his hands on top of his head. "Why? Why are you doing this to yourself?" He turned back to me.

I stood in shock, my face twisted in sorrow, but I didn't let it break me. We stood face to face for a moment, then he pulled me into a hug.

"I'm sorry."

"We can get through this together," he said.

I nodded against his shoulder, my throat tight with emotions I couldn't name. For the first time in a long while, I allowed myself to believe him, even if only for a moment.

* * *

I thought my home would be my safe place, but it had become a broken one. I spent more nights at the local diner than I did at home. I wanted to be away from my mother, and since Jackson found out about the pills I was taking, he kept an eye on me every second. I didn't want him to feel responsible for me. There was no peace left for me at home anymore.

"I found something in your room," my mother said, sitting on the living room couch.

"I just need a break," I laughed, walking into the kitchen. I snatched off my school tie and threw it across the table before drinking a glass of water.

She followed behind me. "Well, I need a break too." She threw a box of condoms in my face. "This is what ya doing now?"

I laughed again. "This is what you were worried about, me being safe? Get a life."

"You are out of control! You went to a fencing camp and came back as a whole new person, acting and talking differently." She leaned against the wall and pulled out her phone. "I'm calling your therapist."

I panicked. "What?"

"I'm getting you help," she said. "I can't handle this."

Jackson walked through the front door. "Christina... what's happening?" he asked politely, dropping his bag by the door.

CHAPTER 15

"Your friend or brother, whatever you call each other, is out of control! I want both of you out of my house."

I rolled my eyes and smirked. "Jackson, just come on, she's crazy!" I gestured towards her with sarcasm.

"Don't come back until I leave!" she shouted as Jackson, and I walked outside.

"Well... I hope you don't come back home!"

Later that night, we decided to get food at Jackson's favorite restaurant in Burn Wood to kill time until my mother left for work. Jackson had to finish cooking my shrimp because I was too busy daydreaming, lost in my worries. All day, he'd been trying to distract me from my nightmares about the Members. I stared ahead until I felt his eyes on me.

"You okay?" he asked, with a spoonful of food in his mouth.

"Yeah," I wiped my face. "How do ya like the food?"

"No, how do you like the food?" he asked back. "I put extra garlic on top of the noodles just for you. I just can't stand the way it tastes." He made a sour face.

"That's why I like it so much, because you hate it," I smiled.

He dropped his head to meet my gaze. "We came all the way to the other side of town, and you're telling me you're fine?" He began chewing his food loudly. "I know when my boy isn't okay. Is this about Drew or your Mom?"

"No, it's about Lyra." Really, it was about Drew catching on to me still being alive, but Lyra had been on my mind constantly. "I just don't want her to leave, you know?" I played with my food. "Then Maxes..."

"Pick the person who's stopping you from loving the one you truly want." He watched me play with my food. "Eat up before it gets cold."

Food stains covered my shirt, and bits of shrimp were still

stuck in my teeth. We stepped outside to the car. The night was late, cold, and foggy. Laughter echoed from a narrow alleyway. Water trickled from the gutters, rats scurried through leftover trash, and then Jackson's smile faded. His hands moved quickly, searching for his keys.

"Keep walking, Acelin, don't make eye contact with any of them," he whispered while still looking for his keys.

A group of boys swarmed out of the alley. It was Johnny. This was my first time seeing him since the last football game when he had torn Tommy's knee. He was taller, stronger, and goofier looking. He moved like he was drunk, and he looked like an upscale druggie with long, nice hair and straight teeth.

"Go home, Johnny!" Jackson shouted, seeming unbothered.

"You still speak to Mandy?" he shouted back, from across the parking lot. "I told you to stay away from her," he laughed out loud.

"The same girl who's been blowing up my phone?"

"That's not what she told me," Johnny said. "She said you asked her to prom."

Jackson stood face to face with him. "Fuck You!"

"When?" Johnny's eyes widened with a goofy smile.

Jackson threw a container of food at his face. The rest of Johnny's boys made their way up to Jackson, trying to hit him. He threw them off one by one into trash cans and cars. Car alarms went off, and we only had a short amount of time to fight them before the police arrived. I ran over and began to fight anyone who got too close to Jackson. "Stay back!" I shouted. I held a pocketknife in my hand. I got struck in the face with a punch that left my face tingling. I chased the boy who punched me into a pile of plants and knocked his head against the ground.

Johnny sat by a car with a bloody mouth, still smiling. I

CHAPTER 15

walked towards him. "That was for Tommy," I said as I spat on him.

He wiped his face. "Just wait until Joe Moss finds out about this!" he shouted as we got into our car.

* * *

Jackson couldn't sleep. He stayed up watching TV until three in the morning. Then, he got a call that changed everything. His mom had died in her sleep from a heart attack. The news left him feeling empty inside. The funeral was in two days, but the pain felt like it would never go away.

The sound of glass hitting the floor broke the silence. I didn't say a word to him. He sat at the table, head in his hands, exhausted from practicing the speech he'd have to give at the funeral. His breathing was shaky, his eyes red from sleepless nights. Jackson felt as if he had let his mom down by not spending enough time with her. I did everything I could to listen to him and understand his feelings. The paper he wrote was full of tears and blood stains from his knuckles.

He fell asleep on the edge of my bed with an ice bucket full of water to stop the swelling. Jackson had a football game coming up against Burn Wood the night before prom. The town was starting to talk about it. There was so much to expect with them coming to our school again.

I stayed in the library, catching up on my missing assignments and finishing Lyra's essay. The quiet was broken when Maxes slammed her sketchbook next to my hand, making me jump so hard I almost knocked over my notebook.

"Okay, hear me out," she said, grinning like she'd just come up with the best plan ever. "I was thinking we should steal Nick's bike. Every morning, he's got this little routine where he rides around the neighborhood for like 40 minutes to stay fit for football—"

"Wait, Nick works out?" I said, laughing. "And why are you even watching him, you creep?"

She sighed deeply. "I know what he did to you in the locker room. So, this could be our revenge, are you in or what?"

The locker room? My chest tightened at the memory. That day Nick and his teammates cornered me, nearly drowning me with their water guns. It wasn't just water—it was humiliation. That moment still haunted me, and it's how I ended up hooked on those painkillers in the first place.

My eyes narrowed. "How do you know about that?" I asked.

She glanced away, tugging her skirt down. "I'm the one who called for help. I stayed after school to finish up some articles for the paper. I saw everything."

My jaw tightened. "Why are you just now telling me this?"

Her eyes flickered with guilt, and she shrugged. "I didn't know how to bring it up. I wanted to get to know you first, and now… well, now you know."

I shoved my books into my bag, heart pounding louder with every second. "Yeah, well, I gotta go."

"Acelin, wait—" she said.

But I was already gone.

I couldn't look at her anymore. It felt like she was always watching me—watching every move I made. My mind was racing with too many thoughts at once.

"Dumb ass! What's wrong with you?" Jamie's voice snapped me back as I accidentally bumped into his arm. I didn't stop to answer him. I just kept moving, pushing through the hallway

CHAPTER 15

crowd until I hit the front doors.

The cold air hit my face as I stepped outside, my breath fogging up in the chill. I made my way to the parking lot. Sliding into the driver's seat of my car, I closed the door and sat in silence, gripping the steering wheel like it was the only thing grounding me. My mind wouldn't shut up.

What if Maxes is the right girl for me? The thought crept in, and I shook my head, trying to push it away. *No, she can't be. She's not.* But my heart wasn't listening. She'd seen me at my lowest, vulnerable in a way I never let anyone see me. And she still liked me. No one had ever done that before.

If she wanted, she could've told the whole school about that night in the locker room. She could've spread the rumors that would've ruined me. But she didn't. She stayed quiet. She saw me, the real me, and didn't run away. My eyes closed as I leaned back in my seat, my thoughts still wrestling with each other. *What if she really is different?*

I drove around town, hoping the movement would quiet my thoughts. Eventually, I found myself at the diner when Jackson was working. He'd picked up a shift to keep busy before his mom's funeral.

At school, he barely spoke to me. I didn't see him at lunch, which wasn't like him. He never missed lunch, especially when they served his favorite snack—milk and Oreo's. It felt off, and now, seeing him here, it all made sense.

He scrubbed down a table with more force than necessary, his jaw tight with focus. Jackson always cleaned when he was upset. He once told me it helped him sort through his thoughts, like scrubbing away the mess in his head.

"Let me guess…" he called over, flashing a half smile that didn't quite reach his eyes. "Strawberry muffin and coffee? Did

I get it right?"

I smiled. "No, it's... it's a blueberry muffin."

"Oh, I was close," he said with a small laugh, but his voice cracked just a little.

I sat down at the counter, watching him stack dishes. "So, how are you?" I asked, even though I already knew the answer.

"Good," he replied too quickly, his hands not stopping.

I didn't press him. I just sat there, letting the silence between us say what words couldn't.

"Do you want to have a movie night later? I can buy the popcorn you always eat," I asked, hoping to lift the mood.

"I can't tonight," Jackson said, wiping down the counter again. "I have work, and by the time I get home, I'll be rehearsing for the funeral."

The door creaked open, drawing my attention. A girl with short hair and blonde highlights walked in. It took me a second to recognize her. "Does that look like Moe?" I asked Jackson, tilting my head. Her hair was usually black.

She wasn't alone. A guy followed behind her—tall, around six feet, with thick, fluffy brown hair. He had that cocky stance, like he owned the place. I squinted, disbelief washing over me as they sat down at a booth. Something wasn't right. Without thinking, I walked over.

"Moe?" I said, pretending to act surprised.

Her eyes met mine, and she smiled, putting her hair behind her ears. "Hey, Acelin. This is my boyfriend, Joe Moss."

I froze. Joe Moss. Johnny's half-brother. A Burn Wood kid. He played football and was known for starting trouble. My jaw clenched so tight I thought I'd crack a tooth.

"Joe Moss, huh?" I said, trying to sound cool, but my voice had a sharp edge. I glanced at Jackson, who was wiping the

CHAPTER 15

counter, his eyes locked on them too.

Joe gave me a slow, smug grin, leaning back in his seat like he knew exactly what he was doing. Moe looked so comfortable next to him, like she didn't see what I saw.

Joe Moss was just like another Nick—but worse. He'd been pulled from the football season to *"get his grades together"* and take anger management classes. Now he was back, and I knew Cherry Hill didn't stand a chance at winning this year's game.

When Nick heard Joe was back, he lost it. It was like hearing his old nightmare had come to life. Back in ninth grade, Joe actually went to our school. He roamed Cherry Hill's halls like he owned them. Teachers were afraid to call him out, and students walked the other way when they saw him coming. But after one too many fights—and a brawl that left a senior kid with a broken nose—they shipped him off to Burn Wood.

On the way home, I stopped at a local store. Lyra had been talking about running low on her box of chocolates—the kind she craved every month during her cycle. I wanted to be the kind of boyfriend who noticed the little things, so I decided to pick some up for her. This was a big night for us. I'd be staying at her house for the first time since her mom was out of town, and it felt like the perfect chance to be with her without all the noise and chaos from my house.

I grabbed a pack of her favorite pads, spotted some funny matching shirts that said, *"I'm yours"* and *"You are mine,"* and decided to get those too. My arms were full, but I still needed to grab her favorite snacks.

"Excuse me, sir! Do you need a basket?" someone called from the end of the aisle.

I turned to answer, but as I did, a couple of items slipped from my hands. I bent down to pick them up and glanced towards the voice. My mood shifted fast. "Maxes?"

She froze too, then gave an awkward smile. "I swear, I'm not stalking you or anything."

I squinted at her, suspicious. "When did ya start?"

"Last week. Monday."

"Great," I muttered, stuffing everything into the basket she handed me. "Now I gotta find a new store to shop at."

She raised her hands like she surrendered. "Sorry." She tilted her head, giving me that sly smile she always did when she knew something. "Is all this for your girlfriend?" she asked, eyes narrowing like she already knew the answer. "She's lucky to have you."

I pulled my wallet from my pocket, glancing up at her just once. "It's for my mother." The lie tasted bitter in my mouth, but it felt easier than saying *"my girlfriend."*

Her face softened, and she smiled like she believed it. "Aw, that's cute. You and your mom must have a close relationship."

I smirked, sliding my receipt into my pocket. "See you at school."

Arriving at Lyra's house, I went straight to her bedroom to see if she was done showering. The sound of running water stopped just as I walked in. I moved to the bathroom door and tried the handle, but it was locked. *She never locks the door around me.*

I pressed my ear to it, hearing her voice. She was on the phone with someone, but the words were too muffled to make out. A minute later, the door clicked open, and she stepped out fully dressed. Her hair was still damp, and the smell of her lavender body wash filled the air.

"Ya good?" I asked, eyeing her.

"Why wouldn't I be?" she shot back, brushing past me.

CHAPTER 15

"Why'd you get dressed in the bathroom?"

Her eyes rolled so hard I thought they'd stay stuck. "I can't?" she said, like it was the most normal thing in the world.

I mumbled, "Never mind," and sat on the bed, trying to ignore the tight feeling in my chest.

We spent the night watching movies. At first, it felt normal—her head on my chest, my arm around her. But after a while, I noticed her phone buzzing under the pillow next to me. Every few minutes, a faint vibration. I glanced down at her. She was focused on the TV, eyes half closed like she was falling asleep.

Carefully, I reached under the pillow, my fingers brushing against the cold screen. I tilted it just enough to see the messages from **Nick**.

"Can I see you today?" one message read. Below it, there were others he'd sent that she hadn't responded to.

My heart thudded harder with each passing second. *Nick. Of all people, Nick?* I sat up slowly, eyes fixed on her.

"So, you still text Nick?" My voice came out rougher than I intended.

Her eyes snapped open. She blinked a few times, confusion on her face. "No?" she said, trying to sound innocent, but her voice was too light.

"Don't lie to me," I said, sitting at the edge of the bed. I started walking to the door, my heart pounding so hard it hurt.

"Please don't do this to me!" she cried, moving in front of the door to block it. Her arms were spread wide, her eyes glossy with tears.

"Lyra, move now." My voice came out low, sharp, and cold. It was the first time I'd ever raised my voice at her. I don't yell when I'm angry—I leave. *I have to leave.* When I'm angry, I don't trust myself to be around anyone.

Her lips trembled. "Please, please, don't do this to me," she begged. "I'll say it, I swear! I'll say I love you! Just don't go to Maxes!"

Her words hit me like a punch to the chest. *Don't go to Maxes?* She wasn't even fighting for *me*. She was just scared of someone else taking me. I swallowed the lump in my throat, my jaw clenching so tight it hurt. "Maybe I will," I said, my voice colder than before. I pushed her to the side and walked out of the room, out of her house, and out of the relationship.

* * *

He scanned his eyes through the loose crowd, noticing all the people who had come out to support him, from family to schoolmates. He gripped the edges of the wooden podium, holding onto a soggy paper with dried blood stains on it, anxious to speak. He took a deep breath in and looked over to me for comfort as he began to speak.

"Thank you all for coming out. I spent days, even nights, wondering what to say about my mom. She was the most talented, beautiful, and even crazy human being that I knew. She always had love for everyone around her, even the people who did her wrong." He cleared his throat. "Those who abandoned her, the people who got another girlfriend and took her money to put into his fucking wine business!" Jackson pulled the microphone closer to him. "Well fuck everyone who just allowed that to happen!" Everyone gasped and held their hearts, concerned for him. "My sorry fucking father, who doesn't give a shit about me and my mother ruined her life!"

CHAPTER 15

I slowly rose from my seat and walked over to the podium by the stage, trying to get Jackson to walk off. "Jackson!" I whispered. "Come down, now!" His dad, Jim, walked up to him, trying to play it off cool like everything was normal between him and Jackson.

"Don't come any closer!" Jackson shouted into the mic towards his dad. "My mom deserved better!" He rushed off the stage and out through the exit doors. Jim took over the microphone as people started to whisper, wondering what was happening.

"Jackson!" I called after him, following him into the alley. "What the hell was that?"

He paced back and forth, his breathing uneven. "Don't ask me anything!"

"What's going on?" I asked, stepping in front of him to block his path. We had practiced this speech for days. It was supposed to be kindhearted, not a disaster.

He jabbed a finger towards the door. "He brought his fucking girlfriend," he said, voice cracking. "She laughed at the flowers my mom loved. Her favorite flowers! And now it's my fault her day is ruined."

"I'm sorry," I said, lowering my voice. "But your mom wouldn't have wanted this. She wanted peace, Jackson. Not this. Get back out there and show everyone what kind of son she raised."

His eyes watered as he tugged at his tie like it was choking him. "I can't."

"Yes, you can." I put my hand on his shoulder, forcing him to look at me. "You can."

Jackson redeemed himself and gave the speech he was supposed to give from the start. His words were heartfelt, and you could tell he was honoring his mom the way she deserved. Afterwards, the tension in the room seemed to ease, and dinner was served. People started gathering their plates, but I slipped away to the bathroom for a moment of quiet. As I washed my hands, I heard footsteps behind me. I turned to see Nick. This was the first time I had spoken to him since I started dating Lyra.

"Sorry for your loss," he said, leaning against the door frame while I dried my hands.

"Thanks. Jackson and I are getting through it," I replied, glancing at him briefly before looking away.

"Hey, um, before you leave…" He rubbed the back of his neck, his eyes shifting. "Lyra and I haven't been in contact with each other." His lips pressed into a thin line. "She told me to go fuck myself after I texted her, so I figured she really wants you."

I raised an eyebrow, not sure if I believed him. "You mean that?"

His face twisted into a frown. "Yeah, don't make it all weird and shit." He pushed off the door frame. "See you at school."

The next morning, school was waiting. I woke up to five missed calls from Lyra and a bunch of text messages from her friends urging me to talk to her. I wasn't sure what to do. Lyra and I definitely needed some space. Even though I still loved her, there was so much going on right now. I had to be there for Jackson. His mom had just passed, and he needed someone to rely on.

The girls were gathered by the bathrooms, all fawning over Joe Moss's flier posted on the wall. It was an article announcing that he'd be playing in tomorrow's football championship game. They were already planning to cheer him on. I couldn't help but think that their loyalty to our school had faded. It felt like

CHAPTER 15

they cared more about supporting him than sticking with our team.

"Hey!" I turned to see Maxes, her hair pulled up into a messy bun. "I'm really sorry about not making it to the funeral. I got caught up with schoolwork, and I felt bad about not being there—"

"It's fine," I said, leaning against the wall next to the bathrooms.

"You okay?" she asked, gently touching my arm.

"I'm good," I replied, but the truth was, I wasn't sure. I was still figuring out everything with Lyra, Jackson, and my messy thoughts.

She stepped back a little, as if giving me space. "I just wanted to apologize for being weird and... you know, annoying. You date Lyra, the cheerleader, and I'm just the book club girl who likes to draw, paint—"

I shook my head, cutting her off. "Maxes, stop. You're not weird, and you're not annoying." I stepped closer to her. "I've been focused on other things and, yeah, taking it out on you. But that's not fair. I'm sorry."

She seemed a little surprised, but there was a hint of relief in her eyes. "You don't have to apologize."

"I know, but I should," I said. "And don't think for a second that being the *book club girl* makes you any less important."

She smiled through watery eyes. "But I'm not important," she said, her voice trembling as she wiped away a tear.

I gently brushed her cheek. "No, no, don't cry," I murmured, pulling her into a comforting hug. She looked up at me with wide, vulnerable eyes.

Without thinking, I leaned in and kissed her briefly on the lips.

She froze and touched her lips. She had pinkish, plumped lips that I had been wanting to kiss for so long. Her lips were cherry flavored. Same flavor as Lyra's lip gloss.

"But... you have a girlfriend," she whispered, her voice uncertain.

"Now you're worried about a girlfriend?" I raised an eyebrow.

She kissed me again, her body pressing against mine as we slipped into one of the bathroom stalls, trying to keep quiet despite the adrenaline rushing through me.

"I've never kissed a boy before," she whispered, her voice shaky.

"Never been with a boy at all?" I asked softly, not sure what I expected to hear.

She nodded, "No."

I gently unbuttoned her shirt, noticing her pink lace bra. I pulled her hair out of the bun as she moaned into my mouth, still kissing me. I could feel her hands shake slightly as they rested on my belt. When she began to unbuckle it, I felt her hesitation. She wasn't ready.

I pulled back a little, my voice soft. "No rush," I said with a smile. "We've got time."

Her eyes met mine, full of uncertainty, but there was eagerness too. I could tell she was nervous about what to do next. "Okay," she whispered, taking a deep breath.

The bathroom door had opened. Jamie rushed in, having a mental breakdown and yelling at the top of his lungs. I covered Maxes mouth to make sure she stayed quiet. I walked out of the stall slowly, making sure she wasn't seen.

"Are you okay?" I asked him.

"It's Moe! She's with dumb ass Joe Moss. I thought she loved me!" He dropped to his knees, grabbing onto my shirt. "Why

CHAPTER 15

not me? I got clean for her, Acelin, I did everything for that girl," he cried with his head down.

I lifted him up. "Look, everyone is upset about her dating Joe Moss but there is nothing to do about it."

He dusted off his pants. "You know what... I'm going to tell her how I feel in front of everyone. I don't give a shit if Moss finds the fuck out, fuck him and fuck you, Acelin!"

Jamie stormed out of the bathroom, slamming the door. Maxes came out of the stall, chuckling and tucking her hair behind her ears.

"I think I should go check on him before he does something crazy," I smiled.

Maxes doe eyes melted as she looked at me. "Okay, goodbye," she stuttered. I kissed her forehead before walking out.

Jamie caused a scene in the hallways once the bell rang. He was drunk out of his mind and begged Moe not to leave him for Joe Moss. The students recorded him as they laughed, but everyone knew how much of a goofball Jamie really was. They didn't actually think he was hurt over a girl. He never gave a shit about one at that. Moe ran into the principal's office as Jamie started to sing on the microphone to her inside the gym, trying to grab her attention. The students followed his every move of entertainment until his show was cut short by the principal.

The principal walked in. "Jamie, my office now. If you don't get there in the next two minutes, you will not play in tomorrow's game!"

On the way down to the office, Jamie was clapping in people's faces and jumping out to scare them. The students did nothing but laugh. I peeked through the office window and saw Jamie holding a trash can to his face. He had drunk so much liquor; he was throwing up constantly.

"Where did you get the liquor from?" The principal slammed the bottle on the desk.

Jamie wiped his mouth. "I don't know! I found it."

"Jamie, I will contact your parents. Where did you get the bottle from?"

I walked in, trying not to cause a big disturbance. "Sorry to interrupt, I just wanted to make sure he got here safely." Jamie didn't make a move to look at me. I didn't know why he was so mad at me. I barely talked to Moe myself anymore.

The principal jerked his hands up. "Oh great! Do you know where he got the bottle from?"

"No sir—"

"I stole it from my parents liquor cabinet, can I fucking leave now?" Jamie said.

"Jamie, watch your language!" The principal shot up from his desk. "Acelin, I know I banned you from the book club, but can you come back just to take pictures for tomorrow's game?"

"Yes—" I hesitated. "Yes, I will." I hadn't taken a picture in months with my camera. I used to carry my camera everywhere. I missed it; I missed being that kid who used to take pictures of everything he saw.

16

Chapter 16

In the middle of the night, Maxes was working a late shift. The town was quiet, the streets empty, and not a single high school student in sight. Who would've thought Maxes and I had a thing going? In the halls, we walked right past each other like strangers. No glances. No smiles. Just two nobodies in a crowd. But during lunch, it was different. We'd meet up with each other in quiet corners of the library or behind the bleachers, far from anyone's view. Nobody knew. Not our friends. Not Lyra. No one. And honestly, I liked it that way. It felt like our secret.

I walked towards the register, hands in my pockets, watching her scan items, her face lit up with a smile.

"Hey," I said, leaning against the counter. "I know it's wild for me to show up at your job like this, but I wanted to see you."

She glanced around, lowering her voice. "I get off in two hours, Acelin. Can't you wait?"

"Nope. Not for you." I gave her a crooked grin. "Come on with me."

Her eyes widened. "Are you serious? You want me to leave

work?" she whispered, looking towards the security camera in the corner.

"Yes." I held out my hand, palm up, daring her to take it.

She glanced at me, then back at the camera. "I'm going to get fired," she muttered, chewing on her bottom lip.

"I'll make it worth it," I said, locking eyes with her.

For a moment, she hesitated. But then, slowly, she reached out, her fingers curling around mine. We rushed through the aisles, trying to hold back our laughter as we swiped snacks off the shelves and stuffed them into our pockets. The crackle of the store's intercom buzzed overhead. "Maxes, return to the register immediately," her manager's voice blared.

We were already at the door, slipping outside before the locks could click. The cool night air hit us as we stumbled into the parking lot, breathless from running. I spotted an empty shopping cart and, without thinking, I put her inside. Her laughter rang through the night as I pushed her across the lot, weaving side to side.

Later, I parked in front of her house, the engine ticking as it cooled. Maxes sat in the passenger seat, eating a sucker. I took it out of her hands and ate the rest.

"You owe me another one," she teased, her voice playful.

"I know, I know," I said, popping the last bit of candy into my mouth.

She wiped the corner of her mouth with her sleeve, the exact way Lyra used to. For a second, it felt strange, but I knew to throw my thoughts aside. She unpinned her name tag and tossed it onto the dashboard.

"Acelin?" she said suddenly, her voice quieter this time.

"Ya?" I replied, leaning back in my seat.

She hesitated, her eyes shifting to meet mine. "You have to

CHAPTER 16

choose between Lyra or me."

"What?" I leaned forward, eyes narrowing. "Where is this coming from?"

"You heard me," she said, her voice serious now. "I'm not gonna be some girl you run to when you're bored or when things aren't right with her."

I blinked, trying to process her words. She sat there staring at me, her brown eyes clear as day despite the foggy windows. "Maxes, I..." I started, but the words caught in my throat.

She shook her head. "Just go home, Acelin. I'll see you at school," she opened the car door and slammed it.

"Maxes, wait!" I called after her but stopped myself from following. I knew that's exactly what she wanted, but this time, I couldn't give in.

When morning came, school was let out early. The game against Cherry Hill and Burn Wood was today. The town went crazy with reports about tight security at every entrance. Cherry Hill High students had bought their tickets days in advance to avoid chaos with the other side of town.

"You okay?" Jackson said, sitting across the kitchen table from me.

I fidgeted with my hands. "My mother never told me where she was going. I think it's odd she's not back yet, ya know?"

"I noticed that too, but maybe she just needed to take her mind off things. What happened between you and her was a little bad."

"But she would've texted me at least," I said.

"Just give it a little more time and see." He began to peel an orange, squirting most of the juice towards my face, landing on my lip. "I've been thinking of something lately."

"What is it?" I licked my lips.

"I'm actually going to cut my hair off."

"Are you kidding me? So, it's final?"

He smacked his lips together. "I already made an appointment."

I laughed. "I'm actually gonna miss dread head Jackson."

"Shut up," he smiled, showing his teeth.

A knock at the door startled me. I walked over, wondering who it could be this early. Peering through the peephole, I saw Nick standing there, adjusting his blonde hair and pulling a toothpick from his mouth. "I know this seems weird and all, but I just wanted to give you something," he called out from the other side.

Curious, I opened the door. From behind his back, he pulled out a helmet. It was the one I had seen in his closet—rusty black, not as updated as the color of my motorcycle. I took a few deep breaths, trying to steady my racing thoughts and excitement. All I could manage to say was, "Why are you giving this to me?" I asked, noticing Tommy's initials on the back.

"I think it fits you," he said, glancing over at Jackson behind me. I never got the chance to tell Jackson about the apology Nick gave me.

"Thanks," I said, starting to close the door as he walked off. But something stopped me. "Wait, have you heard from my mother lately?"

He paused, confused. "No, she hasn't been around us," his voice was unsure.

Then something clicked, I ran upstairs to gather all the letters that had been arriving at my house unexpectedly. I set them on the kitchen table, trying hard to recall where I'd seen the writing before. It was on the tip of my tongue, but I just couldn't pinpoint it. The handwriting on all the letters looked the same,

CHAPTER 16

which meant it had to be the work of one person. It definitely wasn't Drew's; I remembered his letters well, especially not the curved E's. What if the person writing these letters had something to do with my mother's disappearance? Or maybe, I was just overthinking it all?

I needed a distraction, so I tagged along with Jackson. He was going on a date with Frances to a beach that wasn't too far from town. I stayed back on the shore, watching them play in the water. Jackson surprised Frances with a picnic. I sat eating everything they didn't finish—sandwiches, cookies, brownies, and chips—while collecting seashells on a small cover. Frances was pretty, with short red hair, though it was clearly box dyed. Her cheeks were always rosy, and her brown eyes were like the color of the sand.

Soft hands covered my face from behind, making me slightly jump out of fear. "Say thanks to Jackson, he let me tag along."

"Lyra?" I grabbed her onto my lap. "I'm sorry for leaving you, I'm so, so sorry." Was I really sorry because I left her that night, or was I sorry because I kissed Maxes and felt something?

"Just kiss me." She pulled me in to kiss her.

I moved her hair out of her face. "I love you," I said.

Jackson threw his wet towel onto my head. "Took you long enough," he said to Lyra.

I stood up to dust the sand off my body. "Jackson, you are the best brother I could ever ask for."

"Yeah, yeah, whateva," he replied.

Lyra held my hand. "Well… if it's okay with you, Acelin, I saw an ice cream shop passing by. I was thinking we could leave them be and—"

"Yes, of course we can get ice cream," I said. I picked her up in my arms and twirled her around.

We sat at an old, rusty brown table under the trees, leaves falling around us. The area was full of old, damaged homes, most burned or broken down. The neighborhood had a creepy vibe, mostly inhabited by old people.

I got a call from Greek, but the signal was too weak to answer. I knew it was important, likely about Drew, but I had to stay calm for Lyra's sake. She'd start asking questions if she sensed anything was wrong.

"There is absolutely no signal out here!" a man said. He was taking trash out to a dumpster. I ignored him, trying to find a signal with my phone, holding it in the air to get service. "Did ya hear me?" he shouted. He was a heavyset man, and his beard was in a ponytail. He looked sweaty and filthy, like he hadn't had a shower in weeks.

He walked up behind me.

"Can ya let me be?" I stared deep into his eyes. The only thing I could see was trouble, and I felt it.

He aggressively blinked. "You lost? Trying to find your way to that Cherry Hill and Burn Wood game?"

I frowned. "I'm actually from Cherry Hill."

"Acelin, come on!" Lyra said, holding the ice creams in her hands.

I walked over to the car, looking back at the man to make sure he wouldn't follow me. "This place is weird," I took the ice cream from her hand.

"Before we leave, I wanted to talk to you about something."

"What is it?" I said as we got into the car.

She took a deep breath. "My mom is sending me back to therapy. This time I'm getting stronger medication."

I nodded. "You never told me why you go to therapy," I said, taking a bite of the ice cream.

CHAPTER 16

She closed her eyes and let out a sigh. "When my dad died, I didn't know how to handle it, so I acted out by doing things I regret." Once the signal hit, a call from Maxes appeared on my phone. I flipped the phone over before Lyra could read the name. She stopped the car from pulling out of the parking lot. "Why would you just flip the phone over like that?"

"Like what?" I said, guilty.

"Acelin, who is that?" she calmly said.

"It's no one." She knew when I was lying because I started to look down a lot. "Um, it was my mother."

"Get out of my car," she said with a straight face.

I took my seat belt off. "Are you serious?"

"Yes, get the hell out since you don't want to tell me."

"Fine." I had stepped out of the car and watched her drive away. I followed behind her, hoping she would stop. The beach was ten minutes away, and Jackson was on his way home preparing for his football game. I was trapped outside alone.

I returned to the beach, sand filling my shorts as icy water lapped at the shore, sending chills through me. Maxes was my only option to get back to town. I knew I shouldn't be alone with her, but there was no one else to call. Twenty minutes later, she arrived. I was starving and cold, my lips turned purple from the frigid water.

"Hey," I said, getting into her car. I turned on the heat and blew into my hands.

She blushed. "I can't believe I drove far for you."

"I'll make it up to you," we exchanged a look. "About yesterday... at your house—"

"It's fine," she replied quickly. She reached to the back seat and grabbed a bag full of clothes and food. "I hope you can fit the size."

My eyes widened. "You didn't have to do this."

"You're welcome, and if you don't want to talk about why you were stranded in the middle of nowhere, that's fine too." She slapped her hands on the steering wheel.

I began changing my clothes, hinting for her to turn away so she wouldn't see my scars. She quickly looked away. "I hope one day you realize how horribly she treats you," she continued. Then she glanced back at me, noticing the scars I tried to hide—scars from Drew and mostly from my dad.

"Let's just make it to Jackson's game," I placed on my shirt.

When I arrived at the school, there was nowhere to park. It was so crowded you'd think a celebrity was at the game. The loud cheers from the crowds pierced my ears, making me tense with nervousness. I wanted to talk to Lyra before she got back on the field, but she was already cheering. Both towns had their own sections, cheering loudly. I saw we were down by one point on the scoreboard. I went into the locker room to wait for the team's break. My hands were shaking, and the camera around my neck felt tight. I took it off and placed it on my lap.

The football players' voices filled the locker room as they came in, sounding more upset than happy. Losing this championship game meant our school would be considered a pigsty—a saying that haunted losing teams in football.

"Everyone sit down now!" The coach slapped the clipboard down on the bench. "Are you guys scared or what?" he yelled in Nick's face.

"No, sir!" Nick said, looking away.

"Why are we tied with those pigs?" The coach looked over to Jackson. "Jackson, why are you not playing the plays right?"

"Sorry," Jackson said, quickly.

I started snapping photos of the boys. They were caked in

CHAPTER 16

dirt, looking like they had been run over by a truck.

"If we lose this game tonight, all of you can forget about prom. That's over, all of it!" He started to go over the plays on the board one more time. "Everyone pay attention!" The coach wiped his face from the falling sweat. "When we go back out on that field, I want you guys to play like it's your last day living." He paced around, holding his mouth. "Do it for Tommy."

Nick stood up. "Do it for Tommy on three!" The boys cheered and left. I ran behind them, getting every shot I possibly could.

I stayed by the sidelines as they got on the field. I could tell Nick was nervous playing against Joe Moss. He flinched anytime Joe got close to him or avoided trash talk with him. Johnny lingered around Jackson, trying to put fear into him. Jackson always stayed unbothered. Even if he was bothered, he was the type to not let it be shown.

I stood behind the cheerleaders, seeing if I could spot Lyra, and there she was, cheering in the air. The girls placed her down on the ground, and we made eye contact. I snapped her picture before she could react, then she smiled. The crowd got louder by the second.

"Hey Acelin!" Moe yelled, walking over to me. "Where have you been?"

"I just got here," I yelled into her ear. I felt a raindrop hit my forehead that made me flinch. I looked up at the sky, and the moonlight shone down on all of us. More lights lit up around the field, making everything glow.

"Look!" She pointed onto the field. "Jackson is going to make the touchdown!"

I watched him run for his life, trying to get that touchdown. The coaches from the bench cheered him on as the crowd from Burn Wood stood up from their seats, grabbing onto their heads.

I didn't think Moe was on our side, knowing that her boyfriend was playing on the other team.

"Come on, Jackson, you got it!" I yelled, trying to cheer him on.

Burn Wood shouted in madness. They threw their trash at the cheerleaders out of anger, which made me want to run over to save Lyra, but Jackson just won! I ran over on the field to collect pictures for the team, capturing their happiness.

Jackson laid there on the ground, taking deep breaths as his teammates helped him up. They jumped in joy as the Burn Wood team, *the Hawks*, walked away in distraught. The rain started to pour down badly. The cheerleaders ran onto the field to congratulate Jackson, not worrying about ruining their hair. We did it for Tommy. We won for Tommy Graves. Who would've thought us *eagles* would've won again?

"Okay, give him some room!" the coach said, dusting him off. "Congrats, my boy."

"Thank you, coach," Jackson said, out of breath.

There was a tap on Jackson's shoulder. I continued taking pictures, standing from a distance. The coach walked back to his seat packing his bag.

"Hey, good game," Joe Moss said.

"Good game, bro." Jackson held out his hand to shake on it, to squash the beef they had, but no, Joe Moss shook his hand and yanked his arm down to the ground. Jackson dropped, screaming in pain.

"What the hell, bro!" Nick pushed Joe Moss away from Jackson. "Why the hell would you just do that?" Nick said.

"For Tommy, right?" Joe Moss smiled.

Nick punched him in the face. The teams from both sides started to fight in a brawl. I ran over, trying to help Jackson.

CHAPTER 16

It was wet and slippery on the field. The crowd was shocked and trying to figure out what was happening. The cheerleaders were told to leave the field and go back into the school. Johnny watched from a distance, smiling. Jamie punched him in the face for laughing. The coaches ran over to break up the fights.

"My arm, I can't move it!" Jackson said, holding his arm.

I guided Jackson to the locker rooms to grab his things as I ran into one of the coaches who looked familiar. It was like I had seen him before. We both stopped and stared at each other. He hesitated to say something. He was a man who looked like he was in his forties. I could smell liquor lingering on his breath. His hair looked familiar, like my old hairstyle, the way I used to wear it slicked back. "Do I know you?" he yelled as I walked past him. I kept walking, my memory was just blank. That man's voice, his looks, all suddenly went blank.

The car ride to the emergency room was quiet. Nick drove with their trophies in the back of his car. Jackson was still in pain, holding his arm in place, whimpering. I knew something bad would happen tonight, but I didn't expect Jackson to be the one hurt.

While Jackson was being seen by the doctors, Nick and I had words to say to each other.

"This is all my fault," Nick said, scrubbing the dirt from his nails.

"It's no one's fault."

"We won, but at what cost? This keeps happening because of me. Now it's Jackson who has to suffer."

The doctor called us to visit Jackson in the back. Jackson laid with his hand covering his eyes. I walked over, took a cloth, and gently wiped the dirt off his face.

"You alright?" I asked.

"Yes," Jackson replied. "It just feels like my arm is hanging off."

"As much as I want to hurt Joe Moss, I would if prom wasn't around the corner," Nick said.

Jackson said, "I know, I would've bashed his head into the ground."

I didn't care about prom. My life was already shit, so why not risk doing something to Joe Moss? I looked at Nick, then Jackson, and figured why not bash Joe Moss's head into the ground? When Jackson got released from the hospital, he slept all night. But my thoughts didn't stop.

The night was smoky out. The air felt moist, and my hands were sweaty from holding onto the steering wheel, plotting down the street from Joe Moss's house. I was deep inside Burn Wood while these whispered doubts echoed through my mind, thinking if I should hurt Joe or let him be. They say the universe will always do karma, but I needed it to work quickly in my favor.

Moe was sitting in the living room watching television with her back turned towards the window. Joe Moss was nowhere to be seen. He was my target. The urge to just run inside and beat the shit out of him was growing on me. If I revealed myself, Moe would've told everyone what I did. Through the window, he came into the living room with a bowl of popcorn and a tray of drinks. That smile on his face, I wanted it gone.

I hurled a brick towards the window. The sound of shattering glass pierced the air. My heart sank as I watched shards scatter through the moonlight into their home. Glass scraped against Moe's and Joe Moss's faces, landing in the popcorn and drinks they were holding. I crouched in the yard, hunching over as I moved towards the car. I couldn't catch my breath; I couldn't

CHAPTER 16

feel my hands. I blinked repeatedly, trying to grasp reality, but I didn't regret what I'd done.

I was afraid that it felt good.

17

Prom Night

My suit was freshly steamed, my hair neatly trimmed, and my teeth freshly whitened. Everyone around school had heard about what happened to Moe and Joe Moss, but I couldn't care less about feeding into the gossip. I had better things to worry about, like graduation, which I couldn't stop thinking about, and then college.

Lyra had been accepted to two colleges: the one I was going to and her dream college. Maxes had been accepted to the college I was going to since her family was close with the principal. Jackson had a free ride to pick the colleges he wanted. He played football very well, and every college wanted him. Same with Nick. Jamie decided to take music classes; he wanted to join a band after high school and move to New York. Surprisingly.

Jackson iced his arm every single day, pressing the cold pack against his skin until it turned red and raw from the hours of contact. He barely flinched, as if the pain was just another thing he could control.

"How do you feel?" I asked him, my concern obvious.

"Great!" he said, but his frown didn't match his words.

"I just want to make sure you're okay."

"I'm... fine!" he replied, forcing a smile. "Let's just worry about prom, okay?"

I wanted to help, to make sure he wasn't heading down the same path Tommy had, but it felt like I was smothering him with my concern.

"I'll meet you at school?"

"You know it. They've got my favorite snack at lunch. I have to be there," he said, adjusting the brace on his arm like it was no big deal.

When I arrived at school, I went into the library and could smell fresh coffee steaming through the air. There was a stand of refreshments, cookies, cake, and donuts. I had to help myself.

I felt my mouth water as I picked out what I wanted on a small plate. I made a cup of coffee and sat down at one of the tables.

Maxes came up to me. "What are you doing here?" she asked.

I swallowed quickly, my food flushing slowly down my throat. "I don't care if this is a book club meeting," I shrugged my shoulders.

"Sounds like something you wouldn't care about." She looked down at my coffee cup. "Why does your coffee look so black?"

"Just how I like it, black." I covered the cup, feeling embarrassed. I could feel her judging me.

She snatched my cup from my hand, then grabbed two creamers and three packs of sugar from the refreshment stand. "What you do is, mix all these in your cup and drink."

I took a sip and let the taste settle on my tongue. I actually liked it but still wouldn't admit it to her. "It's not all that," I said with a shrug, sliding over a bit as she sat down next to me.

She glanced at me. "What's your deal?"

"A while ago, I got a call from Greek," I said, ignoring her question. "Never got the chance to answer it, though. Think ya could ask him what he wanted to talk about?"

Her expression changed quickly. "Greek doesn't just call people for no reason. You sure you didn't do something?"

"I'm sure," I shook my head slowly.

She fidgeted with the edge of her sleeve. "I'm not allowed in your guy's business. He made that clear, and he doesn't even want me talking to you."

"Why do you always act like he's your dad or something?" I frowned.

She didn't snap back. Instead, she stood up and crossed her arms. "I think you should go before the principal catches you in here."

I stared at her for a moment, debating whether to press her for more answers, but I knew it would've been pointless. "Ya, I should get going," I said.

I walked out the door and made eye contact with the principal. Disappointment lingered on his face. "Acelin. My office, now," the principal's voice rang out.

When I opened the office door, I saw Jackson sitting in a chair. I was confused about why he was even here in the first place.

"Jackson?" I touched his shoulder.

"Acelin?" We both looked confused.

"Let's both take a seat," the principal said as he walked in behind me. He fixed his name tag on his desk that said Mr. Micron. "I called you into my office, Jackson, about your arm. How is it?"

Jackson sat up straight. "Fine!"

"We looked into the conflict. I talked to the coaches from Burn Wood, and Joe Moss stated he didn't mean to pull you down, so there will be no further consequences set for him."

"Are you serious?" Jackson said weakly.

"That's bullshit," I mumbled. "Jackson is not lying!"

"Excuse me, Acelin, but I can't have this school have any more problems. From now on, you will agree that you saw nothing else but an accident, understand?"

"Nick even saw it happen," I said, slamming my hand on his desk.

The principal fixed his glasses from falling down on his face. "Great! No prom for the both of you, you're dismissed."

"Wait! Okay, I'll agree that nothing happened," Jackson said.

If Jackson agreed, then I had too as well. I would miss prom in a heartbeat for him, but it seemed like prom meant a lot to him still. "Okay, Joe Moss didn't hurt Jackson on purpose," I said with sarcasm.

"Good boys, now you both can leave."

Jackson walked out before I could say anything to him. I stared at the principal, hoping he would understand how much of a horrible person he was. I couldn't keep letting Burn Wood play us like sheep or sitting ducks. I had to show them that Cherry Hill couldn't be messed with.

Moe was not the girl who had my back at the beginning of the school year. She had become a traitor, a traitor that I no longer had feelings for as a friend. I tried calling her, even texting her, trying to understand why she still dated Joe Moss. Why couldn't she date someone from our school like Jamie, who actually loved her?

"Acelin," Jamie said as he waited for me by the door.

I raised my eyebrows. "What?"

"Have you seen Moe's face?"

"What about it?"

He laughed. "Whoever did that need to be hurt," he said. "Oh."

He gently pushed me. "I'm playing but I also have connections with people, and I made sure yo ass is going to win prom King," he jerked my shoulders.

I wasn't sure if this was good or bad. Winning didn't feel the same anymore. I didn't care for competition like I once did. "I hope I don't win," I muttered, slamming my locker shut.

Jamie walked in front of me. "You okay, you seemed off?"

Was my face really that guilty looking? "I just had a long night, sorry."

Stands had flooded the halls around the school for King and Queen voting. I never thought I'd vote for myself, but here I was, doing it anyway.

"Yo, Acelin! I heard yo name in the top five, you got my vote, bro," one of the football players called out. I recognized him as one of the guys who had sprayed me with hot water in the locker room.

"Thanks," I said, barely meeting his eyes.

Then, I bumped into Lyra. "Hey," she said, and we both walked into the lunchroom.

I awkwardly glanced around. "Hey." We stepped aside. "We meet again," a smirk tugged at my lips.

"It's my fault," she said quickly. "I treated you like crap that day. It's the medication, I swear."

I let out a breath, trying to keep my cool. "I know how to handle you."

She nodded. "So...? Are we going to prom together?"

I didn't say a word to her. I walked away, cleared my throat, and took the microphone, standing on top of the table. "Hey, um, everybody, if I could just grab your attention, I would like for everyone to listen." Everyone started to get quiet. "I'm Acelin, Acelin Jones, and I'm in the top five for winning prom King, and I hope you guys can vote for me and my girl, Lyra Barns. She's been wanting to win Queen her whole life, and I hope you guys can vote her in. Thanks!" The crowd stayed quiet until Jackson cheered me on. The football players barked and slammed their cups onto the lunch tables. Walking over to Lyra, I saw her polite smile form.

"You know, you didn't have to do that," she gently hit my arm.

"I just want us to win together."

"I told people to vote for me last minute. I think the votes are already in."

"We will see!" I said.

Work had been straight after school. No kids in sight. Only appointments for haircuts, hairdos, and shopping for last minute prom dresses. The whole day I had been nervous with this heavy pressure that sat in the middle of my gut. The night sky was dimming down, the trees were steady. Tonight was going to be one of the best nights of my life. I had never thought I would share it with Lyra Barns. My wish had come true to be with her. The universe had finally answered me.

Outside by the dumpster, rats swarmed their way out. The trash dropped down on the ground. I covered my mouth out of disgust. I couldn't stand the filth of holding dirty things. Every day after work, I tried to avoid removing the trash just to not see the dumpster. Trash was always surrounding the walkway by the back door, making me step on things I had no clue what it was.

I went back inside and washed my hands.

"You have one more customer before you leave," the manager said. I wiped my hands with a paper towel and headed to the front.

"Oh! Maxes," I said, surprised.

"Hey."

"What can I get for ya?"

"A coffee with no sugar and no creamers."

My eyes lit up. "You want to try how I drink mine, huh?" I smiled.

She panicked. "I mean… I just wanted to try it because you said you prefer it dark. It looked good, so I just thought—"

"Okay, I'll make sure to make it how I make mine," I said. "Are you gonna go to prom by any chance?"

She rolled her eyes. "Yes, Nick asked me."

"Nick!" I shouted, almost dropping her coffee.

"Just as friends!" she held her hands up. "It wasn't my idea or his. Lyra told him to ask me. I know it's weird, but I just—"

"No! I'm glad ya did that. I wouldn't want her to think me and you are a thing," I frowned. "Not in a bad way."

She nodded. "I know. Goodbye, Acelin, and thanks for this," she said, holding her coffee up in a cheer.

Home was finally where I went. My suit had been laid out on my bed. I carefully pressed out any wrinkles left over. It was surreal to think that just in a few minutes, I would be exchanging smiles and laughter with my classmates, pretending that my life was back to normal. Jackson had a surprise for me waiting in the living room. His hair had been cut off, his dreads were all gone. He looked different but better, even though he always looked good. I could finally see his rounded shaped ears.

"Wow, you look good, Jack."

He started to pick at his hair. "Yeah, yeah, I just went with something low, not too low." I could see his loose curls even more.

"What did Frances say about it?"

"She loved it, I think," he paused. "She thinks I'm going to find another girlfriend," he frowned.

"No one is as loyal as you. She has nothing to worry about."

He huffed. "Do you think my mom would love my haircut?"

"She's smiling down now."

"I bawled my eyes out getting ready," he laughed.

"Same with me, my mother isn't here still to see me off."

He touched my shoulder. "I'll see you at prom, Acelin."

Arriving at Lyra's house, her mom finally accepted me as Lyra's boyfriend. She took pictures of us and hung them on her fridge. Lyra had worn her hair in a bun to the back with shiny small stones placed around her bun. Her dress was long and dark green with sparkles all over. It matched my suit perfectly.

At the prom doors, I met up with Jackson and Frances. A red carpet guided us to a photo booth. Lights beamed on us as we walked in. Loud music crashed into my ears. Winning was what I was steadily worrying about. Standing on stage in front of a big crowd, knowing I was being judged for something I wasn't sure I deserved, was harder than I ever expected.

As I observed everyone, it became clear that the worries, stress, and problems in this small town had faded away for a moment. But not everyone seemed to be enjoying themselves as well. The couple in the corner, for instance, appeared uninterested in each other. A girl with honey blonde hair sat by herself, looking bored to death, her makeup caked on as if she'd been dipped in a bowl of foundation. Meanwhile, Lyra stood with her girlfriends in a corner, fixing their makeup, laughing, and chattering away.

I sat at the table alone.

"You look good," Maxes said, sitting next to me.

"Thank you! You as well," I yelled into her ear over the loud music.

She wore an all-black dress, and her hair was curled and tucked behind her ears. "Where's your date?"

"With her friends," I said awkwardly. "Where is Nick?"

"Waiting for me in the swim room," Maxes said with a wink. "By the way, Greek wants to meet with you again. He said it's serious this time, whatever that means."

"When?" I asked quickly, my voice tight. "This is really important to me. I need to know when?" I frowned.

Before she could respond, Lyra appeared. "Hey, baby, I'm going to the bathroom, are you okay?" she asked as she saw the look on my face.

"Yes—" She leaned in and kissed me right in front of Maxes. Maxes looked away as I wiped my mouth gently.

"I'll be back," Lyra said, flashing a smile before walking away.

"Okay," I said to Lyra, my voice trailing off. I glanced back at Maxes just as she grabbed her purse from the table. Without another word, she walked away, leaving me sitting there, unsure if I should follow her.

I sat for ten minutes, wondering what Greek was anxiously trying to tell me. I stared at the ground, my hands tucked between my legs. Eventually, I walked out to the hall to get fresh air. My face turned slightly red, and my heart began to race. I ripped the tie off from around my neck. I had this feeling that Drew knew I wasn't dead. That's what Greek had been trying to warn me about this whole time.

A girl came running from the bathrooms towards the gym door, nearly colliding with me. "Hey, have you seen Lyra?" I asked her.

"No, but you need to come back in. We're going to announce

prom King and Queen, come on!" she said, taking my hand and pulling me back into the gym. I could feel a panic attack coming on—I couldn't catch my breath, and my chest felt tight.

Jackson grabbed my hand, guiding me through the crowd to the front stage. "They're going to announce it to you. Are you ready?" Jackson smiled, gripping my arm to keep me close.

Julie Foster, the school president, stepped onto the stage, holding a note in her hands. "Ladies and gentlemen, I know we've all been waiting for this day, and I hope your votes were chosen wisely. Let's start with the prom King!" She opened a black envelope.

Jackson gripped my arm tighter, his excitement loud as he bounced on his heels beside me. The crowd's chatter hushed, the tension building as Julie scanned the paper in her hand. I could feel my heart race, faster.

"The prom King is… Acelin Jones!" The crowd erupted in applause, but everything around me went blank. My vision turned black and white. I stood there, frozen in shock.

"Acelin… you won! Get up there!" Jackson said, nudging me forward. He adjusted his arm brace as he stepped back.

I slowly walked up on the stage, seeing all the students below me, and Jackson looking incredibly proud. I think it was the first time I'd ever seen him smile that much. I forced a smile and gave a slight wave to the crowd.

"And now for our Queen, we have… Moe Hart!" Hearing Moe's name almost made me stumble forward.

"Now it's time for their dance, so everyone please step to the side."

The song "Master of None" by Beach House played as I tried to make sense of everything. I took her hand as we began to dance in the center of the floor. My hands were shaky and sweaty; she could tell something was wrong by the worried look in my eyes. I couldn't face her; I just couldn't. She laid her head on my chest. "Thank you for being a good friend to me," she said. I held her tightly, trying to hold back my sorrow.

The music switched as Julie shouted into the microphone. "Now let's party!" she yelled. I let go of Moe's hand and wandered back out into the hallway, hoping to find Lyra. I called her name everywhere. I took off my crown, holding it in my hands. I checked the bathrooms, locker rooms, and classrooms.

"Acelin!" Jackson shouted, following behind me in the hall. "What is going on with you?"

My eyes widened. "I—I gotta go! I just don't want to ruin your night!" I said, losing my breath.

"Slow down, did you drink something?" he asked, grabbing my hand to calm me.

"No," I said, sweat dripping from my face. "Jackson, I think they found me." I slowly walked away from him, then began to sprint down the hall.

"Acelin, wait!" he shouted. He knew what I meant—the Members found me.

I threw off my suit jacket and placed my crown by the swim room doors. I needed to see Maxes one last time before Drew got me. The swim room was the last place she said she'd be with Nick. I called her name, but there was no response.

A low whimper came from the highest diving board. I called her name again before walking up the steep stairs, hoping not to find anything I didn't want to see.

I reached the top and gasped, finding Maxes sprawled in a pool of blood, struggling for breath with her head against the railing. A deep stab wound marred her right side. Nearby, Nick was slumped over at the edge of the diving board, cold and pale, a broken liquor bottle scattered around him. I dropped to my knees, feeling the rough concrete bite into my skin. "Who did this?" I begged, holding Maxes face steady in an attempt to keep her with me. Her hands were slick with blood; she had fought to stop the bleeding.

Nick's body stiffened, and his arms locked in place as he fell face first into the water. The pool was always covered when not in use—someone must have planned this murder.

Panic went through me as I stared at my blood stained hands, making it hard for me to breathe. I rubbed my hands on my shirt, petrified. I left a smear of blood on the stair rail as I jumped into the pool to save Nick. I pulled him up, desperate to perform CPR, but it was hopeless. White foam bubbled from his mouth. I couldn't save him. All I could do was get help.

I raced through the hallways, frantic to find someone—anyone! My life flashed before my eyes; the blood stained on my hands haunted me. What would they think of me? I couldn't end up in jail for a crime I didn't commit. My head spun, and it felt like I was about to collapse.

Bursting through the gym doors, soaked and trembling, the weight of my wet clothes clinging to me like a nightmare come to life.

"Help me, please," I said, falling to my knees at the entrance door. "Help! Someone… help me!"

Jackson ran over to me, lifting me from the floor. "Acelin!" His eyes were filled with concern and worry, as if he had seen a ghost. "What did you do?" he said. The people around me looked confused and terrified, backing away as if I were losing my mind.

"I didn't do it! I didn't do it!" I cried out, desperation clawing at my throat.

The music cut off. The principal made his way over, pushing the students to the side. "Alright, everyone stand back!" he shouted, making the crowd distance themselves from me. "Oh my Jesus!" His hand flew to his mouth. He saw the blood on my clothes.

The doors burst open with two policemen and a dog. "Is there a student here named Acelin Jones? He is under arrest for the murder of Seulgi Sew," one of them said, shouting into a megaphone. The other policeman held an overaggressive dog, gripping the leash tightly. The students pointed in my direction, and Lyra dropped to her knees crying, falling into Frances arms.

"I think you have the wrong person, sir!" Jackson said as I stood behind him, trying to keep my balance.

I begged, "People need help! They're both in the swim room!"

"Go check the swim room," the cop said, instructing the other officers. More cops surrounded the front entrance. The students looked at me like I was a cold-blooded killer. The voices around me grew louder and louder with lies.

"I need my vote back!"

"I always knew he was a creep."

"He's a school shooter; it's always been true."

"I knew he was killing us off!"

The officer tried to come closer, but I backed away, trying to avoid getting cuffed. I was tasered without hesitation. I dropped to the floor, hitting my head against a metal chair. All I could see was Lyra looking over me and Jackson being held back by more cops. Then, my vision went blurred.

I was known as the *school killer*.

18

Chapter 18

Rain poured down as I stepped out of the police car, water streaming from my hair and soaking into my suit collar. The officers guided me inside the station, unlocked a cell, and shoved me in. The loud clang of the metal door echoed as they walked away.

I couldn't stop thinking about the blood. No matter how hard I squeezed my eyes shut, the image stayed. I kept looking at my hands, afraid I might see it again.

They gave me new clothes—thin, scratchy fabric that didn't keep out the cold. I sat on the hard bench, knees to my chest, leaning against the wall. A damp towel hung around my shoulders, barely offering any warmth.

"Acelin Jones, your bus will be here any minute," a woman's voice called out. She popped her gum and tapped her keys against the cell bars. *Tap. Tap. Tap.*

I looked up, squinting. "What bus?" I asked, my voice rough.

She leaned in with a grin, her eyes knew something I didn't. "You'll see," she said, blowing a bubble that popped loudly. Time dragged on until I heard the rain slow to a soft pattern. The lady unlocked my cell with the same bored look as before. "Out," she said, not even looking at me.

I hesitated but stood up. The towel slipped off my shoulders onto the floor. My steps felt heavy as I followed her outside. The rain had turned to mist. The bus waited at the curb, its headlights glowing like two eyes watching me.

I climbed on, ducking under the low doorway. The air inside was colder than outside, they kept the air on blast. The old leather seats were cracked and worn. A musty smell hung in the air, like my dad's old office where books sat for too long. I ran my hand over the seat, feeling the rough patches where the leather had peeled away.

The driver's eyes stayed on the road, his hands gripping the wheel tight, like it might slip away. We arrived at Dooms Institute for Teens. The building loomed ahead, old, foggy, and isolated. Two statue hawks flanked the entrance, their fierce stares warning off intruders. Security guards escorted me through the towering doors, chains clanking around my wrists and ankles.

Inside, the other kids wore gray jumpsuits and foam slides that barely lasted a week. The place felt like a psych ward; screams echoed from deep within, chilling and unnerving. Eyes followed me from dorm room windows as I was led through the cold hallways. Finally, I was placed in a small office, the door locking behind me.

The doorknob rattled as someone approached. A woman strode in. "Good morning," she said, moving to her desk. Her tight black suit matched her demeanor. She was tall with thick gray hair. She began typing on her computer, the steady clicking sound irritated me as she smoothed her lips together.

I leaned in, the chains cutting into my wrists as I strained

CHAPTER 18

closer. "I was framed by someone named—"

"The things you've done can be fixed with treatment." Her eyes narrowed, her tone clipped.

"No!" My voice cracked, desperate. "You don't understand! I didn't kill anyone. There's no proof."

Her smirk appeared like she had already made up her mind. "Let's get you cleaned up. A hot shower and some food might help."

Anger ran through me. My hands shot out, gripping the lapels of her jacket as I yanked her forward. "Get me out of here!" The words tore from my throat.

She jerked back, her face twisting in alarm. "Security!" she called as she twisted free, stumbling away as heavy footsteps approached me from behind.

Two men rushed in, pulling me back. The chains around my wrists tightened with each tug. They dragged me to the showers. Stripped off my clothes, I clutched them tightly, trying to shield myself as cold water sprayed down on me.

Afterward, I threw on my gray jumpsuit. The number on the suit was #001. I was handed a small bar of soap and a wretched toothbrush with missing bristles. The soap was supposed to last two weeks; the toothbrush would barely survive three days. A bundle of four pairs of white socks was tossed my way. The slides pinched my feet uncomfortably as security escorted me to my assigned room, shoving me inside with the meager belongings they'd given me.

The room was dull and plain, featuring two beds. Someone laid on the other one, messy with covers piled on top. A single pillow rested on top of the dresser along with a picture. The smell of old wood clung to the air, and I hated the way the bed felt beneath me as I sat on its edge, slipping off my slippers.

The door creaked open. "Oh, hello!" a young boy with glasses said, clutching a worn-out bear. He looked about fourteen, and the bear definitely needed a wash. "I heard you're new here."

"I didn't do it," I replied, trying to keep my voice steady.

"Henry said the same thing."

"Who's Henry?" I asked, watching him settle onto the bed across from me.

Just then, another boy slipped in, his pants stuffed with snacks. He dropped half of his stash on the floor, his fluffy blonde hair covered his eyes.

"Cole, get out now!" Henry shouted, shoving bars of soap into his drawer. His blue eyes sparkled with secrets, and I recognized him—he was the lab rat the Members tested on.

I watched as he crammed hand towels, socks, and a toothbrush under his bed, then pulled out a mirror to check his hair, fluffing his curls. I glanced around the room, taking in the peeling paint and the buckets in every corner to catch leaks.

"Hungry?" He tossed me a snack—a pack of crackers with peanut butter. "If you need anything else, just let me know."

I nodded, slowly nibbling on the food. The memory of Maxes and Nick haunted me, especially the feel of her lifeless body in my arms. I couldn't eat.

He hung up another picture of a girl on the wall. "Is that ya girlfriend?" I asked.

"Yeah." He licked his thumb, wincing at the tack that pricked him.

"How long have ya been here?"

"Since I was ten. I get out next year when I turn eighteen." He moved to the edge of his bed. "What about you? Do you have a girlfriend?"

I smiled a bit. "Her name is Lyra Barns."

CHAPTER 18

An announcement blared over the speaker, calling everyone to the entertainment room. Henry quickly changed into a fresh gray outfit—one he must have stolen—and fixed his hair again. "You coming?" he asked.

I followed him as other kids trickled out of their rooms, moving past classrooms and lunchrooms. Everything felt organized, the beige walls mirroring the dull uniforms we wore. The boys had uniform haircuts, while the girls wore slicked back buns. I couldn't believe these kids were trapped here, resigned to their fate.

Henry eyed me closely. "Where are you going? You can't leave the group."

Ignoring him, I stepped away, heading towards Ms. Katy's office—the woman I had met earlier this morning.

As I approached, I overheard her speaking inside. The door was slightly opened, and I caught snippets of the conversation.

"Henry sharing a room with Acelin, I think that's a bad duo," Ms. Katy said.

"He has one more year left, and I think he's doing fine," a doctor replied, her voice low.

Katy shook her head. "No, I'm thinking about keeping him. His parents were found dead last night," she shrugged her shoulders. "He doesn't have a family anymore."

Suddenly, a deep voice cut through my thoughts. "Excuse me, aren't you supposed to be in the entertainment room?" a security guard asked, eyeing me suspiciously.

I touched the back of my neck, swallowing hard. "Ya, sorry. I got lost."

He walked me to the room I was supposed to be in. Pills were handed to me before entering. The doctor used a small flashlight to make sure I swallowed them. The room was filled with board games, coloring books, and a television stand. I stayed off at a table in the corner, watching everyone move in sync.

"Hey," Cole said, walking up to me.

"Why does everything feel like a dream?" I looked down at my hands, examining them.

"Ah, you took the pill." He set his bear onto the table. "What does that necklace mean?"

I looked down at my neck. "It was a gift from someone." I tucked it back into my shirt.

A group of boys walked up to us. One of the boys snatched the bear from Cole's hands and held it in the air, making him jump for it.

"Leave him alone," I said.

"Who are you exactly?" the boy asked, eyeing me hard. He went by the name Benny. Tall, with a normal body and hair that hung just above his ears. He had a look that hinted at both vulnerability and defiance. His eyes narrowed, revealing a look of horror.

I had heard whispers about Benny—how he had been locked up because of his schizophrenia. The rumors flew around the facility like a dark cloud. They said he had killed his little sister, convinced she was going to kill him first because of the voices he heard in his head. It was a tragic story that sent shivers down my spine, but here he stood, just another kid lost in this place.

I pushed Benny away from Cole. He fell to the ground with a slide. He stood back up on both of his feet and threw a tray of food at me. The kids around us cheered on the fight. I picked up the tray and threw it back at him as he dodged my shot. He ran towards me as he grabbed both of my legs and threw me down to the ground. I threw a punch to his left ear.

CHAPTER 18

Henry came running towards us, yanking Benny off me. He locked Benny's arms and shouted, "Acelin hit him!" Henry let me land a solid punch to Benny's face before the security guards stormed in, pulling us apart.

I was placed in a *time-out* center for hours. Sitting on the edge of the narrow cot, the cold stone pressed against my back. The dim light flickered weakly, and the sound of water dripping echoed in the silence. Just when I thought I'd be left alone forever, Cole appeared by the cell, his eyes wide with worry.

He placed both of his hands around the bars. "Acelin!" he whispered, glancing around nervously.

"Cole, ya shouldn't be here," I said, my voice weak.

"Ah, I wanted to make sure you are okay." He gripped the bars more aggressively. "I've been searching everywhere for you."

I looked away from him, my heart pounding. "I'll be out soon, I promise."

"I don't want them to hurt you," Cole said, his voice tight with fear.

Cole clung to people, literally. I'd see it every time someone walked out of a room, the way his shoulders tensed, his hands twitching like he didn't know what to do without them. He didn't cry or beg, but I could feel it in the way he stayed close, too close to Henry. His words always carried this quiet sadness, like he was terrified of being left behind.

I'd catch him watching me sometimes, like he was waiting for me to say something. It made me feel guilty for even thinking about not talking to him, even when I needed space.

My eyes met his, and I forced myself to believe my own words. "They won't."

Cole shook his head, the desperation in his eyes pulling at me. "Promise me that if you ever get out of here, you'll take me with you."

I swallowed hard, trying to ignore the fear gnawing at my insides. "No matter what happens, I promise we'll escape this place together."

Cole's face softened, his eyes lit up with hope. He smiled, a small, fragile thing that seemed too precious for a place like this. We clasped hands through the cold, rusted bars, the warmth of our touch calmed me in the silence that surrounded us.

* * *

For the first time, my thoughts turned dark. Weeks went by, and I started thinking about killing people—not just anyone, but the guards who watched us.

I lied, sometimes people.

I'm not okay. I know that now. This place is to blame. The isolation, the silence—it all played a part in building the twisted fantasy in my head.

Besides that, things started to feel easier—at least on the surface. But I had something else in mind—something I needed to do.

Late at night, when the others were asleep, I sat in the corner of my room. I sketched escape plans on scraps of paper I'd stolen from the staff room. I drew every vent, every hall, every door I'd seen, marking the guards' shifts and where the cameras were. Each line had to be perfect. If I messed up, it would cost me everything.

I hid the plans beneath my thin mattress, careful to fold them flat so they wouldn't be noticed. Every morning, I checked to

CHAPTER 18

make sure they were still there, untouched. Trust didn't exist here. If anyone found out, they'd snitch. I couldn't let that happen.

Every day, I collected what I needed—a loose screw from the bed frame, a broken piece of plastic from the cafeteria, even the metal clip from a guard's discarded pen. They all went into a small box I'd hidden in the crack behind the dresser. Piece by piece, I was building something bigger than just an escape. I was building a weapon.

Then came the night when Henry caught me.

I had just slipped my escape plans back under the bed. He appeared in the doorway, his eyes narrowing. "What is that?" he asked, his voice low, almost too quiet.

I froze, but there was no point in hiding it now. I didn't answer, not right away. He stepped closer, his eyes landing on the scraps of paper tucked underneath the mattress. He pulled them out, his eyes scanning the plans. A cold pit formed in my stomach.

"You're trying to leave, aren't you?" he asked.

"For weeks now."

He shook his head, a slight frown crossing his face. "You know they'll increase the dosage of your treatment if they catch you. They did it to me."

The thought of facing that kind of punishment made my stomach turn, but the need to escape was stronger than the fear.

"There are vents," he continued. "I've seen them in the hallways, but I don't know how to access them. I think it might be worth a shot."

"Can we go together in our free time?"

"Well… during lunch, we'll need a distraction. Something

big enough to draw attention away from the vents. We can use Cole."

Cole glanced at Henry and me, giving us a quick nod. He took a deep breath and marched up to the security guards, his face contorted with anger. "Hey!" he shouted, his voice echoing through the hall. "You think you can just treat us like this?"

The guards looked at each other, choked by Cole's sudden outburst. "Calm down, kid," one of them said, trying to placate him.

"Calm down? Calm down!" Cole's voice rose to a near scream. "I've had enough of this! You can't keep us locked up like animals!" He kicked a nearby trash can, sending it clattering across the floor.

As more guards rushed to contain the situation, Henry and I seized the opportunity. The alarms came on throughout the building. We slipped past the distracted guards and headed towards the vents. I quickly unscrewed the vent cover from the hallway. The vents were on the ceilings, and we both crawled up inside, moving as quietly as possible.

Cole continued his tirade, drawing more attention to himself. "This is a violation of our rights! I won't stand for it!" he yelled, stomping his feet and waving his arms wildly.

Inside the vents, we could hear Cole's voice fading as we crawled further away.

"Look!" Henry said as we both looked at a light from a distance. We made our way to the light and looked down below us. There was a room full of bodies of kids. They were dead. All of them, about ten of them on metal beds. Some were being carried out in bags. Henry was sensitive to the dust mites from the vents. He sneezed, I gasped as the workers from below paused and looked around. They were dressed in hazmat

CHAPTER 18

jumpsuits. Henry covered his mouth as I placed a finger over mine, signaling him to stay quiet.

The walls felt like they were closing in, the shadows creeping in closer, pressing against us. Suddenly, the alarms turned off, but that wasn't our only concern. Soon, the midnight check up would begin, the time when they would deliver our pills to each room. We needed to be back down, fast, before anyone caught wind of what we were doing.

The moment Henry and I slipped down from the vents, everything changed. My feet thumped in my ears as we dropped to the floor. I held my breath, nerves on edge, trying to keep as quiet as possible.

"Over here," Henry whispered, his voice shaky, he looked around the hall. He gestured towards the back hallway leading to our rooms. "We have to move, now."

"I think I should tell you something," I said, lowering my voice. "About where those bodies come from."

Henry frowned, his eyes filled with curiosity. "Okay?"

I clenched my fists, looking anywhere but at him, knowing if I met his eyes, I might reveal too much. "I used to work—"

"Hey! You two!" a voice barked. The sound of heavy boots echoed behind us.

We spun around, eyes locking onto the guard.

"Run!" I hissed, grabbing Henry's wrist and pulling him with me as we ran down the hall.

"Turn here!" Henry shouted, yanking me towards a narrow passageway. I followed without question, my breaths coming in short, shallow bursts. My legs burned with every step, but I didn't slow down. We couldn't slow down.

A sharp *thwip* cut through the air. I barely had time to process it before I saw Henry stumble. His body jerked, his eyes wide with shock.

"No!" I shouted, catching him as he fell forward. My hands shook as I saw the small dart sticking out of his back. His eyes met mine, glossy and confused, before they fluttered shut. "Henry!" I tried to lift him, but he was too heavy.

Thwip. Pain shot through my shoulder like a wasp sting. I slapped at it instinctively, my fingers finding the dart buried in my skin. My heart pounded as warmth spread through my veins, heavy and slow.

"No!" I muttered, stumbling backwards. My vision swirled, everything tilting like the ground had been pulled out from under me. I reached for the wall, but my arms felt like they were sinking into water.

My knees buckled. I hit the floor, face first, cold concrete pressing against my cheek. I tried to lift my head, but my body wouldn't listen.

Boots thudded towards me, steady. "Got them both," someone said, his voice distant, like he was speaking through water.

My eyes fluttered shut, darkness swallowing everything.

* * *

I sat up slowly, my chest rising and falling with slow breaths. It was so quiet. Too quiet. No footsteps. No distant shouts. Just me. I pressed my back against the wall, knees pulled to my chest. I squeezed my eyes shut, still seeing Henry's face, his eyes wide with panic.

Minutes stretched into hours. Or maybe longer. It felt like I was floating in a space too small to move but too big to feel

CHAPTER 18

safe. I didn't sleep. I couldn't. I kept replaying the moment they took Henry away. Over and over.

Eventually, the door swung open. Two guards stood in the frame, faces blank like statues. No words. No warning. Just silent commands. One stepped forward and pointed. I knew what it meant. No fighting. No questions. Move.

A single chair sat in the center of the room; steel restraints bolted to the armrests. My heart kicked in my chest. *No. Not this.*

"Sit," one of the guards barked.

I didn't move. My feet were frozen to the floor.

"Sit." This time, he stepped forward, his hand resting on his sides.

My body moved before I could think. Slow, unsteady steps towards the chair. I sat down, the cold metal biting into my skin through the thin fabric of my clothes. Restraints snapped over my wrists and ankles, locking me in place. My heart was a wild animal in my chest, slamming against my ribs, desperate to break free.

"Subject secured," the second guard muttered into his radio.

A man in a white coat stepped into view. His face was calm in the way that only people without empathy can be. He set down a small tray next to me with a single, round white pill on it. I knew what it was before he even said it.

"Treatment time," he said, his voice as smooth as glass. No emotion. No hesitation.

My breath hitched. I shook my head, pulling at the restraints. "No. No, I'm fine. I don't need it. I'm fine!" My voice cracked. Fear hit my eyes.

"You've shown signs of resistance," he said, his eyes meeting mine like he was looking through me. "We can't have that,

Acelin. The treatment will help you feel at peace. No more fighting. No more fear here." His hand hovered over the tray, fingers pinching the small pill like it was nothing. "Open," he ordered.

I clamped my mouth shut, jaw locked tight. My eyes wandered around the room, searching for anything—*anything*—I could use to get free. But I was strapped down. Powerless.

He nodded at one of the guards.

Before I could brace for it, rough fingers gripped my jaw, forcing it open. I thrashed, twisting as hard as I could, but the guard's grip had me. My jaw ached from the pressure. I heard the clink of the pill being set on my tongue, dry and bitter.

"No—" I tried to spit it out, but they clamped my mouth shut, fingers squeezing my face until my cheeks burned.

"Swallow," the man in white said softly, like it was a simple request. "Swallow," his voice even calmer now. "Or we'll have to do it the hard way."

The guard let go of my face, and I gasped for air, choking on nothing but my own breath. I faked like I took the pill. I couldn't believe I did it. I finally fooled them.

"Good," the man said, wiping his hands on his coat like it had been just another day at work. "That wasn't so hard, was it?" He turned to leave, clipboard in hand. "Bring him to the showers," he ordered the guards.

I stood in the shower, the water beating down on my back as I slipped the pill from under my tongue and watched it swirl down the drain. To stay safe here, I knew I had to pretend it worked. I had to become someone else entirely. So, I did. I let the old me wash away and became someone new. Someone unrecognizable.

Someone who could survive.

19

Eight Months Later

D*ecember 1, 2007*

The room is quiet, like everyone's holding their breath. My words sit heavy in the air. I can feel their eyes on me—some of them curious, some of them doubtful. But I'm not here to convince them. I'm here to tell the truth. My truth.

A boy tilts his head, his face twisted in confusion. "Do you think they're still alive? Maxes and Nick?"

I glance around the room. "I have no idea," I say, looking each of them in the eye. I'm not going to lie, not to them, and not to myself.

"What about the Members?" another boy shout from the back of the group. "Why do you think they put you here if they wanted you dead?"

I shrug, tired of the questions. "I have no clue," I sigh, my voice low this time.

After explaining my story to new people over and over, I head to the lunchroom. It's quieter than usual. Not many people are around. I'm still not cool with Benny. We're not even allowed to be in the same area most days, but today I'm not in the mood to follow rules. I'm tired of it.

Benny and his friend's surround my table. They're not subtle about it either. They're loud, and everyone's watching. I can feel the others all waiting to see what's about to happen.

"What do you want?" I ask, not even looking up as I push the mashed potatoes around my tray. The meat on my plate doesn't have bread today, just a dry patty sitting there looking plain.

"You stole from me," Benny says, leaning in close.

"Okay?" I say, still not looking at him.

"I want it back," his nose flares like he's trying to scare me.

"What do ya want back?" I ask, finally turning to face him. I want him to say it out loud so the guards can hear. I'm daring him to do it. "Go on. Say it."

He looks around, his jaw tightening. "The Playboy magazine," he mutters lowly, but not low enough. A few kids snicker behind him.

"No," I say, taking a bite of my food like he's not even there.

Benny's face goes red. His friends step in closer. I hear the scrape of their slides against the floor. I look up, and Benny's eyes are wild now. He's not laughing anymore. He's serious.

"I'm gonna kill you," he says quietly, his voice steady in a way that's more dangerous than yelling.

His hand moves fast, too fast. A knife slices through my eyebrow, burning as it drags across my face, from brow to cheek.

He tackles me to the ground, pinning me with his weight. Blood drips warm and fast down to my mouth. Kids are shouting, some running for help. My vision blurs as the blood gets in my eye. I grit my teeth, twisting my body and shoving

EIGHT MONTHS LATER

Benny off me. I'm back on my feet, heart racing like it's about to burst out of my chest. I grab a lunch tray off the table and raise it over my head, ready to bring it down on him.

The tray connects with his face. The force of it sends him stumbling back, blood splattering from his nose. His eyes widen in shock before narrowing into a murderous glare.

Before I can react, the guards rush in, dragging us apart. Their hands clamp down on my shoulders, fingers digging into my skin as they yank me away. Adrenaline is running through me like a tidal wave. One of the guards pulls out a needle. I thrash against them, but it's no use—his grip is iron. The sharp pinch in my leg makes me wince. Everything goes quiet. Dark.

When I wake up, my throat feels like sandpaper. My body is stiff, every muscle aching, and my face throbs with pain. I'm lying on a mat—cold and hard against my back. The metallic taste of blood lingers in my mouth. Hours pass, maybe more. I'm not sure.

Eventually, the door creaks open. Two guards stomp in, their boots echoing against the floor. Without a word, they unchain me and haul me to my feet. My legs barely work, but I move anyway because I know they'll make it worse if I don't.

The nurse's eyes soften when she sees me. She's older, with brown hair tied into a neat bun and a calmness that feels out of place here. She's quiet as she works, cleaning the dried blood from my face with something that stings like hell. I wince but don't say anything.

When she's done, she hands me two painkillers and a small cup of water. I take them, pretending to swallow, but slip the pills into my pocket when she turns away.

"You need to be careful, Mr. Jones," she says, her voice gentle but firm, her eyes locking onto mine.

I freeze. My stomach tightens. "What did you call me?" My voice is hoarse, more a rasp than a question.

Her small smile doesn't reach her eyes. "Maybe you've had too much... medication?" she says, her tone light and careful. She tucks her name tag back into her shirt with a quick motion, hiding whatever it says. "Just focus on healing," she adds, patting my arm lightly as the guards start dragging me towards the door.

Her touch lingers in my mind, strangely familiar. Too familiar.

The guards lead me back to my room, their hands gripping my arms like vices. My hand brushes against the wall, steadying me as I shuffle forward, my feet dragging across the cold floor.

"You okay?" Henry asks when I step inside, pulling off his headphones. His eyes flick to my face, scanning it with concern.

"No. Does my eye look bad?" I point to the tender spot under my left eye, still swollen and sore from earlier.

"More like a bad ass scar," he says with a teasing grin, tossing me a sandwich from his stash. "You look like you haven't eaten in days."

I catch it and peel back the wrapper slowly. The dry bread and processed meat don't look appetizing, but my stomach growls anyway. "Yeah, well, I'm starving," I mutter, taking a big bite. It's not good, but it's better than nothing. "What are you listening to?" I ask, my words muffled as I chew.

"The Smiths," he says with a grin, tapping his fingers along to a beat only he can hear.

"Are they, like, a band or something?" I ask, chewing slower now.

Henry's jaw drops like I've just insulted his entire bloodline. "Are you serious?" He yanks the headphones off his head and plops them onto mine without warning. "Some friends are meeting up soon. Want to join?" He pulls the headphones off my head before I can respond.

I blink at him; not sure I heard him right. "What did you say?"

"Do you want to come with me?" he repeats, looking at me like I'm slow.

"Isn't it lock down right now?" I raise an eyebrow, doubt twisting my expression.

"Which means the cameras are off," he says, like it's the most obvious thing in the world. "Why are you acting brand new?" His voice carries a hint of annoyance, like I'm ruining his big plan.

"Last time, you got me in trouble for sneaking your toothpaste when you thought the cameras were off," I shot back. My arms cross as I give him a look, daring him to deny it.

He huffs, rubbing the back of his neck like he's replaying the memory. "Can you blame me? The taste of mint was the only thing keeping me sane."

I snort, shaking my head. "Right."

"Come on, you in?" he says, nudging my arm, his grin practically daring me to say no.

I sigh, glancing at the door, half expecting a guard to burst in. But it's quiet. Too quiet.

"Fine," I mutter. I follow him out, moving quickly and crouching low as we pass the doors of sleeping kids. My heart thuds in my chest, each step louder than the last. The halls are dimly lit, the orange glow of flickering bulbs makes strange shadows.

The office door is wide open. It's never really fully open. Henry doesn't even glance at it. His focus is ahead, his movements quick. I stay close behind, my ears straining to pick up even the faintest sounds. But something doesn't feel right.

The unease crawling up my spine only grows the further we go. The halls stretch endlessly in front of us, empty. Too empty. No guards. No students. Not even whispers. It's like the entire building has been evacuated.

My pulse quickens. "Where is everyone?" I whisper before I can stop myself.

"How would I know?" he says.

We reach a door at the end of the hallway. Henry kneels down, pulling a card from his pocket. It's bent and frayed at the edges, like he's been holding onto it for weeks. He slides it into the crack of the door, jiggling it carefully until there's a soft click.

"Where ya get that?" I whisper, glancing nervously around.

"Found it," he says, smirking as he pushes the door open just wide enough for us to slip through. "Don't ask questions you don't want the answers to."

I frown, caught off guard by the sharpness in his tone. I know he's joking, but it rubs me the wrong way. I hate jokes.

It's colder down here, and the smell of damp concrete fills the air. My nose wrinkles at the musty, almost metallic tang that clings to the walls. The space feels older, abandoned—like we've stepped into a part of the building no one's supposed to see.

"Where are we even going?" I ask, my voice tight.

Henry doesn't answer, he just keeps walking.

The room is bigger than I expected. It's dimly lit by a few old lamps, their small glow barely reaching the corners. Teens are scattered around, sitting on crates or leaning against the walls. The music playing in the background is soft, more like a hum than a song, but it's enough to make the place feel alive. It's nothing like the sterile silence of the halls upstairs.

EIGHT MONTHS LATER

Henry moves ahead, scanning the room. His eyes land on her, his girlfriend, sitting on one of the crates, her curly hair pulled into a loose bun. She looks up, and her eyes light up when she sees him.

"There she is," Henry says, a smile spreading across his face as he walks towards her like he's in a dream.

He throws an arm around her shoulders, pulling her close like they've been apart for weeks. She leans onto him, her smile soft but tired. Together, they make their way towards me, their steps perfectly in sync.

"You guys made it," she says, her eyes locking on me now. There's something sharp in her gaze, like she can see every thought I'm trying to bury.

"Acelin, you remember my girlfriend, Celina?" Henry says, nodding towards her.

"Yeah," I reply. The smell of her conditioner lingers in the air around us. I know she's turning eighteen in two days, but she hasn't told Henry yet. She's too scared. Once she's gone, they won't see each other again, not until he turns eighteen.

I still remember the name they used to call her at camp: *Bloody Mary.* It happened on my birthday, August 25th—the day I apologized to Celina. Henry had secretly thrown a party for me. The smell of cheap cake and candles still sticks in my memory. But the apology? It felt hollow, like trying to patch a dam with tape. What good is *"sorry"* after everything that happened at camp?

The noise in the room dies down, leaving just me and Celina. Henry is helping the others clean, and I'm sitting on a couch, holding the cup she gave me. She's next to me, cross legged, her eyes fixed on me like she's waiting for me to say something.

"I thought you were supposed to leave once you turn eighteen," she says, breaking the silence.

"I decided to stay," I say, staring at the floor.

"Why?"

"I'm not safe out there," I admit.

She turns her head away for a moment, then looks back at me. "This place isn't any better."

Before I can respond, Henry peeks through the dusty door window. "Acelin, we gotta go," he hisses, hurrying towards me. He tightens his slippers, urgency in every movement, as Celina stands up with us. "Security's coming!" he says, grabbing my arm. Celina clings to my shirt as we push through the crowd, but somewhere in the chaos, I lose her.

In the hallway, the noise behind us shifts—a loud pop, sudden and sharp, like a gunshot passing my ear. I glance back, and my stomach twists. Security guards are firing needles, their weapons hissing with compressed air. Kids drop like ducks at a carnival, limp and lifeless as the darts hit their marks. Each thud of a falling body makes my chest tighten even more. Henry and I sprint, weaving through the crowd as screams echo off the walls.

"Shit!" Henry gasps, his hands trembling as he stumbles. "Acelin, help me pick her up!"

I stop and see her, Celina, sprawled on the ground. Her eyes half open like she's fighting to stay awake. My heart pounds as I stand frozen, my gaze darting between her and the guards closing in.

"We gotta go, Henry!" I shout, panic clawing at my throat. "We have to leave her!"

He drops to his knees beside her, shaking her shoulders. "Come on, get up! Get up!" he begs, his voice cracking.

My feet won't move. Kids rush past me, their faces streaked

EIGHT MONTHS LATER

with tears and terror. One of the guards raises his weapon, aiming straight at us.

"Henry, come on!" I yell again, but it's already too late.

I hear the *pop* before I see him jerk forward. His body stiffens, his eyes wide with shock, and then he collapses face first onto the cold, dirty floor.

"Get up!" I scream, the sound ripping out of me, but my legs act on instinct. I run.

I make it a few steps before I feel the sting of a needle in my back. The pain is sharp, but it's the heat that follows, the warmth spreading through my body like fire. It takes me down. My legs buckle, the floor rushing up to meet me.

The last thing I see is Henry's body lying next to Celina's, their hands inches apart but not touching.

* * *

December 2

I wake up, cold. The air cuts through my skin like a blade, and I realize I'm back in the same room where Henry and I saw the kids' bodies through the vents. The sight of it chills me.

I sit up, my bare feet hitting the icy floor, and I shiver. Across the room, Henry crouches in the corner, his face twisted in pain as he digs at the needle wound in his shoulder.

"Why are we the only ones awake?" he asks, his voice weak.

I glance at the metal beds around us. The other kids lie still, their chests rising and falling slowly, almost unnaturally. It's like they're under a spell.

A terrible thought hits me. I walk over to Henry, my heart

pounding. "Listen," I say, kneeling beside him. "I used to work with the Members. They're taking these kids to be bid on."

Henry's face tightens. "What do you mean?"

I hesitate, ashamed. "They're using us, Henry. All of us. We're... lab rats now."

His voice cracks. "They did tests on me? And you're just now telling me?"

"I—" I falter. "I tried. I was embarrassed about what we did to you... all of you."

"No! Stay back!" he snaps, his eyes wild. "You said you didn't remember much about being with those people."

Before I can respond, voices echo down the hall. Henry and I freeze. I motion for him to follow me, and we crouch behind the beds.

Ms. Katy stands in the center of the lab, her eyes fixed on one of the kids. She pulls the cover off him, revealing black veins creeping beneath his pale skin. He's dead.

Name: Cole Locksmith

Age: Fourteen

Number: 002

"This is the last kid," Ms. Katy says, swiping her hair off her shoulders.

The doctor beside her nods silently and walks out of the room. As the door shuts behind him, a group of Members strolls in.

I take a shallow breath, trying not to make a sound. Henry's face is numb by the news of Cole being dead.

Drew walks in last, his eyes scanning the room. His hair is

EIGHT MONTHS LATER

slicked back, longer than before, brushing the back of his neck. He's dressed like he just came from a dinner party. A black shirt and slacks. "Hello again, Katy," he says.

"This is what happens when we test on them for two days straight," Katy says, her tone neutral. Her gaze lingers on Cole like he's nothing more than a failed experiment.

Henry covers his mouth, tears shimmering in his eyes. I feel a knot twist in my stomach as I glance at him.

Drew walks up to her, his expression calm but cold. "This is amazing for us. More kids, more time for testing, and more money for bids." His eyes sweep over Cole's body like he's inventory.

Ms. Katy tilts her head, her face unreadable. "I'm happy we can help," she says with a hollow smile. "But if we keep testing like this, there won't be any children left."

Drew's face hardens. I've seen that look before, the empty, ruthless expression he gets before doing something he'll never regret. I watch him move in slow motion, his hand reaching for his hip.

BANG.

Ms. Katy jerks backwards, crumpling to the floor. Blood pools beneath her head, spreading across the cold tile. Drew lowers the gun, his face frowning.

"Clean this up," he orders the Members. "And find Acelin."

Henry and I exchange a terrified glance. I grab his arm, keeping him from moving.

"We need to find Celina," Henry whispers, his voice frantic.

"No! We have to get out of here!" I argue, panic rising in my chest.

"I'm not leaving without her," he says, his tone final.

I know there's no changing his mind. I look at the Members

leaving the room, and I realize I have no choice but to let Henry go. He starts searching the bodies, lifting the covers off the kids lying on the metal beds.

I sprint down the hall, turning a corner, but I collide with Drew and a few of the Members. Drew steadies himself, his eyes locking onto me in stock. The Members hover behind him, their faces motionless that feels suffocating.

He finally speaks. "Where do you think you're going?"

I fight against his grip. "Let go of me!"

He laughs, a cold, mocking sound. "Woa, look at you all tough." He holds the Members back, stopping them from making a move on me.

"What do you want from me?" I demand, struggling to keep my voice steady.

"You tried stealing from me, faking your death, and you have the nerve to ask me that?" Drew says.

"I didn't mean to steal from you—"

"Enough!" he snaps. Before I can react, they yank me down the hallway, ignoring my attempts to struggle. I try to fight, to break free, but my limbs feel heavy, like I'm already losing.

When we reach the door, he shoves me inside, and the last thing I see before it slams shut is his twisted smile.

He forces me to sit in the cold, metal chair. I glance down and notice the chains on the armrests and legs. Before I can react, the Members move in, locking me in place, securing each chain tightly around me. My wrists feel raw from the pressure as I struggle to breathe.

Drew steps to me, letting out a laugh that feels more like a taunt. "You're like a god, untouchable. No matter what I do, we always meet again and again."

I open my mouth to respond, to fight back, but before the

EIGHT MONTHS LATER

words can leave my lips, I feel the sharp sting of a needle in my neck. One of the Members got me. The pain hits instantly, like fire coursing through my veins. I gasp, my vision blurring, and the heat spreads quickly through my body. It feels like my blood is boiling, my skin on the verge of burning. "No, no, no!" I cry, but it's already too late. I look down, and my veins have turned black, the blood inside my skin thick and heavy, like tar.

The drug is working its way through me, spreading faster than I can stop it. Drew steps back, a twisted smile forming on his lips. "Sorry, brother," he says coldly. He then turns towards the Members. "Let's load all the kids up before someone catches on. Take them through the back doors," he orders, his voice trailing off as he walks out the door.

My body begins to twitch uncontrollably, each muscle fighting against the overwhelming sensation. I try to focus, to hold onto some part of myself, but my mind feels like it's slipping away, drowning deeper. I can't stop it. There's no escape. Before I can think, my head jerks back, and suddenly, I don't feel my pulse anymore. The blood that once rushed through my veins is still.

I no longer exist.

20

Jackson

December 1, 2007

On May 20th, Acelin Jones was taken from me.

It's hard to know where to start, or what to say. Sometimes it feels like there's this weight pressing down on my chest all the time. I'm not sure if I'm carrying it for myself or because of what happened to Acelin.

He's not dead, but it feels that way.

I remember the first time I realized things would never be the same. It's been months now, but I still can't wrap my head around it. Acelin's gone—taken by that damn Dooms Institute. They said they were helping him, that he'd come back *"different"* or *"better."* But he hasn't. He's not coming back.

Every day without him feels like a reminder of what I lost. Graduation came and went. I thought we would be there together, side by side, cracking jokes and taking stupid pictures. Instead, I walked the stage alone. Even when they called my name, I didn't hear it. The whole thing felt fake. Like I was just going through the motions of something that should've been joyful but wasn't.

I couldn't explain it to anyone. Acelin wasn't just my best friend; he was the thing that made life feel real. Without him, everything feels off.

A knock on the door startles me.

"Hello? Is anyone home?" a voice calls out.

I glance through the peephole. "Maxes?" I mumble under my breath, opening the door.

She steps inside, dressed in all black, her hood pulled up. When she pulls it down, her face is tense, like she's carrying something she doesn't want to talk about.

I notice the scars on her stomach when she stretches, rough lines cutting across her skin. They've healed, but the memory of her blood on Acelin's suit still haunts me.

I sink onto the couch, grabbing the beer from her hand. "How's Nick?" I ask, trying to sound casual.

She exhales, leaning back against the couch. "He's been in and out of the hospital since graduation," she says quietly.

My eyes drop to her scars again. "Have you figured out who did this to you?" I ask.

Her fingers trace the edge of her shirt, her eyes distant. "Whatever we drank that night... it erased my memory. Like... it's all foggy, like it slipped away."

Her phone buzzes on the couch, lighting up with a name I haven't seen in a while—*Greek*. My stomach tightens. I move closer without thinking, stopping just short of hovering over her.

Her thumb hesitates over the screen for a fraction of a second before she swipes to answer. Her face grows pale as she listens. *"Greek? What are you talking about?"*

His voice crackles through the speaker. *"It's happening. Now.*

They're coming for you."

My heart skips. I don't know what this is about, but the way his voice sounds—it's like he's talking about something much bigger than either of us. I can see Maxes face draining of color as she listens, her grip on the phone tightening more. She looks like she's about to say something, but Greek's voice cuts her off.

"Remember what I told you?" Greek continues, his voice so quiet I almost have to lean in to hear. *"The Members will not stop, until we are all dead."*

I glance at Maxes, watching the way her expression shifts. She's not just shaken. She's scared, and that scares me. She's always been the calm one—the one who handles the weird stuff, the cryptic calls, the secrets.

She flinches. She doesn't answer me right away, her eyes flicking between the phone and me, her mouth opening like she's going to say something but then stopping herself.

Then Greek's voice cracks through again. *"Get out of there, now!"* he says, shouting.

"We need to go," she says to me.

I stop my tracks. "You hear that?"

She freezes, listening. There's something in the air. Not the usual creaks of an old house, but a low sound. Footsteps. Slow. I know Acelin's house very well. It's upstairs.

We move towards the front door, but another sound stops me in my tracks. I freeze, holding my breath. My hand tightens around the grip of my gun, my pulse hammering in my chest.

The first gunshot shatters through the air, followed by the whoosh of a bullet that barely misses me. The shot came from the stairs, sending debris flying.

I duck instinctively, grabbing Maxes by the arm, pulling her with me. "We need to go. Now!"

JACKSON

Outside the window, I spot them—*the Members*. Men in black suits, moving up the driveway like they own the place. There's at least six of them, their movements calm, calculated. They're heading straight to us. We move towards the back door now.

Maxes reaches for the door handle, but I catch her arm. "Not yet," I whisper.

She nods, waiting for my signal. The footsteps upstairs grow louder, closer. I hold my breath as I crack the door open just enough to see outside. The driveway is lit by the streetlight, and the Members are going inside. It's the perfect moment for us to slip away.

"Go!" I say, and we bolt out the back door.

Maxes is ahead of me, sprinting to the car parked on the curb. My shoes slam against the pavement as I push myself to keep up. Another shot whistles past my ear, too close for comfort. Another shot cracks through the air, it grazes my shoulder. Pain shoots through me, but I grit my teeth and keep moving.

My shoulder throbs as I press a ripped piece of shirt against the graze, trying to stop the pain. We drive off fast, no second thoughts. I keep checking the rear-view mirror, hoping the Members aren't following us.

When we reach the gallery, we head straight upstairs through some doors. The door cracks open, and after a quick glance, we're let inside. The door shuts behind us. The smell of cigars fills the air as we walk in. Greek stands in the middle of the room, tall and still. A light from the art on the walls makes shadows move around him. His eyes lock on us like he's trying to get his thoughts together.

"You made it," he says, his voice calm and controlled. He gestures towards a pair of chairs in front of a cluttered desk, the surface littered with maps, photographs, and half empty glasses of whiskey.

"They're still after us?" Maxes asks, sinking into a chair. Her eyes wander around the room like she's expecting them to bust in any second. "The Members?"

Greek stays still, face blank like he doesn't feel a thing. "They won't stop until they get what they want."

Maxes shoots him a look. "And what do they want?"

Greek's eyes shift towards me for a second before he says, "A cure to stop hallucinations… and Acelin to suffer until he kills himself. But knowing them, he's probably already dead."

Maxes jaw tightens, her fists pressing onto her legs. "Can we just focus on saving him? Start from where we left off?"

Greek narrows his eyes at her. "The reason I stopped trying to save him was because he stabbed you."

"He didn't! I swear he didn't!" Her voice cracks a little.

I lean forward in the chair. "It wasn't Acelin. He would never—"

"How do you know? Were you there?" Greek cuts me off, his eyes squint.

Silence hits us. Nobody moves, and I can feel the tension.

Greek turns to Maxes, his stare steady. "This is your call, Maxes." He runs a hand through his hair and lets out a sigh of frustration. "If Acelin did stab you, and we help him, don't come crying to me when you find out the truth."

Her face burns with doubt and shame. She stays quiet, like she's fighting with herself.

Without a word, Greek walks and opens a door at the back of the room. "Follow me," he says. The air smells stale, like it's been shut for too long as we step in.

Inside, it's modern. It feels more like a high-end spa than anything else. But there's no time to question it. A handful of assistants and stylists are moving around, preparing equipment, organizing supplies. At the center of it all stands a woman in a black suit. She steps forward as Greek enters, her eyes locking onto us.

"This is Natalia," Greek says, introducing the assistant manager. "She's going to help you get cleaned up. I'm sure you'll find it... useful." He stares us down.

Natalia doesn't waste any time. She gestures to the chairs and moves over to the small station set up along the back wall. "Sit. This won't take long," she says to me as she examines my face. She then looks at my arm, sees the graze, and applies antiseptic before wrapping it with a bandage.

The assistants waste no time getting us into separate changing rooms. The shower is already running, the steam filling the room, and I'm thankful for it. I step into the glass walled shower, feeling the heat instantly hit me. The water feels like it's washing away more than just the dirt and sweat. It feels like I'm a new person now.

As I step out, a towel is thrown at me. I catch it automatically and wrap it around my waist. A stylist is already waiting with a fresh set of clothes, a black suit for me. I take a quick look at myself in the mirror. The reflection staring back at me doesn't look like the guy who's been on the run for weeks. He looks like someone who's about to walk into a high-powered meeting.

Meanwhile, across the room, Maxes is going through her own transformation. I can't see her directly, but I hear the sound of water running. A few minutes later, she steps out of her changing room, looking nothing like the woman who walked into the gallery. Her wet hair is now expertly styled, swept back into a neat bun that pulls attention to her sharp cheekbones. Her black suit is tailored to perfection, in a way that speaks of wealth.

We meet at the center. "You look amazing," I say, my voice filled with genuine admiration.

She smiles for the first time, her eyes lighting up. "Thanks," she replies, a hint of shyness in her tone.

Greek stands in front of us, his eyes hard and cold, like he's been expecting this moment for a long time. "Jackson," he says, "You will work for me. I own you now."

I don't have to ask what he means. He's been pulling the strings for too long already. The things we've done, the choices we've made—they've all been because of him. Every move we've made has been to get Acelin out. And now, here it is, the moment he's been waiting for. The moment he wants me to finally join him.

I exchange a look with Maxes, who's standing across from me, her face proud. Her eyes meet Greek, then back to me, before she gives a slight, almost imperceptible nod. She says, "Welcome to the family, Jackson."

Greek takes a needle and pokes my finger, placing it on a paper that looks like a contract. One of his assistants takes a scanner and places it on my neck. I feel a sting, then my picture is taken, and I'm put on the leader board.

After, Greek pours us each a drink—whiskey, smooth and dark—and leans against the desk as he watches us drink. He doesn't seem particularly fazed by the earlier violence, and if anything, it seems like just another Tuesday for him.

"When can we get him out of Dooms?" Maxes asks, breaking the silence as she sets her drink down.

Greek raises an eyebrow, a smirk creeping onto his face. "You and Acelin dating, Maxes?" He pauses, eyes shifting between us. "Jackson, you know if they are?"

Maxes leans forward, her face frowns. "You can't stop me."

Greek tilts his head. "Maybe you should focus on healing a little more—"

"No!" Maxes snaps, letting out a frustrated sigh. "Just because my parents died in a car accident doesn't mean you get to control me, what I wear, how I look, or when I can shave!"

Greek glances at me. "Did Acelin know I was her legal guardian?" Greek doesn't even flinch at her words. He stands there with one leg crossed over the other, like none of this matter. His eyes stay on us like he's watching a show he's seen a hundred times before. "Does he know Jackson?"

"Um..." I stammer, glancing at Maxes, surprised.

"It doesn't matter," she says, leaning back in her chair, her face finally relaxes. "I'll tell Acelin when I'm ready too."

Greek walks over to a cabinet, opens it, and pulls out a small folder. He tosses it onto the table in front of us. "Anyway, I did some digging. Turns out, Acelin's dad works with money. If I have to pay him to help get Acelin out, then so be it."

Maxes eyes narrow. "What about the people who still think he killed those students?"

"I can't win with you, can I, Maxes?" Greek says. He pulls out a cigarette, lights it with a slow flick of his lighter, and takes it in. Smoke curls around his face as he exhales. "Right now, let's just focus on getting him out first." The smoke is still in Greek's face, drifting slowly like he's got all the time in the world. "Acelin's father has been out of the public eye for years, but he's still a powerful figure. Some say he was one of the original founders of the Institute." Greek points to the folder. "The address inside is his last known location. It's an old estate just outside the city, hidden away from the usual eyes. If you're lucky, he's still there. If you're unlucky..." He shrugs.

Maxes doesn't hesitate. She grabs the envelope, scanning the address. "We'll go first thing in the morning."

Greek walks closer to us, almost amused. "Until then… are you both ready for the gallery party?"

A party? The kind Acelin used to tell me about. The kind that always sounded like trouble. I know I shouldn't think so, but a part of me loves this lifestyle—the plans, the edge, the feeling of being untouchable, even if it's only for a moment.

* * *

December 2, 2007

Maxes and I slide into a corner booth, the low noise of the espresso machine in the background is on. The air carries the scent of stale coffee and burnt toast.

We don't say much at first. Maxes pulls her hoodie up, tugging the strings tight until only her eyes are visible. She stares out the window, watching the rain streak down the glass in crooked lines. Her fingers tap on the table, like she's counting seconds.

I glance at the menu, not really reading it, just giving my hands something to do. My eyes focus on her, then back down. "You good?" I ask.

She doesn't answer right away. Her fingers stop tapping. Her eyes shift from the window to me, her gaze heavier than it should be. "Yeah," she says, quietly.

We finally were able to get in touch with Acelin's dad. The man who's spent years hiding. And now, we're hoping he has the key to get Acelin back.

JACKSON

He walks in a few minutes later, tall, broad shouldered, his face more worn than I expected. I don't know much about him—hell, I don't know much about Acelin's family in general—but this guy? This man is different. You can tell just by the way he carries himself, like he's seen things most people wouldn't even believe. To his slick back hair, to his turtleneck shirt, he reminds me of Acelin all the way.

Maxes stands up first, extending a hand to him. I follow her lead, keeping my distance but watching closely as she does the talking.

"I'm glad you could meet us," she says, her voice almost seeming rehearsed.

He doesn't shake her hand right away. He looks at both of us, his eyes sizing us up, like he's deciding whether to trust us. After a long pause, he grabs her hand. His grip is rough, but there's no warmth—just business.

"Jackson, Maxes," he says, his voice catching me off guard. "I hope you understand the gravity of what we're talking about here."

I nod. "We understand," I say, my voice a little shaky. It's the truth. We've been running in circles, trying to get Acelin back, trying to get close to Dooms, but there's always been something missing. That something was him. Acelin's dad.

Maxes sits back down, her eyes never leaving him. She's not asking any questions yet—she knows better than I do when to let silence do the talking. But I can feel the tension in the air, the way it crackles between all three of us, like we're all dancing around something we know but don't want to say.

I finally break the silence. "Do you... own Dooms?" The question feels stupid as soon as it leaves my mouth, but I have to ask. If anyone would know the ins and outs of the institute, it's him.

He sits across from us, his face softening just a little, but there's a coldness in his eyes. His hands come to rest on the table. For a moment, I think he's going to dodge the question or maybe even lie, but he doesn't.

"No," he says, his voice heavy, like he's admitting something. "I don't own Dooms anymore."

I blink, surprised. I thought he'd still have control, pulling the strings behind the scenes. But no. He's not the one in charge.

"Someone bought it from me," he continues, his gaze shifting just past us, as if seeing something in the distance that we can't. "A few years ago. I was out of the picture, too deep in debt, too much pressure from the wrong people. They bought the place, took it off my hands. I couldn't stop them." His jaw tightens, and for a moment, I see something raw and lost in him. "They threatened me. If I didn't give up Dooms, they would hurt my family. I didn't believe them, so they went after Acelin."

Maxes leans forward slightly, her voice low. "Who bought it?"

He hesitates, his eyes flicking to me, then to her, before his eyes drop to the table. "I can't say. Not yet," he says. "I'll help you get Acelin out. Then after, don't ever contact me again."

In the car, I drift off, the hours on the road catching up with me. The car stops, and my stomach growls for food. We pull into a gas station, only ten minutes from Dooms. I stretch as I get out of the car. Maxes is still fast asleep.

"Want anything from the store?" I say, tapping her hand gently.

"No, I'm fine," she mumbles, still half asleep.

I follow Acelin's dad into the store. He heads straight for the liquor and picks up a loose cigarette, tucking it behind his ear. I wonder if he remembers me from when I was younger. I remember him banning Acelin from coming over to my house because my dad refused to work for the Burn Wood football team with him. Acelin's dad was their assistant coach from time to time.

I walk back to the car and say, "Here, I got you some things," pouring the snacks onto the hood of the car. Deep down I know she's really hungry.

She finally speaks. "Jackson," she says, turning towards me, "there's something I need to tell you."

I glance over at her. Her eyes are glossy, like she's about to break. I nod, waiting for her to say more. She steps out of the car, looking for a snack. "You know how my parents died in that crash?" she asks. "One of the Members crashed into them." She's not asking for sympathy, I can tell. That's not Maxes style. But still, her words hit me hard. I don't know how to respond. "I didn't get to say goodbye," she says quietly. Her voice cracks just a little on the last word, but she hides it quickly. "That's why I can't leave people behind. Not ever again. It's why I'm doing this for Acelin."

I exhale slowly. "We'll get Acelin out. We're not walking away from this."

The look she gives me tells me everything. She's ready. She's made up her mind, and no matter what happens next, nothing is going to stop her from seeing this through.

We finally make it to Dooms. The night makes it hard to see much, but what I can make out is enough to put horror on my chest. It's scary from the outside—dark windows like dead eyes staring back. A hawk statue stands by the entrance, its shadow stretching long across the ground. Birds chirp somewhere above us, loud and out of place.

Maxes hesitates. She steps forward, moving with us at first, but then she stops. Her eyes stay locked on the door like it might swallow her whole. "I think I should stay out here," she says. "I can't walk in there."

I glance at her, seeing the conflict in her eyes as she looks back at the car. I want to tell her to stay, to come in with us, but I know this is something different. Something she doesn't need to witness. So, I nod at her. "We'll be quick," I say, trying to reassure her, but I'm not sure who I'm trying to convince—her or myself.

She gives a small, tight smile before turning and walking back to the car, her steps fast, almost too fast. I watch her for a moment before focusing on Acelin's dad.

He doesn't say anything, just gives me a glance that tells me he's ready. No words needed between us anymore. I step forward, pressing the button for the entrance. The doors slide open with a quiet hiss, and I feel a cold shiver crawl up my spine. The place is too quiet.

Just as I'm about to step inside, a man in a suit walks towards us. He's clean cut, a little too neat for my liking. His smile is practiced, like he's been greeting visitors all day, though his eyes don't quite match the friendly tone. There's something off about him, but I can't place it.

"Hello, guys. Come on in," he says with an almost too smooth voice, stepping aside to let us pass. "Your name, Mr.?" he asks, eyes locked on Acelin's dad.

"Aries Graves."

I spot the name on the door: **Ms. Katy**. I pause for a second. *That can't be right.* This man doesn't fit the name. The room feels off too. It's too clean, too perfect—like it's trying too hard to feel normal. But I know better. I glance at Aries, hoping he notices it too. But he's calm, eyes straight ahead, not blinking once. Like he's seen it all before and nothing surprises him anymore.

My heart starts pounding in my chest. The last time I felt this way was the day of the Burn Wood football game. The dread in my gut tells me something is terribly off.

As he taps a few keys on a computer, I notice a clipboard next to him, with names scrawled in black ink. His eyes dart quickly between the screen and the clipboard like he's trying to match up the names with the faces in front of him, but I'm already onto him.

"So, who are you guys looking for today?" the man asks, his voice just a little too forced.

Aries doesn't flinch, like he's dealt with guys like this hundreds of times. "My son," Aries says, his voice hard as steel, "Acelin... Acelin Jones."

The man pauses, his fingers freezing midair over the keyboard. He doesn't look up at first, but I can see the muscles in his jaw tighten. A quick look of something, fear? It passes through his eyes, but it's gone before I can be sure.

"Oh, Acelin," the man says, but it doesn't sound right. It's flat, dismissive. "He told me no visitors."

I can feel the tension snap in Aries voice. "I'm not here for a visit, sir. I'm here to get him out of here."

The man stutters for a moment, like he's trying to hold it together. "He's supposed to be in jail right now—"

"Yes, but he's here, right?" Aries interrupts. "I am his parent, and I did not allow my son to be here without my permission."

I can see it now. His composure is cracking. I watch his jaw tighten more, his eyes darting between the screen and the clipboard again like he's trying to figure out how to get out of this conversation. "I... I can't remove him from this facility," he says, his voice shaky.

We exchange a look, me and Aries. It's a look I can't quite explain, but it says everything we need to know. Aries notices it, his posture tightening. He doesn't flinch, though. He just plays it cool, leaning back like he didn't notice the man's nerves.

That's when I hear it. A scream.

The sound echoes through the narrow hallway, filled with panic, and it sends a jolt straight through my spine.

"Help!" The voice is desperate.

Without thinking, my legs jump into action. I run towards the sound. My heart is hammering in my chest, but I don't stop running.

When I turn the corner, I see him. A boy, maybe 17, with fluffy blonde hair. His hands are shaking, and his eyes are wide as he glances over his shoulder, looking back at me.

"I can't find her," the boy says, his voice breaking. He's practically hyperventilating, looking like he's on the edge of losing it. "And I don't know where they took him."

I frown. "Where do you think Acelin could be?" I ask, breathless.

The boy looks at me like he's unsure—lost—but then he jerks his head, hinting for me to follow him. His eyes are still full of fear. I don't hesitate. I follow wherever he goes.

As we move down the hallway, I hear doors slamming shut, the sound of locks clicking into place. Kids are peering out from behind windows, some wide eyed, others fearful, none of them really understanding what's happening. We dodge a couple of security guards, moving swiftly through the darkened hallways. We reach a small room at the end of the hall. My heart skips when I see it: Acelin.

JACKSON

He's in a chair, his body unresponsive. I swallow hard and force myself to walk over to him. My shoes click on the cold floor with each step, and it feels like time is slowing down, like my feet are stuck in mud. But I push through, the dread growing with every inch I get closer.

I stop in front of him, staring at his face. His eyes are closed, his lips slightly parted, and there's a small trace of blood near his mouth, as white foam is forming from his lips.

"We need to get him out of here," I say.

Without wasting time, we unchain him and lift his body, struggling to support his weight. He's cold and his veins look black.

Henry's panic is clear as he grips the wheelchair's handlebars. "What if we can't save him? There are people in suits everywhere in this building."

He looks at me, waiting for me to say something, but I don't have an answer. We're trapped, and Acelin's dead.

I look at him, my fingers gently brushing the hair off his forehead. Then, I glance towards the door, hoping no one comes in, not yet.

I bend down next to him. "I'm sorry," I whisper, my voice cracking, "I couldn't save you." A tear falls from my eye and hits his cold, lifeless hand. I quickly wipe it away, trying to push the emotion down.

Suddenly, the door flies open, slamming against the wall with a bang that makes me jump. A woman rushes in, breathless, her face flushed like she's been running for her life. Her eyes lock on Acelin, barely glancing at us before she drops to her knees by his side.

Her hands shoot up, palms open. "Trust me," she says, turning to us, her voice serious. Her eyes meet mine, "I can help him.

But we don't have much time before more Members show up."

"Who are you?" Henry snaps.

"I used to work with Acelin," she says, keeping her hands up. "Back with the Members." She pauses, letting that sink in. "I know a way out. But we have to move. Now."

Her eyes shift back to Acelin, checking his face, his breathing. Her hands are quick but careful, like she's done this before.

My heart's pounding, each beat louder than the last. I glance at Henry. He's staring at me, waiting for me to decide.

Do I trust her?

TO BE CONTINUED...

Made in United States
Cleveland, OH
05 May 2025